METROPOLIS

It sounded like there were people everywhere, all over the city, screaming for help or crying. Under the constant rumble of traffic and the distinct blasting of radios, he could hear brakes screeching, gunshots, cries for mercy. Despair crushed him. How many people were there in this city? How many would die before morning? An unfamiliar sensation crept up his spine.

With a start, Clark Kent realized that he was afraid . . .

OTHER BOOKS IN THE SERIES

SMALLVILLE

CITY

by Devin Grayson

Superman created by
Jerry Siegel and Joe Shuster

ASPECT®

NEW YORK   BOSTON

Cover design by Don Puckey
Book design by Charles A. Sutherland

WARNER BOOKS

Time Warner Book Group
1271 Avenue of the Americas
New York, NY 10020
Visit our Web site at www.twbookmark.com.

Visit DC Comics on-line at keyword DCComics on America On-line or at http://www.dccomics.com.

Printed in the United States of America

First Printing: March 2004

10 9 8 7 6 5 4 3 2 1

*For my sister, Jessi,
in admiration of her strength and bravery*

Acknowledgments

It is a true thrill to participate in the legend of Superman. Although the young Clark Kent we get to know in the WB television series *Smallville* has not yet grown into the iconic super hero, the world-renowned story of the Man of Steel informs and heightens the weekly dramatic conflicts so many of us follow so faithfully. Still, what's most remarkable about *Smallville* is that it's not about super heroes. It's about people.

At its heart, so is the legend of Superman. It's a story about hope and potential, and the people who have participated in its creation and propagation over the years are no less remarkable than the characters the legend celebrates. It would take me nearly the length of this entire book to name everyone who has been creatively associated with these characters, but I encourage the viewers of *Smallville* and the readers of this book to explore the rich history of Superman. The character has had a profound effect on the collective unconscious, and he has appeared in almost every creative medium we've established.

I do, however, want to take a moment to acknowledge and thank Superman's original creators, Jerry Siegel and Joe Shuster, as well as the brilliant creators of *Smallville*, Alfred Gough and Miles Millar. They, along with the show's other writers and creative consultants, such as

Gotham's own Jeph Loeb, have done an inspiring job of keeping this legend contemporary and fresh.

I also feel deeply indebted to *Smallville*'s wonderful cast, who have already done the challenging, creative work of bringing these characters so fully to life. It is a joy to watch Tom Welling, Michael Rosenbaum, Kristen Kreuk, John Schneider, Annette O'Toole, John Glover, Sam Jones III, and Allison Mack every week, and having their spirited renditions of these characters available for reference made my work on this book so much easier. My sincere gratitude and admiration to them all.

Additionally, I would like to thank Gibor Bagori for not only knowing how spectrography actually works, but for being willing and able to explain it to me.

Thanks, too, to Chris Jackson of Atlas Comics and his lovely family for showing me the real Kansas.

Thank you to Dad and Linda for your love, support, and use of the farm. Thank you to Mom and Frank for your excitement, encouragement, and willingness to watch most of Season Two with me. Thank you to Auntie Bree for always believing.

Endless thanks to my dear friends for faithfully being there to share the highs and the lows: Arnold Feener, Kaye Jarrett, Janean Langlois, Dave Segale, Dave Kinel, Jay Faerber, Brian Vaughan, Tonya Bowman, Nathan King, Mark Waid, Scott Peterson . . . you guys keep me going, day after day. Even if any of you ever become supervillains down the line, I'll love you still. Same back, right?

Thanks to Steve Korté and Rich Thomas for giving me this great opportunity, and especially to my editor, Chris Cerasi, for setting the bar so high and enthusiastically becoming the muse that I strove to please and impress.

And, last but not least, a special thank you to my brother Max, and to my little love, Moira Kate, both of whom reminded me how enduring the legend of Superman is, and will continue to be.

Devin Kalile Grayson
September 2003

Spaceship. Flying saucer. UFO. Whatever people chose to call it, Mayer Greenbrae was staring at one.

He had studied the photometry and spectra maybe ninety times, and had never been able to see the tiny emission point hidden between three large meteors on the upper-left corner of the chart as anything else. There were the expected color calibrations of the field stars, some as faint as seventeenth magnitude, confirming the photometric accuracy. There were the isolated readings of neutron-rich isotopes on the strangely radioactive meteors that had pummeled Lowell County, Kansas, fourteen years ago, prompting the initial revitalization of space study from which Mayer earned his living. And tucked away among them, practically invisible, emitting electromagnetic radiation of a color and intensity Mayer knew was grossly nonthermal, was an object that could only be a spacecraft. There was simply no other explanation for its spectral slope, or the matching spectral line signatures of short-lived radioactive isotopes in that dot. The obvious Zeeman splitting of highly ionized lines clinched it. An impossibly hot, magnetically channeled, artificial nuclear source was the only possibility. Greenbrae was as sure of it as he was sure that creamed corn didn't grow on trees.

"More coffee, hon?"

Mayer looked up from the spectrograph and found himself blinking in the midday sun. The sun in Kansas had a texture, a density. Mayer swore he could smell it in the air; sunshine you could actually breathe, sunshine that gently seeped into your skin and your lungs and your mood. It permeated the green gingham café-style curtains that decorated the kitchen windows of Annora's Heartland Homestay Bed and Breakfast and created a soft halo around the auburn hair of Annora Washburn herself. Mayer swallowed.

"Yes, that—that'd be fine, thank you."

Annora smiled as she topped off his coffee. The "Homestay" in Heartland Homestay Bed and Breakfast was almost an understatement. Mayer, who was used to motels with scratchy carpets and the occasional antiseptic corporate suite boasting of high-speed Internet hookup options, was a little bit stunned to find himself sitting at a large antique oak table in this fortysomething woman's kitchen. In fact, when she'd first shown him to his room the night before—a frilly riot of pinks and yellows, located, as she pointed out no less than four times, just two doors down from her own bedroom—he'd very nearly thanked her politely and left to go sleep in his car. What stopped him was a sudden scientific inclination to examine the speciology of Kansas close-up.

What did it mean, after all, to be a product of what Mayer mostly referred to as "flyover country"? How had the social rules, principles, and artifacts of this society helped his lurking alien prey blend in all these years, unquestioned and unnoticed? As he lay in Annora's guest bed and stared into the unblinking eyes of a little white kitten photographed peeking maniacally out of a green-painted watering can, Mayer thought about the words and phrases associated with life in the heartland, and how they might have lent some advantage to an alien.

There was "wholesome," of course, which in Gotham almost immediately connoted "naive." But if the alien was masquerading as a pet or a human in a small Midwestern town, "wholesome" could confirm an advantage of predictable social customs and easily mimicked niceties. "All-American Golden Boy"—well, that, Mayer decided, was mostly about the sun, a certain health and vitality and narrow-mindedness that came wrapped in a tan, grinning, masculine package. There was "cow town," which was obviously a reference to the presence of cows, though Mayer was beginning to associate it, too, with a certain high-intensity stench of methane.

And then there was Mayer's favorite, "corn-fed." He was relatively certain it was an agricultural term, but he liked the idea of corn itself bestowing some kind of vivacity or innocent glow. Did the alien eat corn? Mayer couldn't be sure, but it was a reasonable assumption. Smallville, Kansas, the epicenter of the meteor storm, was, before that fateful day (when it hence became known as the "Meteor Capital of the World") known by locals and on road signs as the "Creamed Corn Capital of the World."

Mayer fully intended to eat as much creamed corn while in Kansas as he could stomach.

He in fact had a half-filled, cooling bowl of it next to him as he drank the hot coffee Annora continually refilled for him. She'd produced a slightly chipped, sky-blue cup out of the same cabinet from which she took her own GOLF OR DIE mug, and that confused him, too. Did she golf? If so, where? Certainly Kansas was large enough to accommodate several fine golfing facilities, but Mayer found it hard to imagine Annora traveling to any of them. So far, the only vehicle he'd seen on the property was a tractor, and surely you couldn't take that on the highway . . . Did someone pick her up and take her golfing? Who would that be? What if she had guests? Would she leave them alone in her house?

"That's quite a fancy chart you got there," Annora remarked, snapping Mayer out of his reverie. Instinctively, though he felt confident that she couldn't read it, he held the spectrograph against his chest, hiding it the way a five-year-old might hide a crayon drawing. He was acutely aware that the alien he sought could be anywhere. Somehow, he felt sure, it had hidden itself in Kansas for over fourteen years. Now, as far as he was concerned, his entire professional reputation, not to mention the moral fortitude of the planet, depended on him finding this alien. But not, hopefully, before it found him.

"It's . . . a spectrograph," he informed her, gently lowering it. "It's a type of photograph . . . of the stars."

"Are you an astrologer?" Annora asked, a sudden burst of excitement lifting her voice into a flirtatious coo as she pulled out a chair and sat down, leaning too far across the table toward Mayer for his comfort. "I'm a Leo, myself."

Mayer blinked for a second, then shook his head.

"I'm an engi—I'm a field agent," he answered, moving to push his glasses farther up the bridge of his nose and stopping when he remembered that he no longer wore them.

"Oh, well, what's your sign?"

Annora seemed inflexible in her enthusiasm, reaching

out to pat his hand. *She thinks I'm good-looking*, Mayer realized with a sudden flush of his cheeks. He tried hard to think if anyone had ever told him what his astrological sign was.

"When were you born?" Annora prompted, apparently noticing his confusion.

It turned out that he was a Cancer, but the answer that came to Mayer's head and made him smile was, simply, "today." Starting today, after all, he was a field agent. Today he had woken up in Kansas, and today he was finally setting out to explore a mystery that had captivated him for six years. All that time he had been waiting for his partner-cum-supervisor, Tad Nickels, to clear a field mission to Smallville, but Tad had been distracted by other concerns.

"Mayer, *please*," Tad had pleaded the last time Mayer had asked him about it. "Forget about Smallville. That's not our job. Just build me the spectrometer!"

"I built you a spectrometer last year," Mayer had answered brusquely. He remembered when he and Tad had worked on design specs together at Tad's kitchen table in Otisburg. Those had been good times. Tad was a visionary, full of ambition and extravagant curiosity about the workings of space. Mayer would break Tad's wild speculations down into quantifiable inquiries before coaxing instruments of analysis into being. Their first successful creation, a modest computer program used for predicting asteroid activity in various zoned pockets of space, had earned them both jobs at S.T.A.R. Labs, Gotham.

Mayer had been extremely pleased to join the lauded Scientific and Technological Advanced Research Labs. The job provided him with talented coworkers and the resources he needed to begin building tangible data-collection instrumentation. Tad, however, had reacted strangely to the new development. The better they did at S.T.A.R. Labs, the less content he had seemed to be. He stopped obsessing about space and began to obsess about money. Always handsome and charismatic, even in tattered denim and a stained T-shirt, Tad began to pay for expensive haircuts and even more expensive suits. His shoes were always polished, and his nails always manicured. He was so self-consciously attractive that it made Mayer vaguely nauseous to look at him, especially after Tad took to wearing pastel-colored ties to emphasize the warm blue of his eyes. The partnership might have floundered if not for one lingering, fundamental understanding. More than anything, Mayer wanted to build a prototype for an enhanced spectrometer. And more than anything, Tad wanted Mayer to succeed.

Mayer had been so engrossed in his work that he had allowed Tad his violet neckties and obsessive secrecy. Tad had not wanted anyone to know about the new prototype until Mayer had it completed, and Mayer had been content not to have to fill out incessant project reports that would only slow him down. He had therefore been all the more surprised when Tad broke his own rule to usher in a man he excitedly introduced as Lionel Luthor, majority shareholder and CEO of LuthorCorp, a Fortune 500 favorite and one of the five richest conglomerates in the world. Mr. Luthor seemed very interested in the work Mayer was doing, and the next thing Mayer knew, everything had changed.

First there was the new laboratory. Lionel promoted Tad, making him Mayer's supervisor, before moving both men into a well-stocked but deserted lab of their own. There, they were instructed to do nothing but finish the prototype. If they were successful, LuthorCorp would agree to fund them indefinitely.

Mayer immediately saw the flaw in this logic, but Tad seemed unconcerned. LuthorCorp's financial assistance depended on expense-producing progress, and neither Tad nor Mayer had any money of their own to invest.

"Don't worry about it," Tad assured Mayer when the latter finally shared his anxiety. "You just finish that prototype. I'll handle the financing."

Secondly, there was the spectrograph, which Mayer had discovered while reviewing existing spectrometer capabilities. As he and Tad were moving their belongings from S.T.A.R. Labs to the new LuthorCorp facility, Mayer, who had never so much as jaywalked in his life, stole it. It was an impulsive action, almost accidental, and after Mayer realized he had the spectrograph, he hid it underneath the filter in his air conditioner and lost several nights' worth of sleep imagining what might happen to him if his theft were to be discovered. He figured he'd just tell them he hadn't realized he'd taken it, which was nearly true. What made it untrue was how much he wanted it. Mayer coveted the spectrograph, needed it. As far as he was concerned, it was an actual photograph of an actual spaceship; the most intriguing, terrifying thing he'd ever seen. He loved it the way he loved horror films; it made his pulse quicken and his hair stand on end, sent adrenaline shooting through his body and left him feeling strangely alive. A spaceship had fallen to Earth in the midst of the Lowell County meteor storm.

Maybe somewhere in Kansas an alien was moving freely among the populace.

Admittedly, this last assertion was a bit of a leap, but

Mayer was so attached to the scenario, it was difficult for him to imagine any others.

"Lowell County is teeming with inexplicable happenings!" he told Tad one day, talking enthusiastically as he worked on design specs. "You know Smallville? That little town right on the county border? Someone should subpoena a file on the patients who come in and out of their medical center! Or the local high school newspaper, the *Torch*? Pick an article, *any* article! Mysterious illnesses? Birth defects? That's nothing! There's a story in there about a boy who started mirroring the biology of an insect, complete with molting and matricide! People actually saw this, there are witnesses on record! And that's just one example. There have also been verified reports of fire-starters and ice-makers and a shapeshifter so powerful she was able to frame another Smallville citizen for a bank robbery! Or how about that alien parasite that made it all the way back to S.T.A.R. Labs after infecting at least one Smallville citizen? They still *have* that in Metropolis, we could go *see* that!"

"Town's a freak show, all right," Tad agreed distractedly, peering over Mayer's shoulder at the design specs. "But how do you get from there to an alien infestation?"

"The ship!" Mayer shouted, nearly knocking over a can of soda in his excitement. Tad reached down quickly to right it before it could spill all over Mayer's design, his jaw locked. "We know that those meteors fell there. And we know now that there was an alien spacecraft of some kind among them—"

"A spacecraft too small to hold a humanoid," Tad interrupted.

Mayer nodded. "A full-grown humanoid, anyway. Yes, I've thought about that. I don't think the alien *is* a

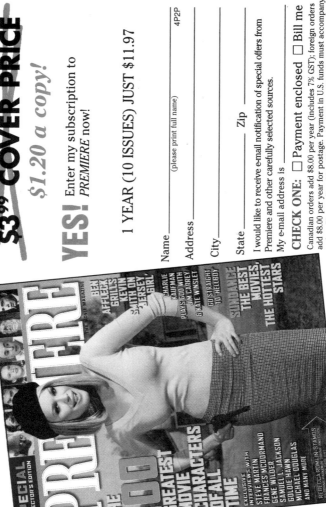

$3⁹⁹ COVER PRICE

$1.20 a copy!

YES! Enter my subscription to *PREMIERE* now!

1 YEAR (10 ISSUES) JUST $11.97

4P2P

Name _____
(please print full name)

Address _____

City _____

State _____ Zip _____

I would like to receive e-mail notification of special offers from Premiere and other carefully selected sources.

My e-mail address is _____

CHECK ONE: ☐ Payment enclosed ☐ Bill me

Canadian orders add $8.00 per year (includes 7% GST); foreign orders add $8.00 per year for postage. Payment in U.S. funds must accompany order. Please allow 30 to 60 days for delivery of first issue.

Visit our website at
www.premiere.com

BUSINESS REPLY MAIL

FIRST-CLASS MAIL   PERMIT NO. 1257   BOULDER CO

POSTAGE WILL BE PAID BY ADDRESSEE

PREMIERE®

PO BOX 55389
BOULDER CO 80323-5389

humanoid—I mean, I don't think it *was*, initially. But that doesn't mean that it can't be *disguised* as one now or, worse yet, parasitically in *control* of one."

"Okay, now you're getting pretty out there." Tad sighed. "We don't even know if this spacecraft was manned. Or aliened, or whatever. Maybe it was just some kind of satellite."

Mayer stopped what he was doing and turned to glare at Tad. He spoke slowly, as if addressing an imbecile. "That wouldn't explain all the weird things that happen in that town."

Tad grabbed Mayer's shoulders and forcibly turned him back to face his work. "Fine. I'm not saying there's nothing going on there, Mayer, I'm just saying it's none of our business."

"It's completely our business! It's the quintessence of our business! How is an extraterrestrial on Earth none of our business?"

"There's no extraterrestrial! It's probably just that LexCorp fertilizer plant wreaking havoc with the environment."

"Come on, you can't believe that. Fertilizer?"

"God dammit, Mayer!" Tad had erupted. "Are you trying to get me killed?"

When Mayer only blinked, taken aback by the sudden virulence, Tad's expression had softened and his tone had taken on an imploring quality. For the first time since they had begun working in the small lab, Mayer noticed that his old friend was sporting dark circles under his eyes. "Mayer, please, I'm begging you, just finish the prototype. That's all I need you to do."

Mayer had continued to stare hard at Tad. "What do you mean, killed?"

Tad turned away, his shoulders slumped.

"Nothing. Just finish. I can't do this without you."

The truth was that Tad couldn't do it all. He was wholly dependent on Mayer to build the machine. When Mayer finally did finish, he was confronted with the third major change in his life since meeting Lionel Luthor. Apparently, while he was working, he had somehow become associated with Japanese gangsters.

"Is this some kind of a joke? Please tell me you're not serious, Tad."

"No joke, Mayer. We needed money, so I borrowed some."

"From the *Yakuza*?"

"Don't worry, we're totally covered. I got the number from Lionel Luthor. I mean, he was on the phone once while I was in his office in Metropolis updating him on our progress. Anyway, he was talking to someone about money, a *lot* of money. But halfway through the conversation, he accidentally dropped the Rolodex card with the phone number on the floor, and I picked it up. I don't think he noticed."

"That doesn't make any sense." Mayer had frowned. "Why would Lionel Luthor be using Rolodex cards? Doesn't he have a secretary to place calls for him? Or at least a Palm Pilot?"

Tad had looked annoyed. "No, no, these guys love having their secret little connection files. Maybe he still pulls the cards before he makes a call out of habit. What do you think, he pulled it out and dropped it just so I would pick it up? You're totally paranoid, Mayer. Anyway, I called the number later that night and set up a deal. But here's the brilliant part—I pretended to be brokering it for LuthorCorp! Get it? Technically, *Luthor-Corp* owes the Yakuza money, not us."

Mayer had not found this distinction comforting, especially not after Lex Luthor came by their lab, scooped up the prototype plans on behalf of Lionel, and handed Tad a check.

"Is that enough to pay back the Yakuza?" Mayer blurted out nervously before Lex had left the lab.

Lionel's son turned around with a raised eyebrow and a slight smile of amusement. "You must be the one who wants to be a secret agent," he commented, looking Mayer up and down keenly.

Tad shot Mayer a furious look and turned apologetically to Lex. "We just . . . borrowed a little, to finish the prototype. It won't effect LuthorCorp at all."

"I'm sure it won't," Lex smiled coolly. "My father is nothing if not a master of plausible deniability."

Mayer's eyes widened, but Tad shook his head, frowning.

"No, no—that doesn't have anything to do with this. It was my idea. It's—really, it's nothing."

"You just keep telling yourself that," Lex replied lightly, once again turning to leave. He wore a pronounced smirk on his face, and Mayer knew that the young scion was laughing at them. "Good luck with your field missions!" Lex called cheerfully to Mayer before letting himself out.

Mayer decided that very moment that he hated the Luthors, hated the Yakuza, and was beginning to hate Tad.

"I want to be like him when I grow up," Tad remarked appreciatively after the door had closed behind Lex.

"He's younger than you are," Mayer mumbled darkly.

"And he doesn't have any hair, so you wouldn't be able to get those prehaircut aromatic scalp massages you love so much."

Tad smiled, turning away from Mayer to sign the back of the check. "Believe me, if that guy wants a scalp massage, he's got no shortage of options. Sorry about the field agent joke, though. I might have mentioned something to him about your future career aspirations. I was just, you know, trying to get in good with him."

"By making fun of me?" Mayer muttered nearly inaudibly.

Tad either did not hear the remark or chose to ignore it. "How fast can you get me the new prototype?" he asked.

Mayer glared at the back of Tad's neatly coifed head. "I'll start on it right after I get back from Smallville."

Tad turned to face him, alarmed. "Wait, what? Smallville's gonna have to wait, buddy. We have monthly benchmarks to hit for LuthorCorp, and if we don't make them, we don't get funded. And if you must know, this is not," he concluded, waving the check at Mayer, "enough to pay back the Yakuza."

"Tad," Mayer continued, trying to force a smile, "let me go to Smallville. Imagine if I find the world's first resident extraterrestrial—imagine how much money you could make then!"

Tad took a deep breath, as if controlling his temper. The look in his eyes was flat-out insulting. "Mayer," he said through clenched teeth, "I'm only gonna say this once, but I want you to really listen, okay? First of all, you're wrong about the alien. It's a stupid theory, and the more you talk about it, the stupider you sound. I will bet my *life* that you're dead wrong, and frankly, that you'd believe something so dumb makes me call into question everything else you've ever hypothesized. Secondly, take a look at yourself, will you, man? You're an engineer, okay? An inventor at best. In no way, in no one's eyes, and in no universe are you a goddamned field agent. Got it? No alien, no field agent. End of story. *Finito*. Move on."

Tad's words got tangled in Mayer's brain like fly tape. He heard them echoing in his skull when he tried to sleep at night and they roused him from bed in the morning. He brushed his teeth to the rhythm of "no alien, no field agent." When he bicycled back and forth to the lab, the wheels seemed to rotate in time to "in no way, in no one's eyes, in no universe . . ." Tad's speech was like a ringing in Mayer's ears that just wouldn't go away. Mayer couldn't take it in.

He understood that he was a good engineer, but he was puzzled as to why he was supposed to be able to see that he was not a field agent. Stumped, he turned his attention from the second prototype—which, after having completed the first one, he had no great interest in building anyway—to a study of quantifiably observable differences between field agents and engineers. The truth was, if you put Mayer's old S.T.A.R. Labs research partners next to the only field agent Mayer had befriended during his time there, you'd get a Central Casting portrait of nebbish brain versus dim-but-affable brawn. But not all field agents were as burly as the one Mayer had gotten to know, and certainly, Mayer didn't think of himself as being as overly scrawny or nerdlike as his former lab partners.

One night at home, Mayer stripped to his underwear and stood in front of the full-length mirror hanging on his bathroom door. He was a little skinny, but there was a wiry strength in his arms, his stomach was tight, and his calves and thighs were muscular from bicycling to the lab every day. At thirty-nine, he still had a full head of hair, thick if an uninteresting brown, and although he did wear glasses, which almost seemed like a prerequisite for engineers in the lab, he had no objections to switching to contacts. He even had a scar on his chin from a bicycle accident four years earlier. Was it possible that it lent him an air of danger, or at least inscrutability?

Mayer stared into his own green eyes and wondered what made some men heroes and others punch lines. His jaw was reasonably square, his shoulders pronounced if not truly "broad," and his posture had always been excellent. Why couldn't he do fieldwork? His took off his glasses and looked at himself again.

All of us, he thought, *are more than we seem to be.*

The next day he saw an optometrist on his lunch break, and a week later he started wearing contact lenses. He moved all of his Smallville files, including the spectrograph, from their hiding place in his apartment's air conditioner into an expandable pocket envelope in his backpack. Then he went to tell Tad that he was going on vacation.

He found his former friend at their desolate little laboratory, sitting with his chin in his hands, staring at the wall. He was unshaven and looked as if he hadn't slept in weeks. Even his suit was wrinkled.

Mayer cleared his throat. "Tad, I—I'm going on a little trip. I'm afraid I can't say for sure when I'll be back, but I'll keep in touch." Mayer paused for a minute, then added, "okay?"

Tad didn't turn to face him, and his voice was a low monotone. "Off to Smallville, are you?"

Mayer hesitated for another second and nodded. "Yes. I'll take unpaid leave, of course."

"Sure," Tad said quietly.

Mayer turned to go, then turned back with a frown. "Are you all right?" he asked a bit impatiently.

"Oh, yeah," Tad answered, a quaver of sarcasm heating up his tone. "I'm just great. Thanks to you and your secret agent fixation, we lost all hope of LuthorCorp funding this week and—oh, get this—all the rights for everything we've developed here automatically revert back to them. That leaves us with, you know, *nothing*. Except an unpaid debt to the Yakuza, of course."

"I thought the debt was in LuthorCorp's name," Mayer offered with a frown. He was trying to be reassuring, but his thoughts were spiteful. *Sleep with the dogs, Tad . . .*

"It is," Tad nodded, still staring at the wall. "It's just that—well, I'm their contact."

Mayer scratched his chin and wished Tad good luck, pretty sure he meant it, before walking out the door.

Now he was sitting in Annora Washburn's pleasantly warm kitchen, eating creamed corn and drinking freshly brewed coffee, the telltale spectrograph on the table beside him. Tad and the Yakuza and the Luthors were far away, and Mayer was a reinvented man.

Yes, he'd been born today. Starting today, finding that extraterrestrial meant more to Mayer than just his professional reputation, his career, or even the chance to make Tad eat his words about field agent work. Starting today, Mayer was a new man, with a new mission, in a new world. Here, in Kansas, he was a field agent. And here, in Kansas, an extraterrestrial was hiding.

Starting today, Mayer thought with a slight smile, *Smallville's alien had better start looking over its shoulder.*

CHAPTER TWO

Clark Kent was seeing stars. Staring out his classroom window at the cloudless blue sky, Clark realized he was unable to reach the boundaries of his own vision. The universe stretched out endlessly beyond the sun-tinted Kansas stratosphere, obscured by refracting light but not truly hidden. Out there, pulsating in the farthest depths of the blue, were thousands of burning orbs, gaseous and strangely beautiful. Was it the clarity of the day that allowed him to see so far, or was it . . . the other thing?

Sometimes, the hardest part for Clark was figuring out what was normal for everyone else. He'd heard the story a hundred times, for example, about lifting his dad's tractor over his head when he was still a toddler, but he doubted that he'd been intentionally showing off. How was a five-year-old supposed to know the expected limits of his own strength? Clark had read an article on-line not so long ago about a six-year-old Korean boy lifting a car off his trapped father, and his heart had leaped with joy. The things he could do—maybe Clark wasn't the only one!

Of course, that was before he knew the truth.

He'd known by the time he woke up from a flying dream to find himself hovering inches above his bed, muddled and prone. Almost as shocking as effortlessly negating gravity was learning that nearly everyone dreamed about flying. How could his thoughts and dreams be so human while his abilities were so . . . alien?

Things that were completely natural for him, like running faster than the speed of sound or lifting tractors over his head, were obviously beyond the scope of his friends and family. They also couldn't see through walls, or shoot heat beams from their eyes. Once he knew the truth about how the Kents had found him, Clark realized the uniqueness of his situation. He couldn't stop hoping, though, that he might someday meet someone else who could do the things he could do, or, better yet, wake up one morning normal. The idea of being the only presence on the planet capable of such feats was too frightening, too lonely. But maybe he should be used to it. After all, he was, as far as he knew, the only being on the planet hiding a spacecraft in the storm cellar of his father's farm.

"This is how you came into our world, son," his father, Jonathan, had explained with undisguised awe. It was the first time he had shown the ship to Clark, the first time he had even mentioned it. "It was the day of the meteor shower."

Moments earlier, during an argument, Clark had angrily stuck his hand in a running thresher and pulled it out unscathed. Apparently that had been enough to make Jonathan decide that it was time to let his son in on the true nature of his adoption.

"This is a joke, right?" Clark had stammered, wild-eyed, backing away from the dark metal craft. When he spoke again, his voice was pitched somewhere between an anguished scream and a roar. "Why didn't you tell me about this before?"

"We wanted to protect you," Jonathan had answered quietly.

"Protect me from what? You should have told me!"

Clark had raced out of the barn, disoriented, furious . . . and terrified. Every teenager in Lowell County woke up sometimes feeling misunderstood and freakishly awkward. Clark knew that. He'd spent a lot of time talking with his best friend Pete about the insurgent mutations of adolescence. Aside from being part of one of the only black families in Smallville, athletic and agreeable Pete Ross was about as normal as they came. Together, Pete and Clark had both survived the voice-cracking and spontaneous bodily hair growth, and they were both still plagued by the mysterious oils that seeped from their skin and the growth spurts that periodically rendered half their accumulated wardrobes useless. Pete said that there were mornings when he felt so physically uncoordinated he wanted to hide in his room until he was twenty, or days when the thoughts in his head were so unfamiliar to him that he felt sure they would seem outlandish and incomprehensible to his peers if he shared them.

But now Pete knew Clark's secret—he was the only one in the world besides Clark's parents who did—and he no longer complained to Clark about feeling different. Pete just sometimes *felt* like he was an alien, completely alone in the universe.

Clark really was.

But it was a beautiful day, the last class before fall break, and Clark didn't want to think about any of that. He wanted to think about the sky and the sun and the way the light brought out an almost endless kaleidoscopic of colors in Lana Lang's dark hair. Lana sat two seats in front of Clark, but that didn't stop him from being sure that he could smell the faint scent of gardenia left over from her shampoo or the warm, gentle musk of her glowing skin. Lana made Clark want to be a certified Earthling with every nerve in his body. She was the most beautiful creature he had ever seen, with long, shimmering hair, luminous brown eyes, audacious, curling eyelashes, and hands so soft he thought he could be happy just holding one of them for the rest of his life.

In fact, it had been Lana who helped calm him that terrible night after he'd first seen the spacecraft. He'd run into her in the woods that ran behind both of their families' properties, in an intimate little graveyard surrounded by elms and elderberries. She was there to visit the grave of her parents, full of smiles and youthful vitality, but also throbbing with unspoken grief. They'd knelt by the headstone together, pretending to converse with the Langs, and Clark had managed to make Lana smile. Helping her, he'd completely forgotten about his own torment. She'd even kissed him on the cheek after he walked her home, and that had been enough to make Clark believe that a man could fly.

But what would Lana think if she knew her blue-eyed farm boy admirer was really an alien from an unknown planet, brimming with powers and loneliness she could never hope to fathom? Clark wanted with all his heart to believe that she could accept him unconditionally, as he truly was, but Lana had suffered a great deal of tragedy and abandonment in her life, and her relationship with Clark was complicated. She seemed to be the most open with him when he was in the role of a dependable, predictable friend, and so he tried to be that for her. Not that it was difficult being her friend. Lana was one of the kindest, most interesting people that Clark knew. The problem was how much it hurt not to trust himself with trying to be anything more than that. It figured that the person who could make him feel completely included was also the person who could make him feel the most alone. He longed to hold her in his arms, knowing, as he did, that he could protect her better than anyone else. But could she ever really feel safe with him? Clark was terrified that he would someday become another trauma in Lana's life, another disappointment and reminder to her of how little control she really had over her future or the people in it.

"Psst!"

Clark was abruptly startled from his daydreams by a wadded-up paper ball that came flying at his head from the direction of Chloe Sullivan's desk. Instinctively, he caught it before it hit him, then turned to blink at Chloe.

Chloe was a spunky, animated blonde who had lived in Smallville less than two years, but had quickly become one of Clark's best friends. Pete even harbored a secret crush on her, and Clark understood why. She was editor in chief of Smallville High's student newspaper, the *Torch*, and her short hair, hip clothes, and endless energy made it clear that she was a city girl at heart. Now she was making faces at Clark urgently, trying to direct his attention to the chalkboard in the front of the room.

"Pay attention!" she mouthed to him with exaggerated enunciation. Clark furrowed his brows for a moment in confusion, then turned to look to where Chloe was indicating.

"Smallville High Science Fair," was written in the teacher's neat cursive on the chalkboard, and under that, "This year's topic: Meteorites." After thirty years of amateur experiments involving the farming and shucking of corn, Smallville High had begun to hold theme-based science fairs. Clark blinked at the board for a moment as a chill darted up the back of his neck, then the bell rang. The teacher's friendly wish for her class to have a great fall break was all but drowned out in the cacophony of laughing, shouting, and sliding desk chairs as all the students rose at once.

Clark did as well, Pete already tugging at his sleeve.

"Man, Clark," Pete whispered into his friend's ear, "could they have picked a worse theme?" Pete was referring to the green meteorites that had littered Kansas since the meteor shower of 1989. So far, they were the only objects in existence that had the ability to make Clark sick—deathly sick. Clark had only to get near them before his skin began to crawl painfully, and his veins swell agonizingly with the sickly radiation the rocks gave off. The only thing that seemed to protect Clark from the deadly meteorites was lead. Both Clark and Pete knew that there was no way Clark could walk into a science fair full of green meteorites. He'd never make it out alive.

"Relax, Pete," Clark answered with the soft, enigmatic smile that punctuated most of his better moods. "There are other rocks I can study."

"Yeah, but—"

Pete's warning was interrupted by Chloe, who was suddenly standing next to Clark with her backpack slung over one shoulder and several books pressed to her chest. If Clark's smile had a tendency to be a bit on the mysterious side, Chloe's was always full-wattage and unambiguous. Pete stopped dead in the middle of his sentence, and Clark realized he wasn't sure if it was because Pete was protecting Clark's secret or because the sheer vitality of Chloe's grin had rendered his friend speechless.

"Meteorites, guys! How excellent is that?" she beamed. "Maybe I can use the science fair to prove once and for all that the Smallville siderites are no ordinary space rocks."

Chloe had a theory that the bizarre events that constantly plagued Smallville were the direct result of meteorite poisoning. Clark had come to realize she was absolutely right, but had to be careful not to appear to know too much about the glowing green stones. There was no question in his mind that Chloe was smart enough to uncover his secret if he wasn't careful.

"Everyone's going to be using those, Chloe," Clark responded with forced calm. "I want to check out those achondrites they recently discovered near Metropolis. I think they're on display at the Museum of Natural History."

"God, Clark, that's so like you," Chloe replied, shaking her head. "There's this major Pandora's box right in your backyard, but *you* want to go combing the country for empty crates."

"Yeah, well I *did* pay attention in mythology, Chloe," Clark laughed. "And how much like *you* is it to want to *open* Pandora's box?"

"Actually, it was a bottle," Chloe mused, turning toward the school library as the two boys rushed to keep up with her.

"What was a bottle?" asked Pete.

"Pandora's box. It was a bottle."

"Get out!"

"No, really. Tell him, Clark. Better yet, Pete, I'll show you."

"Oh, in one of those book things you like to stare at?" Pete joked. "Yeah, I've heard about those."

"Philistine!" Chloe huffed playfully.

Pete turned his attention to Clark. "How much you

wanna bet Chloe's already read every book in the school library?"

Clark smiled and continued following his friends. He didn't know about Chloe, but he had, himself, read every book in the county.

CHAPTER THREE

"Believe me, I could make it worth your while."

Lex Luthor smiled indolently as he paced in front of his jet-black Porsche 911 compact convertible, speaking into his cell phone. His black leather duster was too warm for the bright Kansas sun, and his bald head was far more urbane than the styles usually seen in Smallville, but Lex was the kind of young man who always looked perfectly at ease in his surroundings. Even the dust on his expensive Italian shoes lent him an air of rustic authenticity, whereas everyone else's shoes just looked dirty.

He squinted up at the LexCorp sign to his right, which clarified that the building he was parked in front of was Fertilizer Plant No. 3. It still seemed bizarre to him that in his ongoing efforts to undermine his father he had now managed to diversify into fertilizer production—bizarre and amusingly fitting.

"Why don't you just come see me in the city?" the female voice on the other end of the connection pleaded. Nearly six months ago, Lex had punched her name into his autodial as "Lorilyn," but she had answered as "Lorelei," and half of him couldn't wait for the call to be over so that he could correct the entry. Lex was generally meticulous and accurate, his personal religion being one of graceful triumph over predicted failure. Had she changed her name since the last time he'd seen her, or had he been so drunk when he made the entry that he had misspelled or even misheard it? "I'd never live it down if I told my friends I was going to *Smallville* for the weekend."

Like most people in Metropolis, Lorelei infused the word "Smallville" with so much disdain and aversion, it was a wonder that the little Kansas town hadn't been struck from the atlas maps.

"Come on," Lex urged, and to his credit he could hear Lorelei swallow. Apparently he still inspired longing in her—good. "Fresh country air, a night sky full of stars . . ." Lex strained for a second to think of another one of Smallville's virtues. ". . . Roads almost wholly devoid of traffic," he finally added, good-natured enough to chuckle softly at his own inability to come up with good points where the quiet life was concerned. "Besides, I practically own this town. The possibilities are endless."

"But there's nothing to *do* there, Lex," Lorelei countered.

"What do you mean?" Lex argued lightly. "You can do me."

Lorelei would have hung up on most men after being the recipient of such a self-satisfied *bon mot*, but Lex Luthor, besides being fabulously wealthy and a genuinely enjoyable date, had something about him—in him—that made him strangely irresistible. Lorelei was never sure if it was the world-savvy confidence of his businessman persona or the wounded, lonely boy hidden just beneath the surface of his nearly limitless poise. Most likely, it was the combination. All she knew for sure was that the overall effect was devastating.

Lex listened to the drawn-out pause on the other end of the line and wondered what Lorelei was thinking. It was always a risk to call up anyone from his past. When Lorelei had known Lex in Metropolis—before his father had sent him to oversee ambiguous business ventures in sleepy, Podunk, Kansas—Lex had lived with a dangerous air of abandon. He had wasted time and money, sought after diversion and pleasure with such fierce intensity that she and many others who knew him then seemed to expect he would go out in a blaze of glory. The gang had depended on him to ignite the mundane repetition of their nights with a flash of his wallet or his laughing green eyes, and Lex shuddered to think what they kept themselves busy with in his absence.

"Look," Lorelei said finally, "as pleased as I am to hear from you after all this time, I really just can't see myself in Smallville, even for forty-eight hours. But the next time you're in the city, I'll clear my calendar for you for as long as you stay."

Lex pressed his lips together and nodded in resignation. "All right, Lorelei. You know how to reach me if you change your mind."

He terminated the call and lowered the phone from his ear with a frown, preparing to edit Lorelei's name in the LCD display. The truth was, no one had been more anti-Smallville than Lex himself when Lionel had first sent him here. His only childhood memory of the place was standing in a cornfield at the age of nine, staring up, aghast, at a bare-chested human scarecrow who was pleading with him to be let down mere seconds before a meteorite hurled through the air toward them both. Nine-year-old Lex had run for his life and had always assumed that the scarecrow teen had been incinerated. He discovered years later that some poor freshman was strung up in the fields by Smallville football jocks every October before Homecoming. It was a tradition, a prank—no one had ever died before. But then, the cornfields had never been blasted flat, and never before in the history of Kansas had fiery rocks hurling out of the sky destroyed vehicles and careened through buildings on Main Street.

People all over Smallville lost their lives that day, but Lex had lost only his hair and his previously chronic asthma. There were even a few minutes in the field when, fearing for his son's life, Lionel had called out for Lex with something approximating paternal concern. Lex remembered vividly the moment he heard his father's shoes crunching toward him over the flattened cornstalks. He was on the ground, twitching uncontrollably, unable to speak. Though he hadn't yet seen it, he could feel that his hair was gone. He was sure his father would lift him and carry him out of the ruined cornfield to safety, and waited for the warmth of his touch with what felt like life-threatening need. But Lionel did not carry him, did not lift him, did not even touch him. He called in an emergency chopper and all the best doctors, but not once during the whole ordeal did he touch his son.

In the greater scheme of Lex's existence, it was a powerful memory; one of two times when fate, which he normally didn't believe in, seemed to have singled him out and afforded him extraordinary protection, as if saving him for some greater destiny. Even so, it wasn't the kind of recollection that had made him ever want to go back to Smallville, much less move into some weird castle his father had built there out of rocks shipped over from the ancestral Luthor home in Scotland. And yet, at twenty-three, that was exactly where he'd found himself, organizing to buy out Lionel and run his own farming loans and fertilizer plants.

His first few weeks in Smallville, Lex hadn't been able to sleep. The quiet was unnerving—he could scream at the top of his lungs in his bedroom and not be heard by any of the staff downstairs. The nearest neighbor was over three miles away, and the only means of transportation that ever ventured onto the road in front of his property were horses and the occasional back-road-happy flatbed.

It had taken him less than two months to scope out the entire available female population of the town, and his only real joy had been speeding up and down the winding back roads in his light blue '86 Porsche 911. That had led to fate's second intervention on his behalf, this time in the form of a fifteen-year-old boy.

Lex had been approaching what he later knew to be called Old Mill Bridge. He'd seen the truck in the south lane but had become distracted by his ringing cell phone, which he'd fished out of his coat pocket. There was no question that his driving skills were good enough to keep him on his side of the double yellow line even with his eyes off the road, but he did fail to notice the bale of barbed wire that had fallen off the back of the passing truck until it had already rolled into his path. Lex had immediately dropped his cell phone and slammed on the brakes, but nothing he did at that point could prevent the wire from shredding his front tires as he skidded into it. He had been as frightened as he had ever been—as frightened, certainly, as when the meteor had come hurling down toward him in the Kansas cornfield thirteen years earlier—but as his tires blew out and the Porsche veered sharply toward the bridge's guardrail, Lex had tasted a fear he wasn't sure he could survive. It was one thing to die in a horrible car accident by falling off a bridge.

It was quite another to take someone with you.

There had been a boy there, a teenager—just standing in front of the railing, staring in horror as Lex's Porsche flew toward him. For one awful, endless second, the two young men's eyes had locked. Even hurtling toward him at over sixty miles per hour, Lex could tell that the kid was handsome, healthy, and bright—and directly in the path of his car. *Oh, don't let me kill him*, Lex thought, as panic had sent icy tendrils from his stomach down through his groin. When the Porsche made impact, Lex had seen one last flash of the teenager's jet-black hair and vivid blue eyes before everything had gone dark.

Lex had felt as though he were rising out of the watery depths and had opened his eyes to find himself soaring—wingless but unfettered by gravity—through the tender blue sky over the town. He had felt imbued with the heat of the sun; more free and alive than ever before. *So man can fly*, he had thought joyously to himself, then suddenly looked down to see his own body lying on the bank by the river, his head resting on a rock, the teenager kneeling over him, wet but unharmed.

Impossible.

The sensation of heat left Lex's body, and he had felt himself falling—falling back into the soft blackness of unconsciousness. Awareness seeped in slowly this time, painfully. It felt like someone was rhythmically dropping rocks on his chest, over and over again until Lex felt his own heart begin to shove back in angry protest. He thought he heard a voice, pleading with him from a great distance away. "Come on," it urged, "don't die on me!" He came to all but vomiting water, coughing, sputtering, and freezing cold. And completely confused.

He wasn't dead? He wasn't flying? Oh, man—what had happened to the . . .

. . . kid?

"I could have sworn I'd hit you," Lex had said with wonder as he blinked up at the visage hovering above him. As in the vision he'd had while unconscious, the teenager crouched by his side, soaking wet but completely unhurt.

"Well," the boy replied, his own voice a little shaky, "if you did, I'd be . . . I'd be dead."

Lex followed the boy's gaze as he had turned back to look up at the bridge. The guardrail was wrecked, punched open and mangled, and Lex could only assume that his car was at the bottom of the river.

The boy had shivered and sat down abruptly, his lips parting in some private flash of realization. Lex had forced himself up into a sitting position next to him and tried to keep his teeth from chattering.

"Are you okay?" he had asked the teenager. Instinctively, Lex reached for his cell phone, then remembered that it, too, was probably testing the limits of its manufacturer's boasts of a "waterproof" design. He'd wanted to call 911—not for himself, but for his young savior. Though it made absolutely no sense that the kid was okay, Lex wouldn't have been able to stomach finding out that his new friend had, in fact, sustained injuries.

"Yeah," the boy answered, his blue eyes wide and unfocused. Then he'd swallowed. "Yeah, I'm fine."

Indeed, there wasn't a scratch on him. He looked a little freaked-out, but was otherwise the very picture of unqualified health.

And thanks to him, Lex, too, had been largely unharmed. He had had mild hypothermia and a few nasty bruises, but had been back on his feet and walking around scant moments after the accident.

The kid's name turned out to be Clark Kent, and he remained a source of great pleasure and mystery in Lex's life. Lex had developed a kind of bilateral thinking where Clark was concerned. On one hand he admired the teenager greatly, and had come to think of him warmly as the little brother he never had. Clark had saved his life, and Lex felt, with no sense of resentment, that he owed the teenager a boon. He was frequently tempted to spoil the modest farm boy with lavish gifts (almost always returned) and unusual opportunities (rarely taken advantage of), and even tried to build Clark up in the eyes of the lovesick teenager's crush object, the beautiful and charming Lana Lang. Lex genuinely enjoyed talking to him, finding Clark one of the few people in the world who could actually keep up with his own hyperactive intellect, and did everything he could to be a real friend to the young man.

On the other hand, Clark was a mystery, and in Lex's life, all great mysteries demanded solving. To this end, feeling no guilt and no less affection toward the fifteen-year-old, Lex believed himself entitled to study Clark like a specimen. He tried to befriend Clark's family and friends, managing a reasonable degree of success with Martha Kent and Lana. Pete Ross and Chloe Sullivan were more difficult, as they seemed resentful about the amount of time Clark had begun to spend with Lex, and Lex's relationship with Clark's father, Jonathan, who hated all things Luthor, was a total washout. Lex collected facts and rumors, compulsively tracked the teen's involvement in all the weird Smallville goings-on, and obsessively reviewed the accident that had first brought them together, convinced there was something much greater than luck at play. Strange, inexplicable things happened when Clark was around, and Lex was determined to get to the bottom of it all. Clark was unlike the unlucky victims of the freakish mutations that seemed to plague Smallville's youth. Lex felt sure the boy was made from different stuff altogether. Over time, he'd come to understand less than he hoped to, and more than he ever let on. Clark Kent was Lex Luthor's hobby.

Lex was pulled away from his ruminations by a tinny version of *The 1812 Overture*, sung to him by his cell phone. He glanced down at the LCD only to find the incoming call's number blocked.

"Hi, Dad," Lex answered with a sigh. Lionel Luthor was almost always the last person Lex wanted to talk to, but he felt argumentative and curious enough to field this particular call.

"Son," Lionel cooed silkily from whichever pit of corporate hell he was occupying at that moment. He didn't comment on Lex's ability to guess his identity despite his efforts to impede such detection. "I need you in Metropolis. I've booked you on the five-fifteen commuter, but I can have that canceled if you'd rather take the jet."

"Fine, thanks, how are you?" Lex answered, frowning as he kicked a small stone away from the tire of his car. On the other end of the phone, Lionel's voice hardened.

"Lex, you know I don't have time for tedious civilities. You've got a meeting first thing Monday morning at LuthorCorp, and another one on Tuesday. I thought you'd be pleased that I'm trusting you to fill in for me."

"I'm thrilled beyond measure, Dad."

"You'll use the penthouse, of course, and I'll have a full itinerary faxed there."

"Actually, I hate to break it to you, but I've got other plans." Lex glanced at the fertilizer plant behind him and tried not to notice the knot that always formed in his stomach when he heard his father's voice. Lionel's idea of helpful parenting was to shove Lex's face in humiliation and inadequacy as frequently as possible, and Lex had long ago learned to be on a personal DEFCON 5 whenever Lionel asked something of him.

"What, watching the corn grow? Son, I'm counting on you. Think of it as another chance to prove to me that you've turned your life around."

Lionel had given Lex about nine hundred of these "chances" to prove that he had grown out of the self-destructive phase that marked his younger days in the big city, none of them sincere. Nothing Lex did was ever good enough for Lionel, and the only way Lex knew how to please his father was to lose to him in some insidious little game of corporate espionage. He was about to say as much when Lionel cut in once again.

"You'll do this, won't you, Lex? It won't interrupt anything truly important?"

Lex inhaled sharply, as shocked as if Lionel had just said "I love you," and meant it. His father didn't ask about things like this, he ordered. Despite thinking better of it, Lex felt a sudden twinge of worry.

"You okay, Dad? You sound a little . . . compassionate."

Lionel let out a sigh.

"I've got a lot of balls in the air this week, son. I could really use you here."

Lex swallowed and rubbed the back of his neck as his eyes darted to his car.

"Yeah. Yeah, okay, I'll be there. I think I'm gonna drive, though. I could use a little road trip."

"As long as you're at that meeting Monday morning."

"What's it about?" Lex asked, getting back into his car. Lionel scoffed on the other end of the line.

"Money," he answered, as if this were so obvious as to be beneath comment.

"Right." Lex nodded, turning the keys in the ignition. His Porsche purred to life, teasing another smile out of him. "And you want me to give some of it away, or lose some of it, or—?"

"I'm glad your sense of humor is still sharp, Lex. You can use that in the boardroom."

Lex shifted his car into gear and sped away from the fertilizer plant.

"What do *you* use?" he quipped, but the line had already gone dead. Lex's presence assured, Lionel apparently felt no need to continue the conversation. Lex shook his head and tossed the phone onto the passenger seat. Watching the road unwind before him at over 70 MPH, Lex acknowledged to himself that Smallville really wasn't all that bad.

At least it was way the hell away from Lionel.

CHAPTER FOUR

Mayer woke up suffocating in sunshine. The white organdy drapes fluttering against the guest room windows did nothing to block out the light, and the minute Mayer opened his eyes, they were assaulted by a cheerful insurgence of lemon yellow gingham quilting and baby pink candy-striped wallpaper. On the wall to the left of the bed, the photograph of the white kitten rising demonically from a green watering can still assaulted him, and outside Mayer's window, an unfamiliar cacophony of insects hummed and buzzed in eerie unison. The only thing familiar in the whole room was the smell of coffee, drifting in from downstairs. Mayer sat up with a smile, freed from the monotonous predictability of his former life in Gotham.

Good morning, Kansas.

He put his feet down on the wooden floorboards, ignoring the fuzzy white slippers Annora had thoughtfully left sitting at the end of the bed, and rose with a lazy stretch. Locating a fluffy lilac robe in the oak armoire, Mayer padded down the hall to the communal bathroom, carefully locking the door behind him. He wasn't sure if there were any other guests at the bed-and-breakfast, but wasn't taking chances. He took his time getting ready, then padded quietly back to his room to dress. By the time he sauntered downstairs, entering a number into his cell phone, Annora's kitchen was filled with the enticing scent of flour and cooking oil. Annora herself stood over a large, cast-iron Dutch oven, scooping out rounded cakes with a spatula. She looked up at him with a smile.

"Oh, we don't get cell reception up here, hon. You'll have to go into town."

Mayer blinked at her for a second—was she making *donuts*, in her *kitchen*? Who did that anymore? And what did she mean by no cell reception? Wasn't this her *house*? He caught himself and grinned. *Right. Smallville.* Homemade donuts it was, then he'd stroll into town. Suddenly, he couldn't think of a more perfect morning.

He flipped his phone closed and slid it into the front pocket of his pants.

"Help yourself to some coffee," she encouraged. He noticed the mug he'd used the day before set out near the coffeemaker and helped himself. "So, what does a star-obsessed field agent do with his Saturdays?"

"I'm . . . collecting data," Mayer answered, taking a seat at the kitchen table.

"It's a small town," Annora said, placing a plate of steaming-hot, fresh donuts before him. "Is there anything in particular you're looking for?"

Mayer took a sip of coffee, fearing that the donuts were still too hot to pick up.

"Actually," he answered, twisting around in his seat to smile up at his host, "is there a place in town where young people tend to hang out?"

"Sure," Annora smiled. "That'd be the Talon. It's a coffeehouse right on Main Street. You can't miss it."

"Super." Mayer nodded, turning back around and risking one of the donuts. It was indeed hot to the touch, but it practically melted in his mouth and was well worth the red fingertips.

Four donuts and three cups of coffee later, Mayer headed out to his car, having decided against walking into town after all. There were some things self-respecting Gothamites just didn't do, no matter how nice the weather.

The drive was short and pleasant, and the woods that lined the road surprised Mayer. He'd always assumed Kansas was nothing but farmland and fields, but the surrounding landscape was also full of trees and meadows.

Downtown, parking didn't look to be a problem, and Mayer was steering his forest green rental into a spot just around the corner from the Talon when he was startled by the sound of something falling against the side of his car. He looked up and was shocked to see Tad Nickels pressing his open palms against the passenger-side window.

"Mayer?" came Tad's muffled voice. Mayer hesitated for a second, then rolled down the window. "Mayer, man, I've been looking for you everywhere!"

Without the slightest sign of reservation, Tad reached through the opened window to unlock the passenger door and climbed into Mayer's car. "Go!" he commanded, slamming the door shut behind him.

"Where?"

"*Anywhere*, just go!"

Mayer pulled out of the parking space and continued north up Main Street as Tad twisted in his seat to peer nervously out the back window. "That's good," Tad murmured. "Nice and slow. We don't want to attract any attention."

Mayer frowned in confusion but continued driving. He was not happy to see Tad, but sensed that his former friend was in trouble. Glancing at his passenger, he noticed that Tad's left-hand pinkie was bandaged and seemed to be bleeding profusely.

"What happened to your hand?" he asked, wondering if the rental car company would charge him extra for bloodstains.

Tad was practically bouncing in his seat, as if severely overcaffeinated. "Just a message, this one was just a message. I screwed up, Mayer. I really screwed up. You've gotta help me."

"What do you want me to do?" Mayer's voice sounded petulant, even to him. Tad was ruining everything. He was far too nervous to be a special agent, and he didn't even believe in the alien. Mayer wanted to get rid of him as quickly as possible.

"You've got to finish that second prototype. There's no other way. But I want you to work from here. I've . . . set some things in motion, and I need you to keep an eye on them."

"What things? What are you *talking* about? Is this about the Yakuza?"

"Yeah, listen. The Yakuza were threatening to go over my head, straight to Luthor, you know? That can't happen. I think I came up with a way to get them their money, but it's risky, and I don't know exactly what they're gonna tell Luthor. If this backfires . . ." Tad stopped speaking and shook his head ominously.

Mayer scowled. "Don't you think Luthor knows by now that you borrowed the money in his name?"

Instead of answering, Tad pulled a handgun out of his jacket pocket and checked to make sure it was loaded. Mayer took one look at the weapon and steered off the road, into a fairly isolated gas station called Denehey's

Pitstop. In addition to gas and diesel pumps, Mayer noted a repair garage and a small convenience store. The moment the car stopped moving, Tad looked up from his gun, alarmed.

"Why'd we stop? Come on, Mayer, keep moving!"

Mayer got out of the car and slammed the door shut behind him. He had no plan; he just wanted to get away from Tad—Tad who had called him stupid, Tad who was carrying a handgun and making business deals with the Yakuza.

As Mayer angrily started to walk away from the car, Tad got out of the passenger seat and called to him desperately.

"Mayer, I can't stay here. I've gotta be as far away from the Luthors as possible!"

Mayer spun around to face Tad, his arms rising in a wide gesticulation of annoyance. "What do you mean? Luthor's in Metropolis."

Tad leaned against the car, resting his arms on the roof. He was still holding the gun, which only served to emphasize his bandaged pinkie. "No, not Lionel. His son, Lex. Remember Lex Luthor? He came by once to drop off our first check. He lives here, in Smallville. Practically runs the whole town. Nothing happens here that he doesn't know about."

Mayer was about to turn his back on Tad again, thinking he'd at least go purchase a cup of coffee or some bottled water, when a shiny black Cadillac with Metropolis plates slowly pulled up to one of the diesel pumps. Mayer was admiring the sheer size of the car when it occurred to him that Cadillacs didn't use diesel. He glanced over at Tad, who was scrambling to get back inside Mayer's rental, and heard one of the Cadillac's automated windows slide down.

Tad called Mayer's name the exact moment a sharp crack rang out across the gas station lot. Mayer was too stunned to move as Tad's body slumped suddenly, half-in and half-out of the rental car. The Cadillac's window slid up again as the shiny black car drove back out to the main road. Mayer stared at the license plate as the car rolled sedately away toward town. It bore only the numbers eight, nine, and three.

By then a mechanic had appeared from somewhere inside the convenience store. He took one look at Tad's lifeless body and ran into the garage, presumably to call for help. Mayer swallowed and forced himself to walk forward toward his rental car. A bright crimson stream of blood flowed from Tad's side, and his warm blue eyes were vacant and fixed.

Mayer's mind was racing. At first he could only hold his breath as his brain ticked off half-formed apprehensions and flooded his bloodstream with adrenaline. *They'll come back and kill me too . . . I'll be blamed for Tad's murder . . . The rental company won't take this car back . . . I'm going to be arrested . . . I'm going to be shot . . . I'm going to throw up . . .*

After several seconds of panicked silence, Mayer exhaled and tried to order his thoughts, only to find them full of Tad's voice: *Yakuza* (" *I think I came up with a way to get them their money, but it's risky . . .*") *Luthor* ("*He practically runs the whole town. Nothing happens here that he doesn't know about . . .*") *Field agent* ("*I will bet my life that you're dead wrong . . .*") *Alien* ("*No alien . . .*") *Field agent* ("*No field agent . . .*")

 . . . gun.

Gun.

Mayer reached down and carefully pried the small automatic out of Tad's unmoving fingers. It was a Smith & Wesson, pleasingly heavy in Mayer's hand. Mayer crouched over Tad's body and stared at the gun, trying to stop shaking. He was sure everything would be all right if only he could untangle his thoughts.

Tad borrowed money from the Yakuza, money he couldn't pay back. Tad bet his life that there wasn't an alien in Smallville. The Yakuza killed Tad in Smallville. There is an alien in Smallville. Lex Luthor knows about everything that happens in Smallville. Lex Luthor knows about the alien. The alien might know about the Yakuza. The Yakuza know about me. There is an alien. I am a field agent. End of story. Finito. *Move on.*

Mayer tucked the gun into the waistband of his pants, stood, and walked around the front of the car, getting in on the driver's side. "End of story. *Finito.* Move on," he said huskily to the windshield. It was the first he'd spoken since the shooting, and he was surprised how hard his own voice sounded in his ears. It was a field agent's voice. Mayer leaned across the passenger seat and pushed Tad's body the rest of the way out of the car before pulling the door shut.

End of story. Finito. *Move on.*

His confidence grew as he started the car. There wasn't very much blood on the interior, just a little speck or two on the passenger-side car mat. He could clean that up. Better yet, he could get rid of the car and rent a new one. Maybe under a different name.

As he drove back onto Main Street, Mayer was beginning to realize that bravery was a matter of self-deception; not convincing yourself that there was nothing to fear, which always backfired, but rather convincing yourself that you weren't the kind of person to be governed by those sorts of emotions.

It doesn't bother me at all that a friend of mine is lying dead in the gas station driveway behind me, Mayer told himself over and over as he drove. *He got himself into trouble, and there's nothing I could have done. He bet his life. He bet his life that I was dead wrong. He's dead wrong. He's dead. Tad's dead. And it doesn't bother me at all. End of story.* Finito. *Move on.*

The Mayer Greenbrae who drove south down Main Street while an ambulance rushed past him heading in the direction of the gas station was not the same Mayer Greenbrae who had driven north. He realized that Tad had been an anchor, dragging him down, attaching him to a life and identity circumstances no longer seemed to support. If Mayer was just an engineer, then why had he watched his friend be gunned down by the Japanese Mafia? According to his own list of statistically identifiable variances between engineers and field agents, that didn't happen to engineers. Besides, Mayer didn't want to be an engineer in a world that included an alien and Kansas gas stations full of Yakuza gunmen. He wanted to be somebody grim, determined, and dangerous. The terror he was forcing down into the deep recesses of his guts began to smolder there, heating and turning into a hitherto untapped capacity for violence. He could feel it growing inside him.

New car. New name. What would a field agent call himself? Mayer frowned as his fingers tightened on the steering wheel. A field agent would never give his name. He was just Agent Somebody. Agent Greenbrae. *Agent Green.*

Agent Green nodded to himself, satisfied. The rest was just a shopping list, a matter of rounding up the equipment he might need. His life was now linear, involving, as it did, the pursuit of one, clear objective. That made him decisive. Mayer Greenbrae might have had a lot of things to worry about, but Agent Green's sole priority was the alien.

Field agent.

Alien.

There were other differences, too.

Unlike Mayer Greenbrae, Agent Green didn't let fear run his life.

Women found him attractive.

He could survive outside the city.

Agent Green leaned back in his seat. With his eyes on the road, he could feel the gun pressing reassuringly into his hip. That was another difference, one Agent Green decided on that very afternoon. Mayer Greenbrae was passive and nonconfrontational.

Agent Green was a killer.

CHAPTER FIVE

"What do you think, Clark, one more?"

"I'm good if you are, Dad!" Clark leaned on his trenching shovel, a mattock swung casually over one shoulder, and grinned at his father. Jonathan Kent was still seated on top of the trencher, squinting down at what was about to become the fifth irrigation line in their second cornfield.

"Martha?" Jonathan called to his wife.

Martha Kent shielded her eyes from the sun with her free hand as she stood two trenches back with a low-pressure hose. Her auburn hair sparkled as she turned toward her husband.

"I've got the easy job." She smiled. "Just make sure you guys don't wear yourselves out."

Clark offered his mom a good-natured shrug, and Martha chuckled as she turned her attention back to tamping down the dust with the hose water. They all knew it was pretty much impossible to wear Clark out. Standing in a bright red T-shirt and jeans under the midday sun, and having already leveled out the bottom of four twenty-inch deep, thirty-foot-long trenches, Clark had yet to break a sweat. He still wasn't completely sure why his dad wouldn't let him take care of the digging by himself—that way Jonathan wouldn't have had to rent the unwieldy trencher machine, and Clark could have had the whole field done by dinner.

"Let's make this one a family project," Jonathan had said, winking at his son with undisguised appreciation. Clark had agreed and hauled the irrigation equipment out of the barn as his father and mother reviewed the land survey.

Jonathan dragged the back of his hand across his forehead to mop up the sweat. "Boy, it'd be great if we could lay all the pipe tomorrow." He grinned, then started up the trencher again.

I could lay all the pipe today, Clark thought, but kept it to himself. There was something nice about doing outdoor projects as a team, and he knew that, although farm work was backbreaking and arduous, his dad loved every sweaty second of it.

Jonathan Kent was in his early forties, health and integrity stamped across every feature, from his wavy, golden hair to his boot-tipped toes. He was the kind of man people liked to call "salt of the earth," and he carried himself with an unassuming charisma and effortless dignity that won him trust and friendship everywhere he went, even before he flashed one of his infectious smiles. Although Clark bore no real physical resemblance to Jonathan—their coloring and bone structures were quite different—most of Smallville had long since forgotten that Clark was adopted. The slope of Clark's broad shoulders, his perfect posture, the quiet intensity of his gaze, all were identical to Jonathan's. Jonathan's influence on Clark ran much deeper than familial DNA, and no one doubted Clark's loyalty to or worthiness of his family name. In addition to being self-reliant, moral, fair-minded, and kind, Jonathan openly adored his son. He possessed a natural warmth and affection that touched everyone who came near him. Clark was equally demonstrative in return, and despite Jonathan's headstrong protectiveness and his son's fiery impatience, both of which occasionally led to friction, it was hard to imagine Clark growing up with any other father, or Jonathan raising any other son. The trust and respect between the two men was palpable and deep.

Clark glanced over his shoulder at his mother and felt another wave of appreciation warm his skin. He really did have the best parents on the planet. He was sure of it. For all of Jonathan's affection, Martha Kent was utterly taken with her son. Every look she cast his way was full of pride and gratitude.

Clark knew by heart the story of how badly his parents had wanted a child, especially his mother, who had made no secret of her yearning. Try as they might, however, the Kents seemed unable to conceive. Martha had surprised herself by being unable to accept this fate. She had carried a picture in her mind of a tiny little face, small hands that she could warm in her own. It had felt too real, too powerful to give up on. The sense that something was missing in her life was urgent, an ache. That must have been why, from the first time she held Clark, her heart had been so completely at peace. The circumstances could not have been more alarming, Jonathan's fear more than making up for Martha's calm, but cuddling the mysterious toddler against her breast, Martha knew a completeness she had never before experienced. The meteor storm, the alien spacecraft, the toddler wandering naked and alone through the cornfields, none of these felt insurmountable to her. She knew Clark was her child the moment she took him into her arms.

As Clark gazed at his mother, her bright, intelligent eyes darted up to meet his almost instantly. The smile that crossed her face softened the angular lines of her strong jaw. She was a beautiful woman with a low, melodious voice, and Clark appreciated watching how loving his parents were with one another. As if reading his thoughts, Martha raised the hose she was holding until the arc of water, now fashioning rainbows in the glinting air, was high enough to splash Jonathan and his trencher. Jonathan looked startled for a second as the cold water hit his shoulders, then bent his head back into the stream and laughed.

"Looking a little dusty over there, Kent," she teased her husband. Clark watched their antics with a smile, then turned toward the droning hum of a car heading toward their property. By the time Lex Luthor pulled up in a brand-new silver Porsche, both Jonathan and Martha had also turned their attention to their driveway.

Clark glanced back over his shoulder and saw his father frown and turn back to the trencher. Jonathan hated Lionel Luthor. The billionaire had caused a great deal of heartache and misery in Smallville as he lied and cheated his way into financial control of the town. Although Lex still had a long way to go before he was anywhere near Lionel's level of manipulative deceit, Jonathan didn't feel inclined to stick around hoping for the best.

Martha, who figured Lex could at least be credited for good taste where his interest in Clark was concerned, felt more optimistic about the young Luthor. She turned off the hose, wiped her hands on her jeans, and moved to join her son by Lex's car.

Lex didn't bother to get out of the car, but his eyes sparkled as he smiled up at his friend.

"Hey, Clark! Enjoying fall break?"

Clark had come to stand by the driver's side, hands thrust deep into his pockets as he admired the shiny car.

"Yup. New wheels?"

"What can I say?" Lex grinned. "I've got a weakness for things that move fast."

"It's very nice." Martha smiled, approaching the convertible. Lex hopped out of the driver's seat and stood in the Kent's dusty driveway the moment he heard her voice. He smiled at Martha, then, with a hint of longing, glanced up at the cheerful yellow house behind her.

"Thank you, Martha." Lex's eyes darted back to Clark's mom, and he offered her a grin of practiced charm. "Can I take you for a spin?"

Martha laughed as Clark glanced back toward his cross father, who was getting down from the trencher and preparing to go inside.

"No thank you, Lex," she answered kindly. She had taken it upon herself to treat the motherless magnate with as much warmth and consideration as possible. Her heart told her that despite all his money and fame, Lex would have traded places with Clark in a New York minute. Sometimes she wished that she could shelter Lex at the farm, feed him fresh organic vegetables, and offer him the acceptance and tenderness he so clearly needed. "But Clark might be interested."

"Actually"—Lex took a deep breath as he turned his attention back to Clark—"I'm on my way to Metropolis for the week, and I was wondering if you'd like to join me."

Lex thought the expression on Clark's face could best be described as inscrutable, but Martha saw the spark of delight that lit up her son's blue eyes. He had turned halfway toward her with his "Can I?" grin in place, then had censored himself, shifting his focus back toward the cornfield and the unfinished irrigation trenches.

"Oh, I—I can't," he told his friend, gesturing with his head toward the field. "I promised Dad I'd help him lay some pipe tomorrow."

Lex looked disappointed but nodded graciously, never one to put Clark on the spot where his family was concerned.

Martha, however, couldn't stand it. She held one of her hands up between the young men as she interrupted.

"I'm sure it can wait until you get back, honey," she offered quickly. "That is, if you want to go."

Clark turned toward his mother with a look of sheer delight on his face.

"It's just that we're doing asteroids for the science fair this year," he told her excitedly, "and there's this exhibit at the Metropolis Museum of Natural History I was hoping to catch . . ."

"We'd be staying at my place in the city," Lex added, once again directing his comments to Martha. "I can assure you that Clark will be perfectly safe, and you'll always have a number where you can reach him."

"Let me talk to Jonathan," Martha answered, patting Clark's arm before disappearing into the house.

"Oh, well," Lex said to Clark the minute she was gone from view. "It was worth a shot."

"There's still a chance," Clark argued, but Lex shook his head.

"Your dad hates me, Clark. I doubt a Luthor/Kent road trip is high on his list of parentally approved outings."

"He doesn't hate you," Clark said quietly, without much confidence in his statement.

Lex smiled wryly at the dust between his shoes.

Inside, as Lex had predicted, Jonathan was wholly opposed to the idea.

"Besides," the elder Kent was arguing, as Martha stood in the kitchen shaking her head, "what does a twenty-something want a sixteen-year-old hanging around his penthouse for?"

"*You* like spending time with Clark," Martha countered, "and you're significantly older than Lex."

"I'm his *father*!"

"Well, Lex is his friend. Sweetheart, are you really asking why Lex likes Clark? Clark is the kindest, most intelligent boy Lex will ever know. I have the feeling that Lex doesn't have very many *nice* people in his life." Martha paused for a moment, letting her argument sink in. When Jonathan's expression still hadn't changed she added, "I think Clark's good for him."

"My concern is whether or not *Lex* is good for *Clark*," Jonathan growled, turning away from his wife to lean against the sink. Through the kitchen window, he could see Luthor and his son still laughing and talking outside, and had to admit to himself that they seemed to enjoy one another's company.

"Lex would never hurt Clark," Martha asserted. "He thinks he owes Clark his life."

Jonathan turned back toward Martha with a frown.

"He *does* owe Clark his life," he stated, but Martha could see the hot wind of his temper beginning to leave his sails. Jonathan took a seat at the kitchen table, deflating slightly, and looked up at his wife again. "The Luthors just aren't trustworthy, Martha. Besides, what if Clark . . . slips up in front of Lex? A whole week living together in the same apartment is a long time to hide a secret like Clark's."

Martha approached the table and pulled up a chair next to Jonathan's and took one of his hands in hers.

"If it were up to me, he'd never leave the farm. You know that."

"Then why are you advocating this?"

"Because Clark really wants to go. And because I think he's earned our trust. He's growing up so fast, Jonathan—I don't want to teach him our fears. I don't want to hold him back because *we're* not ready for him to go."

Jonathan's expression softened as he pulled his wife closer, nuzzling her hair as she leaned in against him, resting her head on his shoulder.

"It's a long time to be cooped up in a little convertible."

"Not the way Lex drives."

Jonathan let out a short laugh.

"Great. That makes me feel *much* better."

Martha laughed as well, then spoke softly into her husband's chest.

"When it comes time for him to find his place in the world, how much are we really going to be able to guide him?" she asked quietly, not moving from Jonathan's embrace. It was a subject they had discussed many times before. Their son was stronger than any other human, nearly invulnerable, able to see through flesh and walls. His destiny was incomprehensible to them. The Kents both knew that Clark would one day reach a boundary beyond which their experience would be of little or no use to him.

Jonathan smiled slightly and nodded.

"All right. If that's what he wants."

"I'll go tell him," Martha said. She lingered a moment longer, then leaned in again to kiss her husband.

"You're sure he'll be all right?" Jonathan asked softly when their lips parted.

Martha smiled. "He's got a good head on his shoulders," she affirmed, crinkling her nose as she rose. "Takes after his father."

Jonathan smiled as he ran his fingers through his still-damp hair and watched his wife exit into the afternoon sun.

CHAPTER SIX

Twenty minutes later, Lex's silver Porsche sped down I-35. Lex glanced over at his friend with a grin. In the passenger seat, Clark had been wearing the same tranquil smile since they'd passed Lana outside Chloe's house, hanging laundry in the late-afternoon sun. She'd looked up at them and waved when Lex beeped the horn, offering a big smile. Lex had no doubt that Clark was replaying the moment over and over again in his head as the young man shut his eyes and lifted his face to the wind. They'd barely spoken a word since starting the trip, and neither one seemed to mind. It was enough to be speeding under the sun, occasionally humming along with the CD player, free and young and—at least within the scope of the car—not alone with the weight of their individual intellects.

"What do you have to do in Metropolis?" Clark asked eventually.

"Just attend some LuthorCorp meetings for my father," Lex answered, still smiling at his younger friend. Clark shifted in his seat slightly to face Lex.

"Did you guys ever get along?"

Lex raised an eyebrow, a bemused expression crossing his face, and Clark immediately began to apologize.

"I'm sorry—that was a terrible question. I just meant—"

"No, that's okay," Lex answered evenly, "I know what you meant. And the answer is no. My father and I have always been . . . at odds . . . ."

"Even when you were a little kid?"

Lex shrugged lightly.

"He wasn't around much when I was really small. I think he always liked the idea of having a son, but I was . . . well, I was always a disappointment to him. In fact, disappointing him seems to be the one thing I'm really cut out for, so I might as well take it all the way."

There was no ire in Lex's voice when he discussed Lionel. In fact, aside from an easy smile of amusement that didn't always reach his eyes, there was no indication of any emotion at all. It was as if Lex had learned to cut off his heart completely where his father was concerned, and Clark was torn between sympathy and apprehension. Sympathy because he understood that his friend had been forced to learn how to accomplish this as a means of survival, and apprehension because a man who could silence the counsel of his own heart was a dangerous man indeed.

Lionel's disapproval of Lex was equally disturbing. Clark couldn't imagine what Lionel found lacking in his son, though he'd seen with his own eyes how hurtful Lionel could be toward Lex. It almost seemed malicious. Lex was brilliant, talented, charismatic, ambitious, and, as far as Clark's experience bore out, generous and considerate. Lionel should have been bursting with pride, but instead he seemed to delight in rejecting, entrapping, and belittling his only heir.

"I don't understand that," Clark said finally, shaking his head.

"I know," Lex answered with a smile. "You can barely

even *conceive* of iniquity. It's one of the things I like about you."

"Do you think you'll ever be close?"

Clark didn't want to make his friend uncomfortable, but Lex never shut him out or accused him of prying, and part of him wondered if maybe it wasn't a little bit of a relief for Lex to talk about the problems between him and his dad.

"Become close with my father?" With his eyes firmly focused on the road, Lex shook his head. "I don't know. Sometimes I feel like I'd be better off if I could just . . . forgive him or something. Get on with my life." Lex fell into a thoughtful silence and Clark waited patiently. Lex was both unusually sharp-witted and honest about himself, which Clark found a refreshing combination. Especially since Lex's experiences were so different from his own.

Lex shot a quick look toward Clark and actively had to resist laughing. The sixteen-year-old farm boy was so earnest, so innocent, sometimes Lex thought he himself was absurd to harbor such outlandish suspicions about him. But on the other hand, maybe extraordinary powers of strength and invulnerability were exactly what it would take to allow someone that kind of virtue in this kind of world. Lex turned his attention back to the road and shifted into fourth gear.

"The thing is," Lex continued, "it's hard to forgive someone who's still in your face all the time. My dad isn't *done* with me yet, and that makes it difficult for me to be done with *him*."

"And you probably still want to please him on some level," Clark added.

Lex smirked. "You think?"

"Well, no offense, but why else would you still be working with him?"

Clark watched nervously as Lex shifted into overdrive. The car was about to edge over the 100 MPH mark, but Lex's face betrayed no sign of anger or stress as he watched the rolling blacktop disappear beneath the wheels of his Porsche. The trees lining the highway blurred by them so fast they seemed to form one long, hazy continuum; the idea of a tree, rather than actual trees.

"It's a game, Clark," Lex smiled coolly. "I can't beat him from the outside."

"Why beat him at all?"

Lex's eyes flashed into Clark's with such sudden focus, it was almost aggressive. "Because I can," he answered concisely, before turning his attention back to his driving.

Clark felt his mouth run dry. He'd never been more certain that this wasn't a healthy course for Lex to pursue.

"I think," Clark started carefully, then halted. Lex glanced at him again looking as tranquil and receptive as ever, so Clark braved on. "I think maybe those kinds of games come with a high price. I mean, even if you do beat him, I think it'll cost you something. Something I guess I . . . I don't want to see you pay."

"You're getting downright philosophical in your old age, Clark," Lex grinned.

"Lex, I'm serious," the teenager persisted.

"And I thank you for your concern. I don't think I've had anyone worry over my soul since my mother died." Lex still looked more bemused than anything else, and Clark began to feel frustrated. Lex seemed to notice his disquiet and offered his friend a little more insight.

"Think of it this way: I've got nothing better to do. For all his faults, I can't claim that my father's stupid. He beats me as often as I beat him. He's a challenge, and I believe the only way we can grow—intellectually *and* morally—is to step up to the most difficult challenges we can bare to face as often as possible. There are no limits to what we can do if we hold on to the intention to excel." Lex paused to chuckle. "But look who I'm talking to. *You* know that, don't you, Clark?"

Clark felt a familiar panic tightening around his chest. Lex had been the beneficiary of his special talents more than once, and it was impossible to know what the millionaire had made of what he'd seen. Clark knew he couldn't afford to tell Lex his secret, although sometimes he wished he could. He felt sure Lex would believe him, would probably even help him research the mysteries of his past, but the harder Lex pushed to know, the more secretive Clark became. It was part instinct, part common sense, and partly a promise he had made to his parents. His father had hated counseling Clark to employ dishonesty, but they all agreed that his circumstances were special. The only hope of his having a normal upbringing rested on hiding his extraordinary abilities from the rest of the world, at least until he was old enough not to be threatened with forcible removal from Jonathan and Martha's custody.

Clark wasn't sure whether or not Lex was waiting for a response, but Lex laughed suddenly, alleviating the necessity for Clark to speak.

"Anyway, maybe you're right. Maybe I do still wish I could please him. He's always telling me about this legacy he's leaving me, making me feel unworthy, you know? I wish I could honestly say the whole thing's beneath me, but it's not. Not really. I'm not like you."

"What do you mean?" Clark asked, concern tightening his throat as he brushed his dark bangs out of his eyes.

"Tell me this, Clark," Lex said by way of answer, his eyes bright. "What do you think it means to be a man?"

Clark frowned, turning the query over in his mind, wondering where Lex was going with this line of questioning.

"I don't know," Clark answered honestly. "I guess it has something to do with acting with integrity and taking responsibility for your place in the world. Why? What do you think?" Lex came up behind another car and slid into the lane for oncoming traffic without hesitation in order to pass the slower driver.

"I think it means being willing to push past your comfort zone in order to achieve something," he answered, easing the Porsche back into the proper lane.

"Achieve what?" Clark asked.

"Doesn't matter," Lex shrugged. "As long as you're the first, or the best. Not just a man—*the* man."

Clark didn't know how to respond to that, so he said nothing. The convertible sped on as the light moved across the sky. Lex occasionally drummed his fingers against the steering wheel in time to the music playing from his custom CD player. If he was unhappy, he didn't let it show.

They were silent again for a long time, both lost in their own thoughts, unaffected by the chill that began to seep into the air. The sun was starting to go down when, merging on to I-80 east, Lex's voice startled Clark out of a nearly meditative daydream.

"What's your secret, Clark?" Lex asked softly. "Are you ever going to tell me?"

Lex watched the teenager's bright blue eyes flutter open in surprise, the finely chiseled face turning slowly toward his.

"My secret?" Clark squeaked.

"I'm always honest with you," Lex prompted.

"Are you?" Clark asked quietly.

Lex turned his attention back to the darkening road, grinning as if in compliment of a move well played. The sky turned the color of blood, and the car sped on.

"It's done."

Lionel leaned back in the burgundy chair set behind the huge mahogany desk of his London office. The room was dusky, shades drawn against the outside world, the decorating whispering of old money. "I'm glad to hear that." He smiled into his cordless phone.

"Now there is just the matter of payment."

"Ah, well, that is complicated." Lionel chuckled. "First of all, I don't owe you a thing, and even if I did, you can hardly expect LuthorCorp to write out a check to your upstanding little organization."

The voice on the other end of the phone was insistent, the muted Japanese accent doing nothing to soften the demand.

"You will pay cash."

"Cash?" Lionel spit out the word derisively, the contempt in his voice undisguised. He ran a hand over his well-trimmed beard, letting his index finger rest for a moment on his mouth. His arched brows furrowed into a glower over his dark glasses. "Out of the question."

"Six million, Mr. Luthor. That includes the job fees and absorption of the outstanding debt."

"Nickels's debt? What makes you think I'll take that on?"

"It is your responsibility."

"You know, I'm curious." Lionel regained his composure, leaning back. "How do you intend to prove I owe you a cent?"

"We don't need to prove it. You know, and we know. If you do not pay, things will get very bad for you."

Lionel scoffed, angrily brushing back a stray lock of his meticulously groomed shoulder-length hair. "I'll have you arrested."

"All of us?"

Lionel was silent for a moment, calculating. He was a man capable of frightening stillness and dangerous volatility. His caller pressed on.

"Do not play with us, Mr. Luthor. It will be much easier if you pay us what you owe."

"Are you threatening me?" Lionel's voice took on the honeyed tone of gentle amusement, but whether or not he truly was amused was anybody's guess.

"Oh, yes," his caller answered calmly. "Most definitely."

"Well, this is outrageous! I can't believe you conduct your business affairs so carelessly." One of Lionel Luthor's only failures as a negotiator was a tendency to change bargaining tactics too quickly. Many of his conversations raced by in clipped, staccato dialogues with ever-changing beats; anger gave way to amusement, which in turn gave way to professed innocence, then megalomaniacal confidence. It left weaker negotiators confused and off guard, shrinking from his mercurial wit.

But more practiced delegates sometimes weathered it long enough for Lionel to exhaust his own bag of tricks. Even his son had started out as the former but was beginning to possess the skills of the latter. Lex seemed to have identified his father's tendency toward histrionics and was working steadily to develop an unflappable, icy nucleus in his own heart.

"I think your stockholders would be interested to know about some of the work we've done for you in the past."

Lionel exhaled in frustration, waving a bejeweled hand dismissively into the air.

"That was *years* ago. The public's memory is not that long."

"Ours is."

"Well, what do you suggest we do here?" Lionel leaned forward in his chair, animated with irritation and contempt. "I'd lose much more than six million dollars if I allowed anyone to perceive a connection between my corporation and . . . . yours."

"That is not my problem, Mr. Luthor."

Lionel laughed derisively.

"I'd like to suggest, my friend, that it very much is."

"Six million. In cash. By the end of the week."

Lionel was about to respond when the line went dead. He gritted his teeth and threw the cordless phone across the office. Had anyone who knew him witnessed this action, they would have been alarmed. Lionel Luthor didn't often lose his cool.

Not enough to destroy something he'd paid for, at any rate.

CHAPTER SEVEN

"I can't let you do this." Clark stood before an oval full-length mirror, obediently holding his arms away from his sides as a small, well-dressed man hovered beside him, measuring his waist. Lex's mirthful eyes met Clark's in the mirror from where he stood behind him, hands in pockets.

"How am I supposed to show you a good time if you're dressed like a ranch hand?" Lex asked with an elegant arch of his eyebrow. His amusement was not lost on Clark, who jumped as the tailor went to measure his inseam.

"Hey, what're you—?"

"It's okay, Clark. He's supposed to do that."

"This is too small," Clark sulked, turning his attention back to the mirror. The tailor stood and jotted numbers down on a small pad he held as Lex smiled and came forward to lower Clark's arms and smooth out the shoulders on his suit jacket.

"It looks good. Shows off your physique."

Clark squinted back toward the mirror, doubtful. It was a nice suit, there was no question about that. The blue silk shirt Lex had picked out almost exactly matched the color of his eyes, and the softly textured Italian pinstriped gray wool was so luxurious, Clark was almost afraid to touch it.

"It's just . . . not me." He sighed finally, turning slightly in the mirror to peer at it from another angle. The overly perfumed store was beginning to give him a headache.

"Honestly, Clark"—Lex grinned—"I don't think you have the slightest idea who you really are yet."

Clark fumbled with the price tag, still protesting. His eyes went wide.

"It's over three thousand dollars!" he whispered.

"And that's before the shirt," Lex agreed. "But I promise you I can afford it." The young millionaire reached around his captive model to open the top button on the collar of Clark's silk shirt, then looked approvingly at the overall effect.

"Lex . . . it's too much . . . I just can't accept a gift like this."

"I can't wait to see the look on Lana's face when she sees you in this," Lex teased, mercilessly going straight for Clark's weak spot. "Though we could try it in pincord."

Clark's lips parted slightly, and he shook his head.

"Where would I ever take Lana that I could wear something like this?"

"You never know, Clark. The future's full of surprises."

Clark looked anxiously over his shoulder at the tailor, who was still jotting down notes. Lex's expression sobered slightly as he caught the look of concern on Clark's face.

"You look nervous suddenly. Everything okay?"

Clark leaned in to whisper in his friend's ear, an apologetic wince already dominating his expression.

"Won't he be disappointed when we don't buy this?" he asked, indicating the salesclerk.

Lex threw back his head and laughed. "Mr. Kent will be taking his business elsewhere," he told the salesman evenly, turning from the mirror to face him. "But he'd like me to pay your commission regardless."

Clark gaped in embarrassment, hung his head, and hurried back across the gold and wine red carpet into the dressing room to change back into his jeans as the salesclerk stammered at Lex about how his offer wouldn't be necessary. Clark felt awful as he eased out of the expensive jacket. He and Lex had already kept the store open an hour past closing time, and it was clear from the way they'd reacted that everyone in the shop recognized Lex and were all bending over backward to please him and his country bumpkin friend.

As he changed back into his regular clothes, Clark wondered for the millionth time who he had been on the planet he came from. Obviously, whoever his parents were, they'd been influential enough to send their child off in a spaceship—or was that the kind of thing that everyone on that planet had? If he had been highborn, would he have learned to be as comfortable having people serve him as Lex seemed to be? Did they have servants in his house on that planet, as Lex had in the mansion, or was his family indentured to the service of another? Clark zipped up his jacket, remembering Lex's words.

Honestly, Clark, I don't think you have the slightest idea who you really are yet.

Jonathan always said that knowing yourself was just a matter of really listening. Clark's adoptive father firmly believed that the coding for right and wrong was hardwired into everyone, and that it took actual work to ignore or learn to phase out your own morality.

Clark closed his eyes and tried to listen. In a way, Lex was right—there was so much Clark didn't know about who he was and what his destiny might hold. But what he did know, it was hard to deny. He knew he loved Kansas, and his parents, and in fact this entire planet that had so warmly harbored and fostered him. He knew that Lana was the most beautiful creature in the entire universe, and that any one of her wishes would be worth going to the ends of the earth to make come true. He knew that the allegiance he bore his friends knew no bounds, knew that even if bullets could hurt him, he'd step in front of one for Lex or Pete or Chloe without hesitation. He knew that life was precious, and fragile. And he knew that not doing anything to protect people was just as wrong as hurting them yourself.

Oh yeah, he thought to himself with a smile. *And I know that denim is about ten times more comfortable than Italian wool.*

Lex was waiting for him outside the store when Clark emerged from the dressing room. No one in the store even glanced at him as he hurriedly made his way to the swinging glass door. As he pushed out into the soft darkness of the Metropolis night, Lex turned and grinned at him.

"You can take the boy out of the farm . . . " he started, stopping to shake his head with a laugh.

". . . But you can't take the farm out of the boy. I know, I know. I'm sorry. Should we just go grab a burger or something? I wouldn't want to embarrass you in some fancy restaurant or anything."

Lex pretended to scoff.

"And I wouldn't want to *take* you to some fancy restaurant or anything," he smirked. Clark followed as Lex began walking, though he had no idea where they were headed. "No offense, Clark," Lex continued with a mischievous gleam in his eyes, "but you're not really my type."

"Oh, I know. I'm emotionally available *and* uninterested in your money."

"Ouch!" Lex laughed. "Is this a comment on my taste in dates?"

"Well it's just . . . the girls you pick. They don't . . . they don't really seem to be very . . . *nice*," Clark confessed apologetically. He was remembering one of Lex's last girlfriends, a beautiful brunette named Victoria who had ended up screwing Lex over, both figuratively and literally, with Lionel.

"Maybe. But at least they're not involved with someone else." Lex winked. "*How* long have you been in love with Lana?"

"Since I was five," Clark admitted dolefully.

"And *how* long was she with Whitney?"

"Only freshman year." Clark sighed. The look that crossed over his young face was so heartbroken and dejected that Lex had to laugh. It wasn't so long ago that he himself had been a teenager, and he remembered all too vividly how much it sucked. He reached out and threw an arm over Clark's shoulder as he continued leading him down the block.

"Don't worry, Kent." He chuckled. "She'll see the light. That innocent, reluctant hero thing you've got going is irresistible."

"Even in jeans?" Clark asked.

"Especially in jeans," Lex laughed. For the millionth

time, he thought about how lucky he was to know Clark Kent.

"You're kidding me! Not even a beer?" Not twenty minutes later, Lex sat across from Clark at a small, round table toward the back of a crowded Metropolis bar. Clark could barely hear his friend over the music and laughter, and the agreeable, rolling knock of pool balls. He shook his head.

"No, nothing. Never felt the need." Clark's eyes roved over the crowd, marveling at the sheer number of people packed into the two small rooms. Both the bar and pool-room boasted shiny, oak wainscot and felt green carpets that matched the pool tables. The maroon walls were punctuated with the occasional neon beer sign or frosted ivory wall sconce.

"Well, that settles it." Lex grinned as he pushed his chair back, starting to head to the bar. "I'm getting you a nice scotch. Time you lived a little."

"Lex, no." Clark's hand shot out across the tiny table, grabbing hold of Lex's wrist. Lex looked down at the grip Clark had on him, impressed by his strength, and the younger man quickly let go. Clark leaned forward, wide-eyed and whisper-shouting. "I shouldn't even be in here. I'm underage."

Lex's eyes twinkled for a minute as he watched his younger friend, then, still standing, tall and lean, he shoved his hands in his pockets and let out a long, deep laugh.

"Clark, you're with me. The first time I was in this bar, I was fifteen."

"But I don't—"

"Trust me," Lex said slowly, bending down close to

Clark. He patted the teenager on the shoulder and set off to purchase some drinks.

Clark sighed and leaned back in his chair. The truth was, he liked being in the bar, if only for the people-watching opportunity it afforded, and he appreciated Lex's intention to show him a good time. He was just a little nervous about what that might entail.

A slight commotion at the door caught his attention. Craning his head over his shoulder, he noticed a group of young Japanese men entering, all with long, slicked-back hair and clothes every bit as expensive as Lex's, though somewhat out of fashion. Most of them were wearing tight suits in dark, shiny fabrics over white shirts and under long, black leather trench coats, with pointy, uncomfortable-looking shoes. Those who weren't in suits wore form-fitting muscle tees designed to show off elaborate tattoos that ran all the way up their arms. These were not merely small, singular graphics, but entire, intricate landscapes. Most disturbingly to Clark, three of them were missing parts of their pinkies—two with just the top one-third of their little finger absent, and one with just the bottom joint still in place.

Clark realized he wasn't the only one who had noticed them. They seemed to excite a good deal of attention, some patrons pointing them out to one another with animated whispers, others pointedly getting out of their way. There were seven in all, and something about the way they moved in a choreographed formation made Clark take a closer look. Concentrating on the sweeping, floor-length coat of the one who seemed most intent on surveying the room, Clark focused his X-ray vision. Hovering against their skeletons was an assorted collection of handguns.

"You know, it's not polite to stare." Clark jumped as he heard Lex's voice beside him. As he turned back around in his chair, he saw a flash of Lex's skull before he could refocus his eyes back to their normal vision. Lex had a tumbler of scotch in one hand and was taking his seat. Clark glanced at the table where Lex had left a drink for him. It appeared to be an old-fashioned glass filled with . . . milk.

"See those guys coming in?"

Lex glanced casually toward the door.

"Hard to miss them."

Clark leaned forward again.

"I . . . I think they're armed."

Lex looked unperturbed as he took a sip of his scotch, then nodded.

"I would imagine they are."

Clark let his confusion show on his face, but Lex very subtly signaled to him, raising his index finger a quarter inch off the table. Clark understood the gesture to mean "wait," and carefully turned his attention to his drink as the young men walked past their table. One of them put a bill down on the bar counter, said something to the bartender as he nodded toward one of the men playing pool, then all seven of them disappeared into a separate back room. When the door closed behind them, Lex spoke quietly, his eyes on the indicated pool game.

"*Yakuza*," he said. "Kind of like the Japanese Mafia. The name translates to 'eight-nine-three,' which is a losing hand in their version of blackjack. They go to nineteen instead of twenty-one, so an eight-nine-three hand is worthless—it doesn't fit into the game. Get it?"

Lex grinned and Clark looked uneasy.

"Some historians trace them all the way back to the

kabuki-mono—the 'crazy ones'—of the seventeenth century," Lex continued. Clark listened, always willing to absorb the eclectic information that Lex had at his fingertips. Lex and Lionel sometimes had entire arguments couched in historical allusions. "Those guys were *ronin*—*samurai* without masters and without enough to do in the Tokugawa era. They could get pretty nasty. As you learn all too quickly in my family, nothing's harder on a warrior than peacetime." Lex smiled and took another sip of his drink, then leaned forward slightly, warming to his topic.

"The Yakuza themselves, though, prefer to be linked with the *machi-yako*—civil servants, or 'town servants,' really. The *machi-yako* were the ones who fought off the *kabuki-mono*. Think of them as Japanese Robin Hoods. Much later, when Japan began to industrialize, their role started to change. The guys we think of as Yakuza today are fashioned from the *bakuto*, or gamblers, and the *tekiya*, or street vendors, who began to recruit employees from within businesses like construction and shipping. Politically, they allied themselves with the Japanese right-wing nationalists, taking advantage of growing anti-Western sentiments that were arising in the face of the economic depression. They still considered themselves heroes of the common man, but were actively training members in spying arts like linguists, warfare, blackmail, and assassinations."

"Nice guys?" Clark asked facetiously, but Lex nodded.

"To each other, absolutely. Very, very loyal. The whole structure of the Yakuza is based on family, with 'sons'— *kobun*, taking orders from a 'father'—*oyabun*. Did you notice how some of them were missing parts of their pinkies?"

Clark nodded, his eyes wide and trusting as he listened. Lex reached out and took one of Clark's hands by the wrist, drawing it across the table so it was closer to him.

"It's called *yubizume*, and it's a form of atonement. If you're in the Yakuza and you screw something up, the guy above you in station might hand you a knife and a string. You're supposed to cut your pinkie off at the first joint," Lex used his hand to pretend to chop off the tip of Clark's pinkie, "and present it as an offering to the *oyabun*. Now why do you think they do that?"

"Because they're crazy?" Clark ventured, trying to pull his hand back. Lex smirked and shook his head.

"Because back in the days of the *samurai*"—Lex paused, glancing around their table, which had nothing on it but their drinks. Clark had no idea what he was looking for and was startled when Lex suddenly whipped a pocketknife out of his pants pocket and clicked it open, pressing the smooth, metal handle of it into Clark's palm—"your life depended on your ability to wield your sword." Lex closed Clark's hand around the knife base so that Clark was in effect pointing it at Lex. The whole exercise was making Clark uncomfortable, both because he was sure they were beginning to attract attention to themselves and because every time Lex moved Clark's hand, he had to be careful not to resist Lex for fear of accidentally hurting his friend. Lex reached forward again and pulled Clark's pinkie off the knife. The knife clattered to the table.

"If you're holding a *katana* properly, your pinkie is the strongest finger on the hilt. Compromising a *samurai*'s ability to hold his sword securely would make him more dependent on his master. Sounds like something my dad would do, doesn't it?"

Clark was too distracted folding up the knife to notice Lex's grin.

"Well, what are they doing here?" Clark asked, handing the knife back. He was tremendously relieved when Lex thrust it into his pocket without further incident.

"Making trouble and money, I'd guess." Lex glanced over his shoulder at one of the pool games, then continued. "The aftereffects of World War II created an interesting business opportunity for them. The American soldiers who were occupying Japan were rationing out food, which of course created a vibrant black market, and a new kind of Yakuza—the *gurentai*, or street hustler. The Yakuza are different from the Mafia in that their membership criteria aren't very strict. Once you're in, absolute loyalty is demanded, but they'll take in refugees from Korea and China, orphaned kids, kids who can't hack the high-pressure Japanese school system . . . Those kids go from being all alone in the world to having a loyal family, which includes money, status, authority, camaraderie, and a place in the world where they feel valued and welcome. In that sense, they're more like our suburban gangs. Their activities, though, are pretty hardcore. They're big on meth production—fast-paced culture, though in the states they usually trade drugs for guns—they like gambling, they've got all kinds of control over the sex industry, and they're also masters at corporate espionage and extortion."

"How do you know all this?" Clark asked with wonder. Lex took a long, slow swallow of scotch, then smiled enigmatically at his friend.

"You know how some kids fantasize that they're really

royalty, or an alien or something? You know, somehow special so that someone's going to come and take them away from their parents, who are clearly not real relations? Well, I could always tell that I was really and truly a Luthor. So I used to fantasize about running away, and I studied all the different groups I might be able to hide out with: carnies, the military, cults, the Yakuza . . . anyone I thought might take me in."

Clark shook his head, feeling a wave of empathy toward his friend and thinking once again about how lucky he was to have his mother and father in his life. Just imagining if Lionel Luthor had adopted him instead made his stomach queasy.

"They've got these guys, too, called *sokaiya*," Lex said, tracing invisible patterns on the table with his index finger. " 'Meeting Men,' I guess you could call them, or shareholders—something like that. They buy up a few shares in a company, then dig up all the dirt on the corporation's managers and owners that they can possibly find. Then, before the shareholders' meeting, they'll call up the management and threaten to play show-and-tell in front of the other investors unless they're bought off. Remember, too, that Japan is a shame-based culture. Most Japanese businessmen would rather get hit than have someone accuse them of tax evasion in public."

"Now that definitely sounds like something your dad would do," Clark smiled. He cast a glance toward the back room they'd all disappeared into, then turned back to Lex. "Listen, maybe we should go," he suggested, but Lex was already getting out of his chair. He fished in his pants pocket and pulled out a plastic card key, which he handed to Clark.

"There's a doorman out front all night," he said. "Use this in the elevator to get up to the penthouse."

"Wait," Clark said, alarmed. "Where are *you* going?"

"That many Yakuza in one place mean one of two things; an assassination, or a high-stakes card game. Since I haven't heard any gunfire, I thought I'd go sit in with the high rollers for a while." He paused and offered a chin nod toward Clark's glass. "Drink responsibly."

Clark looked doubtfully at his milk, then back at Lex. He opened his mouth to protest, but Lex cut him off.

"Aren't *I* supposed to be chaperoning *you*?" he asked with a wink, then he sauntered over to the pool game he'd been watching, exchanged a few words with one of the players, then handed him several large bills. Lex smiled graciously at the bartender and disappeared into the closed room.

Clark took a deep breath and looked around the bar. Everything seemed to be perfectly normal. The door to the back room was directly in his line of sight, so after glancing around to make sure no one was paying any attention to him, Clark once again focused on the wall with his X-ray vision.

Four skeletons stood near the door—the ones with the bigger guns, Clark realized. The other three were seated at a round table with four additional skeletons, and Lex appeared to be joining them. It crossed Clark's mind that it was probably weird to be able to recognize your friend's skeleton, but that was the least of his problems.

He had just decided to sit tight and keep an eye on Lex when one of the skeletons got up from the table and was promptly pushed back into his chair by one of the men Clark took to be guards. There was a minor commotion, which Clark was very gratified to see Lex staying out of.

He was just starting to be able to discern individuals in the room when he heard someone addressing him in a slightly husky but crystal clear voice. Clark readjusted his vision and quickly looked up to see a stunning brunette standing over his table, one hand on Lex's abandoned chair. She was smoking a cigarette and didn't appear to be much older than Clark, though she was certainly more comfortable in her surroundings.

"Hey? You alive in there? Helloooo?"

"Huh? Oh! I'm sorry, what was that?"

The brunette exhaled a cloud of smoke and frowned at him with a cross between impatience and amusement. Clark found himself swallowing, entranced by her penetrating gaze.

"I don't mean to tear your attention away from that *captivating* wall, but do you mind if I snag this chair?"

"Sure. I mean, n-no, go ahead."

"Thanks, country mouse," she smiled, dragging the chair to a table several feet away, where she wedged it and herself between five very fast-talking young men who looked to Clark like students of some kind. Clark looked down at his chest to see if he was wearing a Smallville T-shirt, but there was no print on his red tee. He couldn't figure out how she'd pegged him for a non-native unless it was his flannel overshirt. Or his slow response time. Or the milk.

Though her smile still floated in his vision, he shook off the interruption and turned his attention back to the card room just in time to see one of the poker players bring a solid line of metal—a knife, maybe?—down on top of his first pinkie joint, seemingly severing it from his hand. Clark jumped and lost his focus.

No, he had to have seen that wrong. It was just

because Lex had been talking about *yubizume*, and his imagination must be going into overdrive. He had just refocused his X-ray vision when the back-room door opened and another skeleton quickly walked out. The man was unarmed, and as Clark readjusted his vision, he could see that he was also flushed and agitated. Though young and Japanese, he was less extravagantly dressed than the Yakuza who had walked in earlier, his black leather jacket hip length and his shoes unpolished. Clark watched him exit the bar and swore for a moment that he could hear the man's accelerated heart rate.

Absently, he took a sip of his milk, quickly putting the glass down with a wrinkled nose. It was milk, all right, but chemically pasteurized and reeking of suspicious additives. Clark allowed himself a wistful smile. Here he was, quite possibly the strongest being on the entire planet, and all he wanted was to go back to his family farm in Kansas. Lex would no doubt love the irony.

Clark moved to the bar to get a glass of water when the back-room door opened again and one of the Yakuza cardplayers marched out holding a bloody cocktail napkin against his right hand. The man's face was pale and his eyes were red and shiny with controlled pain, but he was moving normally, heading swiftly for the door.

Clark swallowed and used his X-ray vision again. The man's pinkie had indeed been cleanly severed off at the top joint, and what was worse was that the tip was wrapped up in his left pocket near a gun he had stuck into his belt. A quick glance into the game room established that Lex was still all right. Impulsively, Clark snatched his jacket off of his chair and followed the gunman out.

As noisy and crowded as the bar had been, Clark found the Metropolis night even more overwhelming.

People were rushing in every conceivable direction, on foot and in cars and taxis. The occasional bike or skateboard whizzed by, and helicopters dotted the skyline. Only the chill of the darkness itself provided relief from the chaos of car horns, neon lights, blasting radios, cigarette smoke, and conversations crowding the air in every tongue known to man. Clark stopped outside the bar doors and swallowed. He felt strangely excluded from the dizzying assembly of humanity—a rational notion trying to penetrate a viscosity of sensation.

The crowd had already swallowed up both the gunman and the unhappy gambler who had left before him. Clark had to use his X-ray vision to find the gun the Yakuza guard still carried under his sweeping duster. Despite being able to run faster than he knew how to calculate, Clark had a hard time catching up with the bleeding gunman. He started out at accelerated speed, dodged to avoid one of fourteen people in his way and accidentally brushed his shoulder against a bus stop sign that promptly bent at a sixty-degree angle. He'd never had to worry about running into anyone in the rural cornfields of Smallville. Doubling back at superspeed to straighten out the bus sign before anyone noticed, Clark realized that he was in very real danger of hurting someone if he tried to move through a crowd hyperaccelerated. When the Yakuza turned into a narrow alley between two towering skyscrapers, though, Clark was glad he'd made the effort to stay with him. The gunman had closed in on the unhappy gambler, culling him from the surrounding herd of humanity the way a predator isolates his prey.

"Watanabe," the Yakuza gunman called, all but disappearing into the dark alleyway. Farther down the passage, Clark could hear the footsteps of the gambler stop, then break into a run, heading frantically for the other side of the alley.

The gunman paused to twist what Clark figured must be a silencer onto the end of his weapon, wincing as he tried to hold his newly butchered pinkie aloft, then took aim at the running gambler's back.

Clark heard the click of the Glock's safety and realized he had to act. Though narrow, the alleyway contained only himself, the Yakuza soldier, and Watanabe, the soon-to-be-victim. As the gunman fired, Clark shot by him in a blur of color.

From Clark's perspective, the world around him was instantaneously robbed of movement and speed. He saw an expanding ring of light slowly emerge from the gun's muzzle and watched the bullet ease out of the barrel of the Glock, as if pushed by a child's measured exhalation. He had plenty of time to follow the bullet's trajectory with his eyes and note that it seemed very likely to strike Watanabe between the shoulder blades.

His blue eyes wide, Clark reached into the air and wrapped his hand around the bullet. Everything he'd grown up seeing—the news, the movies, the intermittent crime scene—told him this couldn't be done, that he was about to blow his fist to smithereens. And yet all he felt in his hand was the smooth heat of warmed alloy metal and the vague throb of momentum halted.

To his right, the gunman was squeezing off another shot. To his left, Watanabe continued to run with excruciating slowness. Neither was aware of Clark, and he thought it would probably be best to keep it that way. He was also conscious of the need to dissuade the bleeding gunman from continuing the chase. That would probably require a witness.

Still moving faster than either of the two men could see, Clark waited for the second muzzle flash, scooped that bullet out of the air with his free hand, let both pieces of ammunition drop, and retreated back toward the entrance of the alleyway. There he slowed his speed back to normal, noisily cleared his throat, and stepped into the alley as if entering it for the first time.

"Hey," he called loudly. "I thought I heard gunshots. Is everything all right?"

As he had hoped, the gunman spun toward him, the weapon hidden from view, then turned and ran as fast as he could. Clark pressed his lips together, brow furrowed as he thought for a moment. He shot down the alley at superspeed, passing the Yakuza soldier, who noticed a gust of wind blow by him but didn't know what to make of it. At the end of the alley, Clark turned left and pressed against the side of the building, trying his best to hide himself in the shadows. A quick glance down the street confirmed that Watanabe was still uninjured, on his feet, running, and soon to be lost in the crowd. The Yakuza gunman turned right at the end of the alley and also sprinted off into the crowd, though in the opposite direction. Clark exhaled and stepped away from the wall. He'd saved a life, and although he'd had to use his special gifts to do it, his instincts had led him there. He even allowed himself a slight smile as he joined the heavy foot traffic on a street he didn't know, but he had taken fewer than three steps before he stopped again, the smile vanishing as quickly as it had appeared.

He was lost. He remembered where Lex's apartment was, more or less, but realized that only did so much good if he didn't know where *he* was. Using his X-ray vision, he could see the subway lines running beneath the streets, but didn't know enough about where they went to follow any of them. He headed back into the alley with the idea of at least getting back to the bar, but that didn't do much to calm him. He was probably just hearing things—his ears weren't as good as his eyes, were they?—but it sounded like there were people everywhere, all over the city, screaming for help or crying. Under the constant rumble of traffic and distinct loud snatches of radios, he thought he could hear brakes screeching, gunshots, cries for mercy. Despair crushed down on him like the proverbial safe falling out of the sky. How many people *were* there in this city? How many would die before morning? He swallowed and kept walking down the alley, telling himself over and over that he was imagining things. And yet, an unfamiliar sensation continued to creep up his spine.

With a start, Clark realized that he was afraid. *Don't be ridiculous*, he told himself sternly. *Even if someone jumped out of the darkness right now, they couldn't hurt you*. The minute the thought crossed his mind he stopped dead in his tracks.

But they could hurt Lex, or themselves, or each other. *And that's what I'm really afraid of.* How could people be strong enough to build a city like this, with ninety-story skyscrapers and lights blaring twenty-four hours a day, and yet still be so fragile that their safety relied on the goodwill of every single stranger they passed?

By the time he walked back into the bar, Clark's hands were shaking. A pretty redhead now occupied the table he and Lex had been sitting at. The brunette who had stolen Lex's chair had apparently left with her friends. Clark sat on a stool at the bar, hoping he wouldn't get carded. Concentrating, he squinted through the back-room wall. Lex

was still sitting at the game table, every bone in place.
Clark felt so grateful for his friend's presence that he almost teared up.

Lex knew how to navigate the city. Lex knew how to
keep himself safe. Lex would be able to remind Clark
how people like Watanabe protected themselves with
alarm systems, 911 calls, and pepper spray.

He ordered a cup of coffee and hoped there would
never be a day when he'd have to face Metropolis without Lex there for support.

CHAPTER EIGHT

Agent Green was on a roll. In his former life as Mayer Greenbrae, he'd been tracking an alien he had no idea how to find and depending on others to provide him with work equipment and assignments. As Agent Green, however, he had spent almost no time in Smallville before realizing the identity of the extraterrestrial. It came to him in a sudden flash of insight, mere hours before the creature left town with a friend. At that moment, Agent Green understood that universal forces were on his side, working to help secure his victory. The alien had to be stopped, it was preordained.

Now he was combing through an unoccupied S.T.A.R. Labs storage bay in Metropolis, taking what he wanted. His backpack was full of state-of-the-art spyware, and the gun he had lifted off of Tad's dead body still rested comfortably between his waistband and his hip. Earlier that afternoon, he had tracked his prey to a flashy penthouse in Metropolis. All that was left for Agent Green to do was observe the alien until he could identify either a weakness or a chance opportunity that would allow him to strike.

Agent Green noticed a shadow fall across the doorway behind him but did not bother to turn around.

"Are you finding everything you need?"

The question came from the young lab assistant who

had let him into the storage bay. Agent Green didn't answer. He was busy studying a handful of microcameras. "It must be exciting, working undercover. Not that I don't love my job here, but . . . well, you know."

Agent Green pocketed the microcameras and moved on to a shelf littered with universal adapters and circuit breakers. He had watched the penthouse until the alien and his friend had gone out for the evening, and now moved quickly in the hopes of returning to the building before they did.

"I looked up your ID like you asked," the young woman continued, now leaning casually in the doorway, watching Agent Green. "Everything's in order. It says you don't even work for S.T.A.R. Labs anymore, but that you spent three years in Research and Development improving on astronomy tools. I wouldn't have looked twice at it if you hadn't told me to, it's totally boring. It doesn't give anything away. Well, except your name. *Is* Mayer Greenbrae your real name?"

Agent Green slipped a small spy camera into his backpack, then turned to frown at the lab assistant. "No," he said, after a moment of silence.

The young woman nodded and backed out of the doorway as Agent Green strode out of the storage bay toward the elevator bank. "Um, you do have to sign that stuff out, though," she murmured timidly.

Agent Green stopped in front of the elevators, then turned and walked back to the young woman. She was holding out a clipboard with a sign-out sheet on it and a pen. Taking both from her, he scribbled out a signature before handing them back and returning to the elevators.

"Thank you . . . Tad Nickels!" the lab assistant called after him, grinning as she read his "real" name off of the sign-out sheet. Agent Green offered her the very slightest smile before the elevator doors closed behind him.

He lit a cigarette on his way into the garage, enjoying the way the smoke forced him to squint. He was in a good mood as he approached the shiny red coupe he'd rented that morning in Tad's name after trading in the green clunker he'd originally picked up in Gotham. No one had bled on the interior of this car, and Agent Green intended to keep it that way. He was, however, prepared to make exceptions if necessary.

It took less than half an hour to get from the downtown Metropolis S.T.A.R. Labs facility to the building the alien and his friend were occupying. Agent Green started to pull into the complex's underground garage, then thought better of it, circling the block three times until he found parking on a nearby side street.

He walked around to the lot behind the imposing high-rise carrying a duffel bag and his backpack, then crouched between two trash bins to review the equipment he'd taken from the lab. As he fingered the spyware appreciatively, imagining how he'd put each piece to use and musing over what he might be able to invent later to improve the range or efficiency of any given apparatus, Agent Green slowly realized that he hadn't thought to grab anything that would help with a break-in. He wasn't even sure what that might be. Still crouching between the trash bins, he frowned and shoved his hands into the pockets of his jacket to warm them. His right hand closed around the cold steel of Tad's gun. Tossing his tenth cigarette of the day to the ground, Agent Green closed the duffel bag, rose to his feet, and pulled on a pair of thick suede gloves.

He stood perfectly still in the gathering darkness,

running his plan through his head. Only when he knew exactly what he intended to do did he move, heading straight for the left side of the building.

Years full of city apartment living told Agent Green that a building the size of the one he now circled would most likely have all of its main fuses and utility meters located in a centralized control room. Such rooms were often structurally uninspired and, therefore, tucked away where they wouldn't interfere with the greater architectural scheme of the high-rise to which they belonged. Agent Green located the room on the lower northwest corner of the building in less than two minutes and quickly used the handle of Tad's gun to break the medium-sized hopper window that afforded it a small amount of natural air circulation. With his gloved hands protected from stray glass shards, Agent Green pulled himself up to the shattered window and pitched headfirst into the building.

The control room was dark. As Agent Green had anticipated, his less-than-subtle entry summoned an armed guard, who promptly opened the door to the control room, flooding the entryway with light from the lobby. Somewhere in the back of his head, Agent Green understood that to stop and think about what he was doing would be the end of him. That was precisely why he had been so careful to think it all through in advance.

With his mind blank, Agent Green took aim at the center mass of the man's dark silhouette without bothering to get up from where he'd landed beneath the window. He squeezed the trigger of Tad's gun three times before the guard had even finished asking who was there. It seemed to him that the sound of the shots echoed in the dark for a long time, vanquished, finally, by the soft thud of the guard falling to the tiled floor.

All Agent Green wanted to do was sit on the cool tiles of the dark control room and think about what it meant to have just taken a man's life. Such meditations, however, were not factored into the plan he had rehearsed in his head, and Agent Green knew enough to stick to the plan. He scrambled up to his feet and studied the main control board in the dim light for a moment before deftly cutting power to the building's security cameras and elevators. Next, he cut the main light sources in the lobby and penthouse and waited for the inevitable approach of the doorman, who would, of course, have heard the gunshots.

It didn't take long.

"Ralph?" Agent Green heard a voice calling as heavily soled shoes rushed toward his location. "I thought I heard gunfire, are you—"

The words froze on the doorman's lips as he detected the unmoving form of the security guard splayed out in the opened doorway of the control room. With his eyes more adjusted to the semidarkness, Agent Green was able to see the doorman's eyes flash into his own.

"Please," the doorman started, the fear in his voice evident. "I don't—"

"Come inside," Agent Green heard his own voice command, though he hadn't thought he'd have the guts to speak to either of them. The directive made sense, though. If Agent Green shot the doorman outside of the control room, he'd have to drag his body inside before he left the lobby, which would take up precious time and potentially leave a blood trail. Shooting the doorman inside the control room would eliminate both of those problems.

The doorman complied quickly and quietly, stepping carefully over the prone body of the security guard and thrusting his hands up in the air for good measure, no doubt hoping to be spared for his cooperation.

Despite the doorman's acquiescence, Agent Green suffered a brief moment of panic. For a second it seemed to him that he was Mayer Greenbrae again, and the thought that raced wildly through his head was *What did you do!? You talked to him! You can't shoot a man you've talked to!*

He wanted to run from the room in fear as he heard two more gunshots fired in the dark, but then as the doorman slumped to the floor beside the security guard, he slowly realized that he himself was still standing, that the gun that had been fired was his own.

Or, more precisely, Tad's.

Agent Green closed his eyes and exhaled. He imagined his old self, Mayer Greenbrae, and when he had every detail perfect, he imagined shooting him. *Bang, bang you're dead, don't want to hear you in my head.* Then he opened his eyes again, knelt to take a master card key off the doorman, rose, stepped out of the control room, and closed and locked the door behind him. He moved through the darkened lobby until he found the stairwell, then ran up all twenty-four flights to the penthouse. His hands were shaking, but he didn't stop once until he reached the top, spurred on by the memory of Tad's voice chanting in his brain: ... *You're wrong about the alien. It's a stupid theory, and the more you talk about it, the stupider you sound. I will bet my life*

that you're dead wrong . . . No alien, no field agent . . .
No alien, no field agent . . .

He was sweating by the time he entered the rectangular access hall that separated the penthouse living quarters from the elevator bank, but his breath rose and fell evenly. With every passing moment it became increasingly obvious to Agent Green that he was, in fact, a field agent, and so equally obvious that he was right about the alien. The mirrored walls of the hallway reflected his own image back to him, and Agent Green cocked his head to one side to examine his reflection, feeling sure that there was something different about his appearance. Maybe it was the small splatter of blood on the front of his shirt.

An entire wall of mirrors created an interesting surveillance opportunity. Agent Green placed a camera—smaller than the head of a match—on top of the elaborate molding that surrounded the front door before using the master key to enter the domicile proper.

The Luthor penthouse looked like an advertisement for modern minimalism. Polished concrete flooring ran from the entranceway to a wall of clear glass, which framed the Metropolis skyline magnificently. Floating almost magically from the wall were upturned bowls of frosted glass, perching on swan-necked chrome stems—light sconces, Agent Green realized after studying them for a moment. The entire space was streamlined and clean, and it was difficult to imagine anyone living there despite a few obvious signs of recent occupancy, such as a crystal tumbler cradling a puddle of melted ice on the breakfast bar that separated the kitchen from the living room, and a high school geology textbook left sitting conspicuously on a glass-and-chrome coffee table otherwise wholly devoid of reading material. Agent Green went to work.

He placed microcameras in the light sconces and, pleased with his own inventiveness, on a slowly swirling mobile hanging on the living room ceiling. He refitted the wall sockets in the living room and both occupied bedrooms with outlet surveillance transmitters and switched out the telephone outlet in the master bedroom with a line-powered socket transmitter before installing an Infinity receiver on the main phone line. A microwave transmitter pen camera was slipped into a penholder on the desk in the master bedroom, and the screw head on the kitchen clock was used to conceal yet another microcamera.

Before exiting, he pulled out an expensive spy camera and photographed the contents of two overnight bags he had found on the floors of the master and guest bedrooms respectively. He was hoping to discover some clue as to the alien's powers. The varied reports and articles he had collected indicated that the alien was very strong and very fast, but for all Agent Green knew, he might also be able to turn invisible or, more likely, bend weak human minds to his will. To stop the alien, Agent Green was going to have to find a weakness, a chink in the extraterrestrial's armor. That would require some patience, but Agent Green decided then and there that he was a patient man.

Once he had everything in place, Agent Green slipped out as quietly as he'd slipped in and made it back to the stairwell undetected. He was frowning as he walked down the stairs, through the darkened lobby, and back into the control room to turn the power on again and begin stripping the uniform off of the doorman, but it wasn't because he was unhappy or dissatisfied with his work.

It was because he figured that field agents didn't gloat.

CHAPTER NINE

"Clark, what're you still doing here?"

Though his enunciation was perfect, and his eyes still looked sharp, Lex swayed ever so slightly as he spoke.

"Are you drunk?" Clark asked with an amused smile, collecting his jacket off of the stool next to him and rising to stand next to his friend.

Lex frowned. "Drunk? Nah. Maybe a little tipsy, but certainly not drunk. Sturdy Luthor constitution and all that. . . ." Lex pounded his chest lightly with one fist to emphasize his point. "You've got to keep your wits about you when you're playing cards with guys with guns."

"How'd you make out?"

Lex, who already had his coat on, put an arm around Clark's shoulder and started leading him out of the bar. The crowd had been steadily thinning out since a little after one, and now, at a quarter to two, only three alcoholics, two couples, and one game of pool players remained. The bartender winked at Clark as Clark slipped a few dollars onto the counter as thanks for the four cups of coffee and six glasses of water he'd drunk while waiting.

"I lost eighteen thousand dollars," Lex said without blinking. "It was a great game. Do you play poker?"

Clark shook his head. "Last card game I played was Go Fish."

Lex laughed and led Clark back outside into the city night, where he let go of him long enough to saunter confidently into the middle of the street and hail a taxi. Clark stayed on the sidewalk and shouldered on his coat, watching Lex with the strange mixture of admiration and apprehension that seemed to war in his heart every time he was alone with his friend.

"Lionel and I used to play that," Lex confessed, as a yellow cab pulled up inches away from his polished shoes. Clark stepped off the curb and waited while Lex slid into the taxi's backseat. "Only we used corporate holdings instead of cards. 'I know you've got thirty-six shares of Byline Pharmaceuticals, son, you couldn't have already dumped those . . .' "

Clark slid in after Lex, smiling at his friend's impersonation of Lionel, which included a glower that Clark didn't think he'd ever actually seen on Lex's father's face and a conceited wagging back and forth of the head that definitely looked familiar.

"Luthor Tower Two," Lex told the driver, leaning forward. Clark closed the door behind him as Lex sank back against the tattered leather seat.

"I'm surprised you don't have a car service in the city," Clark commented.

"We've got three," Lex answered, turning his head to grin at Clark. "But every time I use any of them, my dad gets a full report on my comings and goings. Besides, the drivers are all LuthorCorp employees—I'd rather spread the money around a little."

Lex exhaled contentedly, turning his head to look out the window to his left.

"You know, you really didn't have to wait for me, Clark," Lex remarked after a minute of silence. "I'm a big boy. I can find my way back to my penthouse all by myself."

"I know," Clark said quietly, staring at the litter on the cab floor and wondering about the people who might have left it there. He prodded a mustard-stained napkin with his shoe. "It was me. I got kind of lost."

Lex closed his eyes and nodded slowly, reaching into his coat pocket. He pulled out his wallet. Eyes still shut, he pulled out a bill at random and offered it to Clark. It was one hundred dollars. Clark's eyes grew wide.

"What's that for?"

"Cab fare. I wasn't thinking. I should have hooked you up earlier."

Clark smiled and shook his head.

"Put your money away, Mr. Luthor." He meant it as a joke, but realized his miscalculation when Lex's eyes snapped open and the corners of his mouth tightened slightly. Clark rushed on as Lex stuffed the bill back into his pocket. "I had enough money for a taxi," Clark continued, "It wasn't that. It was the city. I just . . . there are so many people here, you know? It's nothing like Smallville. How does . . . how does everyone stay safe?"

"They don't." Lex shrugged. "People get hurt. Some even get killed. But more take their place." Lex turned toward Clark again with a quiet smile. "I'm sorry if that offends your 'all men are created equal and every life is sacred' sensibilities."

Clark watched the streetlights smear against the dirty window of the moving cab and tried to explain.

"I know everyone's not equal, exactly, but no one deserves to die."

Lex sat forward, pressing his hands in between his knees as he stared off into space.

"Let me tell you a little story, Clark. Legend has it, when the first Navajo arrived on Earth, they wanted to know whether or not they'd live forever. So they went to the edge of a sacred lake, and one of them picked up a piece of wood, and said, 'If it floats, we will live forever. If it sinks, then our lives will be finite and in time each one of us will die.' He threw the stick into the lake, it floated, and they were all very pleased. But then the trickster Coyote appeared and said that as a distinguished spirit, he'd be better able to divine the truth of their destinies than they. The guys on the edge of the shore weren't too happy about that, since they liked the answer they'd gotten, but they knew that, as much of a pain in the ass as he was, Coyote was a powerful spirit, and could in fact divine the truth. So they watched as he picked up a rock and, under the same terms they had laid out before, tossed it into the lake. The rock sank, and the Navajo were pissed. But then Coyote told them that it was unwise to have infinite lives in finite space. 'Eventually,' he told them, 'if you all live forever and have children and they have children and so on, there will be no room for the children to play and no room for the corn to grow.' The Navajo understood Coyote's logic, and begrudgingly accepted their fate."

Lex paused and turned toward his friend.

"So you tell me, Kansas boy—which is more important? People or corn?"

"That's a good story," Clark answered. He didn't feel like pointing out that if there were no people, there'd be no particular need to grow corn. He understood the message of the tale, but thoughts of mortality always made him uncomfortable. He wasn't sure whether or not he himself was mortal, and reminders of the transience of his family and friends were nerve-wracking. Lex sat back again with a sigh.

"My mother told it to me," he said quietly. There was a hint of sadness in Lex's voice, and Clark turned back toward his window with furrowed brows. He felt like Lex had just proven his point. Lex's life would have been so different, so much better, if someone had been able to save his mother.

"Take her situation, for instance," Lex said, ostensibly thinking along the same lines but arriving at a different conclusion. "Nobody attacked her. Nobody put her life into jeopardy. She just got sick. It wasn't anybody's fault, and there was nothing anybody could do. It's just part of being alive."

"Here?" the cab driver asked from the front.

"This is fine, thanks," Lex answered, and the taxi came to a stop. Lex handed the driver the hundred-dollar bill Clark had refused and smiled at him politely.

"Got change for a twenty?" he asked.

The driver looked at the bill in his hand, looked back at Lex, and quickly tucked the money away.

"Sure," he said evenly.

"Lex," Clark started, alarmed, "that's not a twe—"

Lex turned his head ever so slightly, offered Clark a quick wink, and accepted four dollars and twenty cents from the cab driver before sliding out of the taxi. Clark followed him out, confused. Lex was smiling as the cab pulled away. He put a hand on Clark's shoulder and started heading toward his building's front door, unceremoniously dumping the change in his coat pocket.

"Let that be a lesson to you, Clark. There's a reason people don't trust each other. And while we're on the sub-

ject, you had better remember that no good deed goes un-
punished, and that people are *not* really good at heart."

"Some of them are," Clark said quietly, as they
approached the awning-covered entranceway of the
building.

Something about the doorman looked wrong to Clark.
He wasn't the same man who had been there when they
had left, but Clark realized that it was much later and
shifts had probably changed. This man was thinner, probably in his late thirties, with brown hair and green eyes.
There was a scar on his chin, and his uniform didn't seem
to fit correctly.

"Welcome back, Mr. Luthor," he said, moving to open
the door for Lex and giving the rich young man a rather
unsubtle once-over. Clark glanced at Lex, but Lex wasn't
even looking at the doorman as he entered the ornate entrance hall. Lex had said many times before that he was
used to people staring at him, and Clark realized that he
must have learned to tune it out. Clark tried to make eye
contact with the doorman as he thanked him, but the
doorman now held his gaze low, and Clark was forced to
follow Lex in without making any kind of real connection.

"Did the doorman seem weird to you?" Clark asked, as
the elevator doors closed behind them. Lex looked deep
in thought, but lifted his head with a slight frown and met
Clark's eyes.

"Didn't notice. Why?"

"I don't know," Clark admitted, "he just looked at you
kind of strangely, and his uniform seemed like it was the
wrong size."

Lex surprised Clark by reaching forward to push the

emergency stop button on the elevator, his expression completely serious.

"Want to go back down and check it out?" he asked. Clark felt shyly flattered that Lex had so much faith in his instincts, but he didn't want to trouble his preoccupied friend.

"No, that's okay," he said, reaching across Lex to push the penthouse button. "I'm sure it's nothing."

"I hope that doesn't disappoint you," Lex said with a smirk as the elevator started up again. Clark shot him a quizzical glance. "I know how much you like solving problems," Lex clarified with a wink. Clark shook his head, smiling slightly, as the elevator doors opened to the top floor.

Lex stepped out into the entrance hall, and Clark followed him, hands in his pockets.

"Believe me, I'm perfectly content when things are calm," he asserted, as Lex used his card key to unlock the doors that led to the living space. "It's just that when they're not, I feel like I should try to help."

"I've noticed," Lex said with a wry smile.

"Oh, like you're not always ready to lend a hand whenever my family's in trouble." Clark laughed, following Lex's lead and tossing his jacket over the back of the black leather couch.

"You Kents are a special case." Lex grinned. He was moving toward the back balcony, casually shedding his shoes and shirt as he went. "Believe me, I'm not usually so altruistic."

"I'm not sure I believe that," Clark answered with a soft smile. The smile turned into a laugh as Lex removed his socks and pants, then slid open the hidden door to the balcony. "What are you doing?"

"Hot tub," Lex said. "Join me?"

Outside on the balcony, Lex was already sliding the top off the tub. Clark became dimly aware of an electronic buzzing noise in the apartment, but didn't think anything of it as he made a quick pit stop in the guest bathroom to grab a pair of towels, then joined his friend.

Steam was coming off the bubbling water as Clark stepped out onto the balcony, leaving the glass door open behind him. Lex was leaning back in the hot water with his eyes closed as Clark slipped in across from him. Liquid warmth seeped into every muscle, the buzzing sound from the apartment unheard over the nighttime city noises, and Clark found himself beginning to relax. Until that moment, he hadn't realized the extent to which he was still carrying the tension of the narrowly avoided Yakuza assassination with him. He was tempted to tell Lex about it, but didn't know how to do so without alarming his friend. It was difficult to figure out how to share the story without mentioning his own invulnerability to bullets.

Turning his head to admire the view, the cool night air contrasting deliciously with the heat of the water, Clark suddenly understood the difference having money could make in the scope of urban living. The city lights glittered below the balcony like stars reflected in a deep, still lake, and from this height the teeming life of Metropolis—the struggles and despair and frantic rushing he'd felt closing in on him in the alleyway behind the bar—seemed natural and enduring.

"This is nice." Clark sighed, sinking farther into the roiling water. Lex opened his eyes and stretched.

"I was thinking about this on the whole drive down. Can I get you a drink?"

"No thanks, I'm fine," Clark answered, letting his own eyes close. Without moving much, Lex reached into a cooler behind him and pulled out a chilled bottle of sparkling water.

"You know, Clark," he started, after taking a long swallow of the mineral water. Clark opened his eyes to see Lex peering at him through the steam. "It's a little easier to help people in a small town than it is to help people in a big city. I know you can take care of yourself, but—" Lex paused, thinking for the millionth time of the day they'd met. He took another swallow of his water and continued. "Just . . . stay aware of your surroundings. There are a lot of people getting into trouble all over this city, and most of them don't want to be helped." Clark was watching him with such concentration and worry that Lex had to smile. "I know," Lex went on, "because I used to be one of them. Oh, I'd get so pissed when someone tried to help me." He chuckled to himself as Clark sat forward.

"What finally happened?" Clark asked.

Lex shrugged. "I grew out of it. Saved myself. That's usually the way it happens around here."

Clark nodded, knowing that Lex's advice was well intended. But how could he let someone get shot when he knew he had the power to stop it? That was what threw him off about Metropolis. In Smallville, he had a pretty good sense of what he could and couldn't help with. But the city felt like a domino effect waiting to happen. How many other people got shot while he was saving Watanabe? If he held himself responsible for saving that one life, didn't he have to hold himself responsible for them all? It was almost easier to take Lex's counsel to heart and stay out of it. But that wasn't how Clark Kent had been raised. He struggled to find a way to explain this to Lex.

"I can understand that," Clark said carefully, "but think of it this way. You've got a lot of money, right? So, for example, when my family is having trouble keeping up payments on the farm, it's the most natural thing in the world for you to offer to help us out." Clark furrowed his brows, feeling Lex's unwavering gaze on him and knowing he had to proceed with caution. "I . . . feel inclined to help people in trouble. It's just in my nature, it makes me feel . . . well, connected to everyone else. And I'm not a different person when I'm in the city than I am when I'm in Smallville. Just like you're no less rich when you're here than you are at home—" Clark had more to say, but Lex had lifted up a hand and was shaking his head.

"Gotta disagree with you there, Clark. I have the same amount of money tonight as I had this morning—well, give or take a few thousand—but this morning I had that money in a town with a median income of twenty-nine thousand, whereas tonight I've got it in a city with a median income of fifty-two thousand. Just like this morning you were one guy trying to help out in a town of forty-five thousand, but tonight, well, you're one of ten million, nine hundred and twenty thousand. Makes a bit of a difference, don't you think?"

"So what do you suggest I do?" Clark asked. "Be less of a moral person in the city than I am on my dad's farm?"

Lex let a slow smile spread across his face as he thought through the implications of Clark's insincere proposal. There were times when the young Kent was so naive it was damn near heartbreaking.

"I suggest you go to bed, Clark," Lex said as he

averted his gaze. "It's late, and I feel confident that the city of Metropolis—known, after all, as the City of Tomorrow—will be safe without you at least until dawn." Lex smiled again and placed his empty water bottle on the tiled side of the hot tub before reaching around to grab the towel Clark had left for him. "Besides," he muttered, "your mother would kill me if she knew I kept you up this late."

"On that point, we're in complete agreement." Clark grinned, rising and stepping out of the water. He hoped his friend would follow his own advice. Lex still looked content and alert to Clark, who wasn't used to seeing the young industrialist show any vulnerabilities at all, but he knew that he had to be tired. "Good night," he offered cheerfully.

Lex turned and offered him a lazy smile. "Sleep well, Clark," he answered, watching the teenager head back into the penthouse, water beading on his powerfully built body and a red towel hooked around his waist. Lex wondered if Clark's desire to do good in the world was anything like his own ambition to be an unqualified success. Somewhere under all that genuine kindness and morality, was there an abandoned child's need to prove his own worthiness lest he be abandoned again? Lex, who considered himself an excellent judge of character, sensed no egoism in Clark, but there was some kind of weight on the young man's shoulders, something darker, or at least heavier, than the simple inclination to be helpful.

Lex shut off the jets, stepped out of the water, and toweled himself dry as he stared out over the view Clark had found so captivating. The high-rise to the left of his building, Luthor Tower One, was almost completely dark, the bluish light of TV sets flickering in only a few of the visible windows. Lex dragged the cover back across the hot tub and went in, wrapping himself in a robe of black satin he'd left hanging in the master bedroom.

On a whim, he intercommed to the doorman, but no one answered. That in and of itself was odd, but nothing Lex was going to lose any sleep over. He'd look into it in the morning. With one last glance around the apartment, he turned off the lights and headed into the master bedroom. The solid veneer birch panel headboard gleamed in the soft light of the reading lamp Lex had left on before he and Clark had ventured out to the bar, and the crisp, linen sheets looked cool and inviting. He had one more objective to accomplish, however, before he could allow himself the luxury of sleep.

Grabbing his cell phone, Lex flipped it open and speed-dialed a local number.

Across the way, in Luthor Tower One, Agent Green dialed in on the Infinity receiver the minute he lost visual contact. The living room had gone dark, and although he had grabbed both night-vision goggles and a photo-sniper camera from S.T.A.R. Labs, the apartment he'd infiltrated offered him a view of only the living and dining areas. Both the alien and his companion had now retreated into bedrooms, and Agent Green was hoping to be able to hear whether or not the alien slept. Instead, he picked up one half of a cell phone conversation.

"Hey, Lorelei, it's Lex . . . A little after four I think, why? . . . Well, you said to call you when I was next in the city, something about clearing your calendar? . . . I just thought you might want to get an early start on that . . . That's not Charlie, is it? Put him on! . . . I just wanted to say hello to him, Lorelei, relax . . . Look, I'll pick you up tomorrow evening at nine. Tell Charlie I said 'hi' . . ."

Agent Green heard what must have been the phone snapping shut, then a soft chuckle. There was the gentle clack of something being put down—the cell phone on the nightstand, he guessed—the click of a switch, a slight rustling of sheets, then silence. Agent Green listened for nearly twenty minutes until he heard slow, rhythmic breathing coming from both bedrooms. He dialed out of the Infinity reception, thinking it would be smart to rest while the alien and his friend both slept. The couch would have to do for tonight, though.

Agent Green had managed to shoot the elderly couple in the apartment he needed without much trouble, but the idea of sleeping in their bed made his stomach turn.

CHAPTER TEN

Jonathan rolled over in bed to frown at the clock on his nightstand. It was half past four, way too late to be awake still, yet early enough to give up trying and get out of bed. Careful not to wake Martha, he slipped out from under the covers, put his bare feet on the cold wood floor, and stretched. The sun was still at least half an hour away from rising, and after the cozy warmth of the bed, the dark air around him was bracing. He turned to gently pull the quilt up around Martha's shoulders before padding quietly into the bathroom to wash up and get ready for the day.

Once outside, he felt more at ease, but all the more absurd for being worried in the first place.

"I know he can take care of himself," he told the chickens as he tossed their feed to them in large handfuls. Only the rooster resisted the lure of scattered corn kernels and scratch pellets long enough to feign interest in the conversation. "Hell," Jonathan told it with a slight smile, "there's probably no parent on the planet who wouldn't trade places with me in a heartbeat. I mean, as long as Clark stays away from those green meteorites, there's really nothing that can hurt him at all, right?" The rooster rotated his head eighty degrees to watch for the still-absent sun, then turned his gaze back on Jonathan.

"Although I'm not sure how he'd feel about his father talking to poultry," came his wife's voice.

Jonathan jumped, then turned around with a sheepish smile. Martha stood by the henhouse wrapped in a quilted robe, shivering slightly in the dark.

"Sorry, sweetheart," Jonathan said, coming toward her, "I didn't mean to wake you."

"I couldn't sleep either," Martha confessed, as Jonathan took her in his arms. "Aren't we a pair?"

Jonathan rocked her slowly in his embrace, and neither of them started when the rooster caught the first gleam of sunlight and let out a sudden triumphant crow. His cry had been their alarm clock for years.

"You know what I think it is?" Jonathan whispered into his wife's hair. She tipped her head back to look up at him. Behind him, the sky had just begun to blush with the sun's first rays. "It's that when things *do* happen to him, they're so outside my realm of experience, I . . . I'm just so afraid that if he ever *does* need me, there won't be anything I can do to help him."

Martha nodded, hugging him tightly.

"I feel exactly the same way," she admitted softly, her voice still throaty and warm from sleep. "I thought I'd be kissing scrapes and bruises better and putting bandages over skinned knees, but instead . . . even when it *is* something within the range of what I expected, like his feelings for Lana, all the good advice I thought I had to give seems completely beside the point. What am I supposed to tell him, Jonathan? 'I'm sure she'll like you if you just be yourself'? We've forbidden him just to be himself!"

Jonathan swallowed, nodding.

"I know. Living on a farm forced me to address the birds and the bees early on, but I never took it beyond the barn with him. I just have no idea what to tell him when it comes to *people*. And he has so much faith in us . . ." Jonathan paused, looking over his shoulder at the glowing horizon. "I feel like I'm perpetually about ten minutes away from failing him completely," he admitted. "It would be such a . . . *relief* if he called and told me he'd had a little too much to drink and was afraid to drive the truck home. But I just know that one of these days he's going to call and tell me the world is about to come to an end and ask what he should do."

"Save it," Martha said with sudden confidence, gently pulling away from her husband's embrace. "Tell him to save it."

Jonathan watched her for a moment in the glow of dawn, then nodded.

"I'm sure he's fine," he asserted.

Martha smiled at him and nodded back.

"I'll go make breakfast," she said. "We can give him a call at Lex's tonight."

Jonathan watched his wife turn and head back into the house, her head held high. He smiled as he turned to lock up the henhouse, feeling his love and gratitude for his family run through his veins like caffeine. Sometimes it gave him the shakes, but it always woke him up and made him feel ten times stronger.

Lionel was awakened from a dead sleep by the ringing of a telephone. Brushing his long, wavy hair out of his eyes, he glowered in the general direction of the clock and reached for the phone, sure that it was not yet five in the morning. Unforgivable.

"This had better be good," Lionel snapped, half-expecting to hear a confused broker from the Tokyo

Stock Exchange begin making obsequious apologies. The voice he heard did have a faint Asian accent, but it wasn't anyone calling from Tokyo.

"Your son is in Metropolis," the voice stated flatly.

Lionel frowned and rubbed the scratchy stubble on his cheek.

"Lex? Yes, I know, I sent him there."

His confirmation was met with patient silence. Lionel sat up in bed and rubbed his temples. He felt like he'd just come in in the middle of a chess game being played by mail and was being asked to defend a board he'd never seen. He took a deep, slow breath, collecting himself, then ran the conversation over in his head once more.

Your son is in Metropolis . . . This, of course, from the group who persisted in claming he owed them money, who were themselves based in Metropolis. Lionel straightened, and laughed suddenly, his shoulders relaxing.

"Are you threatening to hurt Lex if I don't pay up?" Lionel's entire disposition had changed. He suddenly couldn't think of a more amusing wake-up call.

"If you value your son's safety—" the voice began, but Lionel cut him off, his eyes narrowing as his tone took on a hard, sardonic edge.

"You have no idea what I value. Shall I tell you? I value competence, and ruthlessness, and achievement. As far as I can tell, my son possesses none of those qualities. I suppose he has potential, but that's of negligible worth. If you want to kill Lex, you go right ahead. His participation in LuthorCorp is nominal, I can have a qualified headhunter replace him in less than twenty hours. Would you like an address for him?"

Lionel smiled menacingly as he noted the confused

silence on the other end of the line. Finally, his "creditor" spoke once more.

"I find it very difficult to believe that you are so unconcerned with the safety of your only son, Mr. Luthor."

"You've got to do your homework, my friend. If you'd called and told me that you'd talked to Lex and *he'd* agreed to work with *you* to kill *me*, well, then I might be worried. But calling me to say you might destroy *him*? I could destroy my son more effectively than you can possibly imagine."

"Be assured," the voice on the other end of the line continued, and Lionel smirked to himself imagining the man reading off some kind of script, "that we have no intention of hurting the younger Luthor, providing that you agree to cooperate with our plan. We have devised a way for you to give us the money you owe without compromising the public relations image of LuthorCorp. It will cause your son only minimal inconvenience and discomfort, and you will come away looking like a hero."

Lionel leaned back against his goose-down pillows and smiled.

"An opportunity for self-promotion, then? Why didn't you say so? Now that's something I do value. Go ahead. I'm listening . . . ."

CHAPTER ELEVEN

She stood with her back to him, then turned suddenly, her face lighting up with a brilliant smile that he somehow understood was meant for him alone. Clark felt his whole body tighten in anticipation, every nerve on edge.

"Lana," he whispered. "What are *you* doing here?"

"I'm always here," she answered, still smiling, the bridge of her nose wrinkled in amusement. The statement made no sense to Clark, who for a moment wasn't even sure where "here" was, but Lana said it with such easy confidence, he let it go.

She sat down on the edge of the bed in the guest room of Lex's Metropolis penthouse and crossed her legs, still smiling up at him. It seemed to Clark that she was the only source of light, incandescent and framed by a radiant halo that did little to illuminate the murky corners of the room. Cocking her head to one side, she looked up at him from under a fringe of dark lashes.

"I've known all this time, you know," she said, holding his gaze. "We all know. You don't have to go through this alone."

"You—you do?" he asked, amazed. Noticing that he was leaning against the wall across from the bed, he began to move slowly toward her.

"Of course, silly." Lana laughed lightly, then shook her head, still smiling. He knelt in front of her on the rug, gazing at her with longing that went well beyond the physical, longing that made him ache.

"What do you know?" he asked carefully, afraid to hold too much hope.

"You're supposed to be here, Clark," Lana said seriously, leaning forward to take his face gently in her hands as her smile was replaced by an expression of intense thoughtfulness. "It isn't an accident. You were sent to us, to me. I won't pretend to know anything about where you're from, but I know where you belong. You know, too, don't you?"

A cloud of worry crossed her face, and Clark rose on his knees to take her hands in his own.

"Yes. I've known since the first moment I saw you, when we were five. I've known all this time."

"Why didn't you tell me?" Lana asked with a small smile. "I've been waiting so long for you to tell me how you feel."

Clark thought about Whitney, the boyfriend she had had until he left for the Marines, and he thought about the few times he'd tried to say something to Lana, and how it had always felt like the wrong time. There was always too much at risk, and he felt that his secrets would burden her life in some unfair way.

"I was afraid if I told you one truth, I'd tell them all," he heard himself saying.

"Oh, Clark . . ." She leaned toward him, lowering her face toward his, her soft lips grazing his own. Clark surged forward, desperate to receive the kiss, but she pulled back, and it remained ephemeral, a suggestion of a kiss. A wish.

"How did you find out?" he asked when he opened his eyes again. "I've tried to be so careful."

"I told her."

Clark craned his head and looked over his shoulder as Lex emerged from the corner closest to the door, hands in the pockets of his slacks, head held at the usual high, watchful angle. "You didn't honestly think I wouldn't figure it out, did you, Clark?"

Clark swallowed and rose unsteadily to his feet, still holding one of Lana's hands as he turned to face Lex. Lana remained perched on the side of the bed, seemingly unsurprised by Lex's presence in the room.

"I—wanted to tell you," he started, but Lex cut him off.

"No, you didn't. You're afraid of me. All I ever wanted was your trust, Clark. That's all any of us ever wanted. You say you care about us, but you lie to our faces every day."

Lex took a few steps forward and reached out to Lana, who let go of Clark's hand to take Lex's, rising to stand between them. Clark felt the room constricting. The galvanizing rush of inclusion that had come with Lana's confession was growing cold around him, twisting in Lex's mouth into something dark and lonely, something that isolated him from everyone in the world with ever-increasing finality.

"Well, no more," Lex continued, his jaw tight and his eyes flashing menacingly. Clark wanted to go down on his knees before him and beg his friend not to do this, not to give up on him. "I'm looking out for you, as usual. I told everyone, Clark. Everybody knows. That's what you wanted, isn't it? *Isn't it?*"

Isn't it?

Clark woke with a start, his mouth dry and his heart pounding in his chest. He sat up with a long exhale, trying to shake off something that felt like a cross between panic and grief. He had left the blinds open in the room and could see the Metropolis sky absorbing the first light of morning, the color of clay.

The strange electronic buzzing sound that had annoyed Clark the evening before hummed persistently in his ears again, setting his teeth on edge. He knew he wouldn't be able to go back to sleep, so he threw the sheets off and rose with a stretch. He made the bed carefully, trying to be a respectful houseguest, then went into the guest bathroom to shower. Once dressed, he walked barefoot into the living room and sat down at the sleek, modern desk placed before the all-glass wall. He picked up the phone and dialed, listening as it rang twice. He sat up straighter, alert and needful, as a woman's voice answered.

"Hello?"

"Mom?"

Clark imagined his mother smiling at the sound of his voice and caught himself smiling back in response, as if she were right in front of him.

"Clark, honey! Is everything okay?"

"Yeah, it's fine. I didn't wake you, did I?"

"No, no," she assured him, chuckling. "Your father's been up since five measuring the irrigation tubing."

"Don't let him lay the pipe without me. I don't want him to hurt himself."

"I promise, I'll make him wait. Oh, I'm so glad you called. We were going to try to reach you tonight. We miss you. Are you and Lex having a good time?"

"Yeah, it's—the city, you know . . ."

Martha laughed.

"Yes, I know. It can be a bit overwhelming, can't it?"

Clark smiled, relieved that she understood.

"Yeah. But Lex's place is amazing. I love the view. You can't see very many stars at night, but if you look down at Metropolis, it's almost the same effect, like you're flying over it. You know, all these twinkling lights, and some of them are hiding the most amazing stories— a galaxy of them, just waiting to be discovered."

"Yes, I remember. I remember always wondering where everyone was going. Oh, wait, here's your father. I know he wanted to talk to you. Hold on a minute." Clark could hear his mother lower the phone, then the muffled sounds of his father taking over the line.

"Hey, son!" Jonathan's voice was enthusiastic and full of affection, and for a moment Clark wanted more than anything to be home. "How's life in the big city?"

"Hi, Dad! Well, it's not like the farm, that's for sure."

"Yeah, you can say that again. Listen, is everything all right?"

"Yeah, fine, Dad, I just wanted to say hi. Hey, um . . ." Clark paused, looked over his shoulder at Lex's closed bedroom door, and dropped his voice slightly. ". . . Do you think there will ever be a time when I won't have to, you know, hide everything?"

There was a tense silence on the other end of the line, and Clark could imagine his parents, both huddled close to the phone, exchanging an uneasy glance.

"Why are you asking?" Jonathan asked suspiciously.

"No reason. It was just on my mind."

"Son," his father started with a warning in his voice, "we've discussed this. Is Lex giving you a hard time?"

"No!" Clark exhaled noisily, irritated with his father's relentless misgivings about Lex and the weird buzzing noise in the apartment. The last thing he wanted was an argument. "No," he said more calmly, "he's been a perfect host. I just . . ." Clark trailed off, not sure what exactly it was that he wanted.

"Lex Luthor is the last person in the world you should be confiding in, Clark. I know you consider him a friend, but the Luthors have proved to be very untrustworthy."

"Jonathan," Clark could hear his mother gently admonish.

"Never mind," Clark mumbled. He heard his father take a deep breath.

"Clark, look," Jonathan started more softly. "Eventually, it's going to be up to you, son. Your mother and I will support you in whatever decisions you make. You know that, right?"

Clark swallowed, nodded, then realized he had to speak.

"Yeah. Yeah, I know. I just—I have no idea how I'm supposed to decide."

"Well, don't worry about that right now. That's exactly why your mother and I wanted to give you some time. Clark, I know the . . . secret you keep is a tremendous burden, but having it out there would just be another kind of responsibility. I wish I could take on those burdens for you, but . . . it's just not possible. All your mother and I can do is give you a safe, supportive place to come home to and try to buy you some time. The hard decisions are gonna be yours. But you don't have to make any yet, okay?"

"Thanks, Dad." Clark exhaled again, feeling better. The sky outside was growing lighter, and as always, Clark felt somewhat cheered and strengthened by the warmth of the sun. "Well, I should get off the phone. I don't want to run up Lex's long-distance. But I'll be home soon, okay, so just wait on those pipes."

Jonathan laughed.

"Yes, sir," he chuckled.

"Good-bye, honey. We love you!" his mother called from the background. "Call anytime!"

"Bye, Mom. Bye, Dad. I love you, too. Talk to you soon!"

Clark hung up the phone and looked out over the city again. What had Lex said, ten million, nine hundred and twenty thousand? That was a lot of people to tell a secret to, and this was only one city . . .

Lex woke up to an unfamiliar smell. He got out of bed, threw on his robe, and strode into the kitchen to find Clark showered, fully dressed, and washing dishes.

"There's a warm plate for you in the oven," he said with a smile, barely looking up from the pan he was scrubbing as Lex came into the room. "It's just eggs and toast, but even a lame breakfast is better than no breakfast."

"I don't eat breakfast," Lex replied, still looking a little dazed.

"That's not good for you," Clark frowned. "Breakfast is the—"

"—most important meal of the day," Lex finished, his tone singsong and mocking.

"Well, it is," Clark said, pretending to be wounded by his friend's irreverence.

Lex chuckled. "All right, I'll make you a deal, Clark." Clark grinned as Lex fully awoke, bargaining, teasing, and taking control of the situation all at once, as was his special talent. "You make some coffee, and when I get out of the shower, then maybe—just maybe—I'll try your twice-warmed toast and soggy eggs."

"Don't do me any favors." Clark winked, but he set about making coffee as Lex went off to shower.

When Lex emerged a short while later, groomed and fully clothed, Clark already had a place set for him, complete with a place mat, linen napkin, glittering silverware, oven-warmed breakfast plate, and a steaming cup of coffee. Clark himself was sitting at the table sipping his own mug of coffee as he read the *Daily Planet*. Lex took his seat at the head of the table, mildly amused that Clark had put him there and wondering if any thought had gone into it. He lifted the steaming coffee to his lips gratefully and reached for the business section.

"You know, cold scrambled eggs are really gross," Clark warned teasingly, still half-hidden in the Metro section.

"More so than hot scrambled eggs?" Lex asked lightly, also now obscured behind the paper.

Clark laughed, but Lex looked up as the laugh died in Clark's throat too abruptly.

"Did you see this?" Clark asked, thrusting his section of the paper toward Lex. Clark watched as Lex's composed expression gave way to a dark frown. After reading for a moment, Lex put the paper down and stared at Clark.

"What, exactly, did you see?" he asked. Clark shook his head.

"Just exactly what I said. His uniform looked a little too small, and he was looking at you funny. It was a vibe more than anything else."

"Why the hell hasn't anyone called me?" Lex asked tightly, rising abruptly and heading into his room. A minute later he strode back into the dining area with his cell phone already pressed against his ear. A quick glance at his watch seemed to make Lex even more agitated. "Now I'm going to be late," he mumbled.

"You have a meeting this morning?" Clark asked.

Lex nodded curtly and focused his attention on the person on the other end of his cell phone.

"This is Lex Luthor calling from Tower Two—why am I reading about compromised security for this building in this morning's *Planet*? Yes, I'm talking about the murders . . ." Lex glanced at Clark and shook his head at the stupidity of the person he was talking to. "He did? When?" Clark watched with sympathy as Lex let out a frustrated sigh. He could guess what turn the conversation had just taken. Lex ran a hand over his smooth head. "Isn't he in Europe? I see. Well, next time, if I'm the one in the building, I'd like to be informed *before* my father. Thank you. By the way, when were the bodies discovered? All right. Double the security shifts on both towers until further notice." Lex snapped the phone shut and took another quick look at his watch.

"I've got to go," he told Clark, almost apologetically. "Make yourself at home."

"What did you find out?" Clark asked.

"Nothing we didn't already know. They found the bodies around five in the morning, which was after we came in. Both of them were in the control room, but only the doorman had been stripped. It's possible that the doorman who let us in was involved somehow; a lookout, or even the murderer dressed in the dead man's uniform. Just . . . keep your eyes open, okay?"

Clark nodded.

"You too," he said quietly, and was gratified when Lex

nodded in return. Lex had started for the door when he stopped suddenly and turned to face Clark once more with a snap of his fingers, as if just remembering something.

"Oh, and we've got dates tonight. Separately. Yours starts at six."

"Wait, what?" Clark asked, eyes wide. He'd fully expected Lex to hit the town with a lady friend or two, but what was this "we" business?

"Dinner's part of the package, and you'll want to dress nicely, but nothing extreme. Just show up ready to have a good time. Everything's all taken care of."

"Lex, you—you didn't . . . ."

Lex had to press his lips together to keep from laughing. Clark looked so utterly horrified as he flashed his open palms at Lex, at an obvious and total loss for words.

"What, you think I want you hanging around here while I do my thing? No, you're gonna be across town. And you're going to have a good time, I promise. So please, just relax, and make sure you're ready by five-thirty. There'll be a car waiting at exactly six."

"That's . . . really . . . um, *generous*, Lex, but I—I don't want—"

"Sometimes your friends know what's best, Clark. Trust me on this one."

"Actually, I thought I'd hit the museum today," Clark said quickly, pushing his chair back and rising to clear away Lex's untouched breakfast plate. "Start getting some notes on those achondrites and everything. I could be there kinda late . . ."

"The museum closes at five. But it opens at eight, so come on, and I'll give you a ride," Lex offered, distractedly frowning down at the LCD display on his cell phone and taking one last sip of coffee.

"Oh, um, okay. Cool."

Clark hurriedly cleared Lex's plate from the table as Lex snatched up his briefcase and shoved his cell phone into his coat pocket. Going with Lex would buy Clark at least ten more minutes to try to get Lex to cancel this disastrous date idea, as well as getting him out of the apartment with its strange buzzing noises, so he was all but moving at superspeed as he hurried to get ready.

"Thanks for breakfast," Lex said with a wink as Clark dumped Lex's eggs and toast into the garbage disposal. Clark rolled his eyes, smiling, and grabbed his backpack, following Lex out toward the elevators.

"Do you have enough money to get yourself some lunch and get back safely and everything?" Lex asked, as they rode the elevator down to the lobby. He was already reaching for his wallet.

"You're underestimating the public's demand for organic vegetables," Clark replied, his blue eyes sparkling. "I'll be fine."

Lex chuckled as the elevator announced their arrival in the lobby with an electronic chime.

"About this date thing, though," Clark continued. The doors slid open, and Lex swept out toward the building's front doors, Clark hurrying after him.

"It's too late to cancel it, Clark, sorry. You'll just have to suck it up this time."

They both gave the doorman a hard look as he held the door open for them, then went back to their individual brooding as they rushed toward Lex's waiting car. This morning it seemed that Lex had decided to let the LuthorCorp drivers do their job.

Clark waited as Lex climbed into the back of the town car, pulling his briefcase in behind him. Still fretting over the impending date, Clark glanced over his shoulder again at the doorman, and then across the street, where two men were standing outside smoking. He was about to climb in after Lex when something made him look at the smokers again. One of them was grinding a butt out under a pointy-toed shoe and seemed to be watching Lex's car. Both men were Japanese, one wearing a shiny silver suit and the other dressed in expensive-looking slacks and a tank top that showed off the elaborate tattoos that covered both of his arms. The tattooed one noticed Clark staring and turned to say something to the other.

"Come on, Clark," Lex urged from inside the town car. "I've really gotta get moving here."

Clark stuck his head in the car and began stammering at Lex.

"I'm, uh—I think I'm gonna take the subway after all."

Clark glanced up again in time to see the second man clap a hand on the shoulder of the first, then a bus passing on the opposite side of the street obscured both of them from his sight.

"You sure?" Lex was asking. "It's no problem to drop you off. We have to go by the museum anyway—"

He stopped midsentence and sighed. Clark had already shoved his backpack into the car and broken out in a run, darting across the street through traffic, heading southwest. Lex rolled down his window and shouted after him, pointing northeast as his driver got out and closed the passenger door.

"Clark, uptown's *that* way—"

"Sir?" the driver asked, getting back behind the wheel and closing his door behind him. Lex shook his head.

"Let's go," he said with a dismissive wave of his hand. "We'll send a search party out for him after the meeting."

"Yes, sir."

"Clark, Clark, Clark . . ." Lex sighed, settling back into the seat as his driver nosed the car into traffic. "This is just great. What are the odds he'll be back before six?"

Clark had made it across the street without damaging himself or anyone's car, but as he'd feared, the two Yakuza *kobun* had vanished into the crowd without a trace. There was a subway station two blocks ahead, and Clark decided that since they hadn't appeared to be in a car, there was a reasonable chance that they were trying to catch a train.

He ran down the steps, stopped to hurriedly purchase a pass, slipped his card through the gates, and raced down to the subway platforms. A northbound train identifying itself as the "Uptown E" was closing its doors just as Clark hit the landing. As the train rushed by, he watched the windows slide past as carefully as he could but saw no sign of the two Yakuza he was pursuing. He knew that the subway cars connected to one another, so conceivably they could be walking through a few of them ahead of where he'd been able to start watching, but there was no way to be sure. Were they even still running? They'd seen him notice them, and from what Lex had said about the Yakuza, not to mention what he himself had witnessed in the alley the night before, they were up to their necks in illicit activities. Still, did that really mean they would let themselves be chased into the subway by a sixteen-year-old farm boy? *Plus which, you're making the whole thing up,* Clark thought to himself hotly. *What would the Yakuza want with Lex?*

Lex said he'd dropped a large sum of money at their game, and seemed perfectly cheerful about it to boot, so it was unlikely that he owed them a gambling debt. If it was the corporate extortion angle that Lex had mentioned, it seemed to Clark that the Yakuza would do better to go after Lionel. Lex did own personal shares in LuthorCorp and had an official title, but even when surrendering control of subsidiaries like the fertilizer plant in Smallville, Lionel kept his son on a short leash. Clark couldn't imagine Lex buying drugs, or selling arms, or being involved with any kind of sex scandal. Could it be something from his past come back to haunt him? Lex had alluded more than once to being a bit of a hellion during his younger days. Had Lex run afoul of Japanese organized crime?

It seemed far-fetched, even to Clark. He was about to give up on his chase altogether when he was distracted by a group of young Japanese boys spilling noisily down a staircase to his left. There were five of them, mostly around the age of fourteen, but one or two possibly as young as twelve. They all wore matching orange-and-green windbreakers and similar variations on high-topped sports shoes, and they were all carrying and playing small portable video games in brightly colored plastics. Clark watched them as they positioned themselves in the clump of people waiting for the Downtown J and realized that although they each carried their own game devices, they were linked up with one another in sets of twos, the youngest leaning unsteadily against an architectural support beam, playing by himself.

Clark thought about his own solitariness and

wondered how tempted he might have been to form a gang of some sort with other aliens, had he ever found any. The boys on the platform with him were boisterous and took up a lot of space, but they in no way seemed menacing or dangerous. Still, it was clear that they considered themselves more than a group of friends—they sought some sort of deliberate conformity, a sense of belonging that presumably eluded them elsewhere in their lives. Was it that very sense of cultural isolation that made so many gang members vulnerable to criminal leanings? Clark's own outsider status always made him want to try harder to fit in, to follow the rules and maybe even at some subtle level ingratiate himself to others. He felt more apologetic about his uniqueness than affronted by those who might ostracize him for it, but, of course, his circumstances were very different from those of most urban teenagers. Clark really was someone who could be accused of being abnormal and reclusive, whereas the boys he was watching now perhaps felt unduly disenfranchised for reasons of race, economics, religion, age, or any number of factors that influenced other people's perceptions of them. That made theirs a righteous anger, and one to which Clark felt he had no access. As long as he remained on Earth, he would always be legitimately alien.

Glancing at the boys again, Clark noticed two tall, lanky figures appearing suddenly behind them, also waiting for the J. They were the men Clark had seen outside of Lex's apartment building, and his heart skipped a beat as he edged closer, apologizing softly—to no noticeable effect—as he eased through the crowd.

The focused rush of wind and rumbling tremor of noise from an arriving train came rushing at Clark's back as he continued inching his way toward the Yakuza. Looking up indifferently to glance at the oncoming train, the Yakuza with the tattooed arms noticed Clark and narrowed his eyes. Without so much as a nod toward his companion, and with his eyes still locked on Clark, the tattooed Yakuza smiled slowly, displaying one flashing gold tooth in the middle of his otherwise orthodontically neglected smile, before shoving his flattened hand into the back of the young boy leaning against the support beam.

Clark's first instinct was to tear toward the boy at superspeed as the twelve-year-old lost his footing and pitched toward the subway tracks with a startled gasp, but the crowd around him was too dense; if he rushed forward, the airstream he left in his wake would only knock another dozen or so people onto the tracks. As the train's horn and screeching brakes began to dominate even the gasps and shouts from the crowd, Clark remembered the execution he'd stopped outside the bar the night before and realized with a tightening in his chest that the men he was hunting were cold, unapologetic killers.

With no way to move through the impenetrable mob, Clark leaped over them, acting more on instinct than thought as he willed himself forward toward the boy while avoiding the low ceiling beams. The jump was so fast and so complexly controlled that Clark couldn't even allow himself to think about how he was doing it without feeling nauseous. Only the small distance traveled and his own insistence separated it from the act of flight, that in itself being a power so associated with the recognized limits of human ability that at sixteen, Clark was simply not willing even to consider it.

As if to prove he was not flying, Clark landed on the

train tracks in a crouch behind the boy. With the train
bearing down on him, Clark scooped up the terrified boy
and bounded back up on to the platform's edge, just in
time to feel the train's airstream hit his back. He'd saved
the boy, but what he hadn't had time to do was frame a
plausible scenario for the rescue.

Now back to normal speed, Clark watched the seemingly frozen masses roar to life again.

"Whoa, careful!" he said with a weak smile, quickly
maneuvering the boy so that he was holding him by one
backpack strap rather than both arms. The boy was staring at his sneakers and the platform beneath them with
obvious confusion and disbelief. "You almost fell, there!"

Gasps of panic from those nearest the incident
morphed almost comically into expressions of confusion
and relief. Clark watched them carefully for a second,
remembering something his dad had told him once about
the great lengths people would go to not to acknowledge
the implausible. It certainly seemed to be true.

The subway car doors directly behind Clark slid open,
and he was pushed backward into the car as the few people exiting began to file past the massive inflowing
swarm. Alarmed, but unwilling to push for fear of hurting
someone, Clark looked up in time to see the Yakuza
kobun with the tattooed arms pulling the other one away
toward the E train side as public transit officials approached the J from the other direction to verify that no
one was injured.

His mind still racing, Clark sat down on a bright or-
ange plastic seat and tried to formulate a plan. Most of the
crowd seemed to have already forgotten the near tragedy,
or at least the part Clark had played in averting it, and
were chattering about their individual adrenaline rushes

or beginning to unfold newspapers as the policemen on the platform signaled something to the train operator and the doors slid shut. Only the twelve-year-old and his friends continued to watch Clark with what he took to be a combination of suspicion and amazement. The train started moving, and although dimly aware that he had no idea where he was going, Clark felt some relief in simply putting distance between himself and the scene of his latest superhuman act, not to mention the dreaded blind date meeting site.

"Dude, that was *awesome*!" one of the boys suddenly announced, breaking the strained silence as the others followed his lead and started beaming in Clark's direction. "That was, like, totally Samurai Shodown!" The teen mimicked a superfast martial arts move, complete with sound effects, and Clark realized that the world these kids lived in was filled with speed and motion and excuses for the inexplicable.

"Are you all right?" he asked the boy he'd rescued. The kid looked up at him with a slightly dazed expression and nodded.

"Thanks," he said weakly.

"Did you see that, Jack?" another one of the young gang members asked the boy Clark had saved. He had jumped out of his seat to perform a one-man re-creation of the save as he narrated. "You were all, 'whoa!' and he was all, bzzzzzooom! And you were like 'huh?' and he was already BAM!"

"You play King of Fighters?" a third boy asked Clark, thrusting his video game device in Clark's direction. Clark shook his head.

"Jack's Ryo Sakazaki is unbeatable! His HSDM toasts my Iori Yagami every time!"

"I keep telling you," Jack smirked, obviously pleased by the compliment, "It's just jump d, d, f plus a, q-c-f times two a-c, then jump d, c, f plus a, q-c-f-h-c-b-t-a! *But* he's got to be at low life to do it!"

Clark laughed. "Wow, that sounds like algebra."

"You ever seen one of these?" The fourth boy was also thrusting his game player toward Clark. "My big brother brought them back from Japan. You can get the NGPCs here, but these are the *N*NGCPs."

"*New* Neo Geo Color Pocket," the second boy translated.

"Pretty cool," Clark nodded.

"Where are you from?" asked the eldest coolly, eyeing the flannel button-down Clark wore over his red T-shirt. Clark's eyebrows raised in alarm for a moment, then he relaxed into a grin.

"Smallville," he answered. "Does it show?"

"Not unless you've got eyes," the eldest smirked.

"Would it help if I knew how to play King of Fighters?"

"It's easy!" Jack piped up, suddenly animated. "Here." He handed Clark his Color Pocket and slid into the seat next to him, pointing at the monitor and at various buttons. "That's you," he said, indicating a flat but colorful animated figure on the screen. "For now you should just learn how to fight. We'll help you assemble a team later. So like, for instance, if you want to kick that guy you're fighting, you press that, that, and that."

Clark smiled gamely and gave it a go, but about three stops in he realized he did best when he just pushed as many keys as he could over and over again in no particular order. His new friends positioned themselves around him so that they could see the screen he was playing on, with Jack sitting next to him, sporadically shouting out nearly incomprehensible advice. A few minutes later, casually and with his eyes still on the monitor of the electronic toy, Clark tried to change the subject.

"Hey, do any of you guys know anything about the Yakuza?"

Clark hadn't quite noticed just how loud the boys were until they all fell silent at once. He looked up to see them staring into space, staring at their shoes, or staring at their fingernails—looking anywhere but at him or each other. A Japanese girl of about nine with pink-ribboned pigtails and a pink plastic daisy-covered backpack sat by herself in a seat near the boys, and she was staring at Clark with wide, dark eyes that were somehow even more censuring than the furtive evasiveness of the boys.

"This is our stop," Jack mumbled suddenly, grabbing his Color Pocket away from Clark and rapidly getting to his feet. The other boys also stood en masse, as did the little girl and a few other people on the subway car. The train was slowing down, and the markers on the platform read NEO-TOKYO. Clark rose as well.

"Bye, Smallville," the eldest called, pushing ahead out onto the platform the minute the doors opened. The others started to follow suit, but Clark, who had exited the train with them, grabbed Jack by the arm.

"Isn't there some kind of proverb that says if I save your life, you owe me a favor?" Clark asked him quickly, bending down to try to speak directly into one of his small ears.

"That's not a *Japanese* proverb," Jack said with the kind of vehemence that usually masks fear. "And anyway, it goes, if you save my life, you become *responsible* for it." He shrugged away from Clark and hurried to join the other boys.

Clark stood on the platform and let out a deep sigh. Metropolis was so different from Smallville, it was hard to believe that they were part of the same country. The doors of the train he had just departed were closing behind him. Not that it mattered, he realized as the train left without him. He had no idea where that particular train was going anyway, and no reason to be on it unless it would help him find the men who had been stalking Lex. Clearly they had not been on it. He was deciding whether or not to catch a train going in the opposite direction in an attempt to at least get back to where he'd started from when he felt a weak but urgent tugging at his sleeve. He turned around to see the nine-year-old girl with the pigtails staring up at him soberly.

"You have *very* blue eyes," she practically whispered.

Clark smiled and deliberately slouched slightly so that he wasn't towering above her quite so much. "And you have very pretty bows in your hair," he answered, still smiling.

The girl looked down with an undisguised blush, then looked back up at him with an expression he often dreamed about seeing on Lana's face. He shoved his hands in his pockets and waited.

He felt sure the girl was going to say something else, but she continued to stare at him for an uncomfortably long time, as if drinking him in, committing his features to memory. Finally, she looked down, almost miserably.

"If I tell you a secret," she started in the same whispery voice, "do you promise to be careful?"

"Cross my heart," Clark replied, taking one of his hands out of his pocket to do just that. He wasn't sure if the humanness of his features and physiology was intentional or a lucky accident, but Jonathan and Martha had established early on that every hair and finger was in place, his heart was beating where it was supposed to be, and unless he was in the process of using one of his special gifts, no one would ever guess he was anything other than a strong and healthy country boy. Still, he sometimes had nightmares about waking up to find himself transformed into some kind of monster—green, maybe, or amorphous, or scaled. He had no way of knowing what other members of his original planet looked like, and his curiosity and terror ran pretty much neck and neck.

With a small wave, the girl with the pigtails indicated that Clark should come closer to her, so he leaned in until she stood on her tiptoes and brought her face to his, cupping a hand next to his ear.

"Takashi Plaza on Collyer," she whispered. Then she pulled back, peered into Clark's face for another minute, and exhaled very slowly and quietly. Clark was still processing what she'd told him when she turned from him and broke into a run, heading toward the escalator that would take her up to street level.

Even Clark, who could, as Chloe would happily attest, often prove a bit dense where other people's (especially females') feelings were concerned, didn't miss the little girl's obvious and deeply felt adulation. It filled him with the strangest sensation, almost a tingling. It took him a moment to put his finger on it, but when he did, he broke out with a huge, unbidden grin. Her sweet infatuation with him had made him feel as if he counted in her world. He hadn't scared her, hadn't had to act slower or weaker or stupider than he really was in front of her, but nor had he done anything terribly impressive. She was just drawn to him because she liked the color of his eyes, and she trusted him and wanted to help. The idea that she might think about him later, or write a silly little entry about him in some fuzzy pink diary somewhere warmed Clark with a desire to prove himself worthy of her confidence in his goodness. It wasn't that he craved adoration, it was that the idea of making himself deserving of it inspired and energized him.

Armed with a street address and a renewed sense of purpose, Clark bounded up the escalator and exited the subway, convinced that he could find the two men he'd seen outside of Lex's penthouse. If they weren't at this stop, well, he still had a few dollars left on his subway card. Metropolis's Japan Town—it was so obvious, why hadn't he thought of it earlier? How hard could it be to locate a couple of pinkieless Japanese gentlemen in a clearly demarcated sector of the city?

The smile on Clark's face died the moment he stepped out onto Swan Boulevard. Smallville didn't even have a sushi restaurant. But Metropolis's Neo-Tokyo covered over thirty city blocks. For the dozenth time since arriving in Metropolis, Clark had the strong sensation of being lost in a sea of desperation and need. So much human life teemed around him, vibrant and fragile all at once. He had to do something.

He began moving through the crowd, watching street signs. Twice he tried to stop people to ask for directions, but no one even slowed down for him. The streets were not in any predictable order he could discern, but they were, at least, laid out on a pretty standard grid that he began to search methodically.

By the time Clark crossed onto Bridwell, mentally marking off each horizontal cross street he passed, he was enveloped by a completely foreign landscape. The sounds of the English language had been replaced by the even, staccato vowels of Japanese. The sweet, smoky scent of aloe incense competed with the sharp, marine reek of raw fish for supremacy over occasional undercurrents of tea, ginger, human sweat, boxed sweets, and steamed rice.

The smaller streets offered tiny shops brimming with tatami matting and flowing kimonos in every imaginable hue from deep charcoal ebony to soft pastel yellow. These hung alongside low shelves crammed with ironware teapots and brightly colored origami paper in patterns of increasing intricacy. Furniture shops were saturated with the intense warmth of polished rosewood and the calming glow of bamboo. The cool, earth tones of ash-glazed pottery complemented the glossy but muted brilliance of raku enamels in sweet grass greens and sky-blues. Clark found his eyes darting from the sudden brilliant flash of polished, red lacquer to the milky gleaming of inlaid mother-of-pearl. Bold calligraphy scrolls on textured rice paper twisted in the slight spring breeze over the glinting silver scales, pink flesh, and translucent gray entrails of freshly sliced fish.

The larger avenues boasted clean, modern high-rises and sprawling cultural centers of ivory stucco, with the gentle, creamy pink of cherry blossoms hovering like storybook clouds over an endless rush of shiny ebony hair, softly bronzed skin, and bright, contemporary clothes. Moving swiftly through the streets, Clark could just barely pick out the plaintive strains of a flute soaring over the clicking of high-heeled shoes and the laughter of schoolchildren darting about in the glory of the fall day.

The idea that this place was always here, in the middle

of the city, running at its own restless tempo even as the rest of Metropolis throbbed with action and life was astonishing to Clark. It reminded him of Lex's family castle back in Smallville, a structure and disposition so shockingly out of place with the rest of the town, one had no choice but to accept it utterly in all of its extraordinary incongruity.

Clark had been walking in a daze for nearly forty minutes when he realized with a start that he was on Collyer Street. The Takashi Plaza was unmistakable. A plaque in the center of the square that led to the main opening indicated a nightclub, bookstore, noodle restaurant, gift shop, and tattoo parlor within the center. Thinking it might be a little early for the nightclub to be open, Clark headed for the tattoo parlor. Maybe he could get a lead on the strange tattoos worn by the men he'd seen in the bar with Lex.

The plaza's main doors opened into a cool hallway with high ceilings, dim lighting, and gray flooring made out of shiny squares of fake-looking stone. To Clark's immediate right was an unlisted gift shop, now closed, full of Japanese tableware, teapots, sake service sets, and lacquered chopsticks. The noodle shop was to the left, open but not very busy. Clark saw the neon sign of the tattoo parlor in the far corner and quickened his pace. Something about the entire center felt off to him.

The tattoo parlor was dark, but since no sign indicated whether it was open or closed, Clark pushed on the swinging glass door and entered.

"Hello?" he called. His attempt at making his presence known was aided by the tingle of a small brass bell attached to the door, but no one appeared to greet him. The floor of the tattoo parlor was carpeted in a deep burgundy, and the walls were covered with hundreds of tattoo options, each design identified with a small letter and number combination just beneath the graphic. In addition to the expected *kanji* characters, dragons, *koi* fish, and *oni*, Clark noticed several cartoon figures, animals, abstract patterns, astrological signs, and religious symbols.

"*Nani ka osagashi desu ka?*"

Clark spun to see a tall, heavyset Japanese man in his midforties behind the counter, staring at him impassively. He wore a black silk shirt, and his left eye didn't move when his right one did. Clark realized with a start that it was fake. Though he had no idea what had just been said to him, Clark sensed that the tone wasn't angry or challenging. If anything, the clerk looked and sounded bored.

"Hi. Do you—um—do you speak English?"

"What do you want?" the man answered in the same indifferent tone, reaching into his shirt's front pocket for a package of cigarettes.

"Oh, good!" Clark smiled, relieved to at least be past the language barrier. "Actually, I'm interested in those really ornate, landscape tattoos. The kind that cover up your whole arm or back. Do you do those?"

The man's right eye looked Clark up and down, and he frowned slightly, raising a cigarette to his lips.

"Those take a long time. And they're expensive. Not recommended for beginners." He flicked on a lighter, lit his cigarette, and squinted his right eye as he let out a large exhale of smoke. "How about something smaller?"

"Oh, uh, it's not for me!" Clark blushed. He thought about the time his mom had tried to take his blood when he was still a little boy and subsequently broke seventeen needles on his skin before giving up. "I have a . . . weird skin condition." Having arrived at that not entirely untrue statement, Clark smiled weakly.

The man behind the counter took another slow drag off his cigarette, folded his arms across his chest, and exhaled with a frown. Something still felt strange to Clark, but he had to acknowledge to himself that he was no detective. Chloe had sharpened her intellect in the service of investigative reporting and seemed able to use those skills to pinpoint elusive details. Maybe that was something he could learn to do someday.

"I . . . have a friend, though. Who's interested. In getting one of those. You . . . you can do those, right?"

The man smiled, or maybe it was a sneer. Clark was about to give up when he realized that there was no actual tattooing equipment on display anywhere, which meant there must be at least a back room. Focusing, he looked past the man at the counter and through the wall behind him. The store was so quiet that Clark was a little surprised to see a bevy of activity in the back. Past a wide hallway that seemed to serve as the tattooing area was some kind of high-ceilinged, cement storage room, currently being used as an elaborate science lab, complete with someone hunched over a Bunsen burner and someone else standing nearby counting what looked like packages of powder. Bones came through very clearly when Clark used his X-ray vision, and so did metal. With a swallow of alarm, he realized that the counting man had a gun in his hand.

"Send your friend in and we will talk," the glass-eyed man said with cold finality. Then he glanced over his shoulder as if trying to figure out what Clark was staring at. Clark snapped his attention back to the man in front of him and knew it was time for him to leave. He started to back out of the store, but his mind was racing. He didn't know exactly what was going on, but he was worried that someone was in trouble.

"On second thought, I think I will get something small," Clark heard himself say before he'd fully worked through the implications. Well, he'd get into the back room anyway, and ad-lib it from there. The frown of the man with the glass eye deepened. Clark looked quickly around the shop. "How about that one?"

Clark found himself pointing at a small graphic of planet Earth and winced inwardly. He was self-aware enough to know that the selection, although unconscious, had not been completely arbitrary. He would love some sign that he truly belonged on this little planet, some indelible badge of integration. Although he knew it wasn't possible for him to get a tattoo, he wondered if he might actually have gone through with it if it were.

The man behind the counter turned and opened the door that led back toward the storage room.

"That will be fifty dollars," he said loudly. Clark realized he was warning the others. A door shut, closing the storage room-cum-laboratory area off from the hallway that held the inking equipment. *Next time I do something this dumb*, Clark thought to himself hotly, *I'm definitely going to have an actual plan.*

The man with the glass eye seated himself on a leather stool in front of a larger chair that was apparently meant for Clark. He began pulling ink and needles out of a metallic lunch box with grim concentration. As Clark had guessed from his previous glimpse, the room they were in was essentially a wide hallway leading to the square, high-ceilinged storage area in back. Clark concentrated again to see through the now-closed door and into the lab. The man with the gun had come up behind the man working at the burner and was pressing the muzzle of his pistol into the back of the other man's head. Clark felt his own pulse quicken.

Holding a needle, the tattoo artist flicked on an articulated desk lamp, illuminating the chair Clark wasn't sitting in, and stared up at Clark with his good eye.

"Where do you want it?" he asked. Clark had his hands in the pockets of his jeans and was standing near the chair, still squinting with all his concentration at the closed door leading to the storage room.

"I . . . think I've changed my mind," he said abruptly. The man with the glass eye stood up, a needle still in one beefy hand. Clark realized he was out of time. Whatever he was going to do, he had to do it immediately.

Out of desperation, he decided to attempt something he'd never tried before. Focusing the heat he had learned to force from his eyes with the same concentration he normally brought to his X-ray vision, Clark began to burn two small holes through the door. His idea was to ignite something on the lab table, thereby hopefully distracting the guy with the gun. He started to feel a little elated as he realized that he could, in fact, burn through walls with his eyes.

Unfortunately, it would have been better to do so without anyone watching him.

"What are you staring at?" the tattoo artist demanded, peering at him from across the room. It was only a matter of time before he smelled smoke, or, worse yet, looked past Clark and saw the two smoldering holes in the door.

Clark doubled his concentration and suddenly realized he was looking into the laboratory without the use of his X-ray vision. Rippling heat from his eyes continued to surge into the room beyond the door, and before he fully realized what he was doing, the blaze beneath the Bunsen burner had intensified tenfold.

The tattoo artist moved to restrain Clark when the two were knocked back by a fiery explosion so intense it blew the storage room door clean off its hinges. Clark was immune to the effects of the fire, but not of the concussive blast, which sent him flying back five feet, his ears ringing with the shriek of cleaving metal.

He landed on top of the tattoo artist, who was burned and seemed temporarily stunned. Oily, black smoke billowed out into the hallway, stinging Clark's eyes and obscuring the storage room from view. He scrambled to his feet, his nostrils filled with the scent of burning chemicals.

Oh, no, he thought desperately. *What have I done*?

Coughing as he waded through the smoke toward the back room, Clark found the entire area ablaze. Whatever they had been making in the laboratory had proven to be highly flammable, and what Clark had intended as a small distraction had turned into a major conflagration. Could this be the Yakuza methamphetamine production Lex had mentioned?

Clark found the man who had been huddled over the Bunsen burner lying unconscious across the lab table, and used his considerable strength to pull the man from the flames toward the back of the room. He kicked open a fire exit door, wondering belatedly if the influx of fresh oxygen would make the situation inside the laboratory worse, and carried the man outside, where he laid him gently on the asphalt ground of a small parking lot. That accomplished, he ran back and pulled out both the dazed tattoo artist and the man with the gun, who was out cold.

As he feared, the addition of fresh oxygen had stoked the now-towering flames.

Thick, black smoke poured from the fire exit door, rising into the air to smudge the pristine beauty of the cloudless sky. Though no fire alarms were ringing, Clark felt sure that the smoke would soon attract attention. He had no idea how many more people might be inside the complex, or whether the fire would spread past the concrete walls of the storage room. He hesitated for a moment, glancing apprehensively at the three men he had rescued.

Endangered. And then rescued.

"Is this what we can now expect from the DEA?" the tattoo artist groaned quietly, then muttered something in Japanese, interrupting himself with an irrepressible coughing fit. Clark frowned and dashed back into the burning room to search for a fire extinguisher.

By the time he had the flames under control, the fire department had arrived. The three men from the tattoo shop had all vanished into the city.

CHAPTER TWELVE

Clark decided not to make his presence known to the Metropolis Fire Department or the MPD. He hid out of sight long enough to learn that they'd determined it was indeed methamphetamine being produced in the lab and that no one was hurt in the fire. They also seemed to assume that the combustion had been an accident caused by the volatile nature of the chemical components in use. No one was looking for a teenager from outer space by way of Kansas who could shoot heat from his eyes. Well, no one with the exception of the Yakuza.

Though relieved that the fire had caused no casualties, Clark felt restless and disheartened. It seemed obvious to him that he'd brought about more problems than he'd solved. He remembered what Lex had said about the Yakuza trading drugs for guns and wondered if he had cost the Metropolis Yakuza branch an arms shipment. Among the rubble, he'd found a piece of shipping crate bearing a stamp that indicated passage through Pier 42 of the West River's Ordway Docks. It seemed likely that the Yakuza had other drug-manufacturing labs in the city, and that there would be some kind of standing date with their gunrunners. Maybe he could check it out later. Now he had to find his way back to the penthouse and clean up before his dreaded date.

Clark wasn't entirely sure why he was so opposed to

the idea. Though the possibility for something truly shocking and ribald did exist, Lex had most likely set him up with some very nice, age-appropriate city girl, someone like Chloe maybe, and made some interesting plans for them. He knew he should be grateful, both for the trouble Lex had obviously gone to and for the opportunity to see the city in another context. But no matter how entertaining an evening Lex might have set up, Clark knew the whole thing would just make him frustrated and sad.

Where Clark's heart was concerned, it was Lana or bust.

It would be a struggle even to be polite to another girl for the several hours it took to get through a proper date, and Clark was naturally as polite and agreeable as they came. Still, he just didn't have Lex's ability to make everyone he met feel included and at ease. And who knew what Lex had told this girl about him. Clark groaned as he realized that people were staring at him. He looked like . . . well, like he'd just walked out of a chemical fire. It was time for a taxi.

Remembering Lex's easy nonchalance the night before, Clark stepped out in the street and nearly got plowed into by a speeding Corvette. Though he knew the car couldn't have actually hurt him, Clark was too tired and depressed to try to explain why steel folded when it hit his body, or why he looked like he'd just caught several exploding grenades. He was relieved when he managed to scramble back up onto the curb in time and didn't even mind that he'd seen and waved to at least eight empty taxis before one finally stopped for him.

"New Troy, please," he sighed as he closed the door behind him. "Luthor Tower Two."

The driver glanced at him in the rearview mirror, not bothering to disguise his skepticism. Clark tried to think of what Lex would say but knew that Lex would never have to say anything. Not only would he never stumble into a cab soot-smudged and smoldering, but even if he were somehow forced to, he'd manage it with so much dignity that no one would question him even if he requested to be taken to Buckingham Palace.

Clark, on the other hand, felt he'd do best to rely on an oldie but goody.

"Mr. Luthor's expecting me."

The cabby's eyes widened, and he nodded quickly, expertly steering the taxi into the rush-hour traffic.

"You sure you don't maybe wanna see a doctor or somethin'?" he asked with concern. When Clark shook his head, the cabbie reassured himself. "Yeah, I guess Mr. Luthor's got one waitin' at the tower, huh? Or a couple, huh, like a whole team? That's what I'd do if I was him. I'd have me a whole team. Like the lawyers, you know, but with doctors. The Doctor Dream Team."

Clark offered a weak smile, unable to imagine how strange it must be to have that level of renown. Or was it notoriety? Lex's face and name were known almost everywhere, as were the golden letters that symbolized his father's company, LuthorCorp. People judged him before they met him, feared him, revered him, assumed he could do favors for them, had passionate opinions about what he should be doing and what they'd do if they were him, and followed his personal life with unapologetic curiosity and entitlement. Even Chloe, defending her right to publish in the *Torch* a less-than-flattering piece about his getting temporarily mixed up with a pheromone-emitting black-widow type, insisted that Lex had forfeited his right to privacy the minute he'd been born into the Luthor clan.

"That wasn't his fault, though!" Clark had protested. Chloe had just shrugged.

"Nobody's destiny is their *fault*, Clark. But that doesn't mean it's not their *responsibility*."

Her words echoed back at him as he watched out the window of the taxicab where the colorful streets of Neo-Tokyo were giving way to the slightly more familiar landscape of New Troy. They hit some traffic and arrived at their destination too late, Clark feared, for him to get in a good shower and still have time to hit the museum before his date.

He thanked and paid the cab driver and nodded at the doorman on his way in. Clark recognized him as the one he'd seen with Lex when they'd first arrived, the legitimate one before the imposter. He wondered if the guy was scared, and might have asked had his own appearance been less conspicuous, but as it was, he headed quickly toward the elevator, rode it to the top floor in silence, and let himself into the penthouse.

"Clark, are you on fire?"

Clark had feverishly hoped he'd beat Lex home, but no such luck. Lex was sprawled out on the black leather couch, laptop open, still dressed in the clothes he'd worn to his meeting that morning, his tie, suit jacket, and shoes nearby.

"Not anymore," Clark said weakly, heading toward the guest bathroom.

"Jesus, Clark!" Lex, having clearly taken in the full extent of Clark's dishevelment, got up from the couch, placed the laptop on the coffee table, and followed after

Clark with an appalled look on his face. "What *happened* to you?"

Clark stopped and turned to face Lex. He shifted his feet, unable to meet his friend's eyes. He hated lying.

"I was in this shopping center that kinda caught fire and I . . ." He let his words trail off, but already knew that Lex wasn't going to let it go. Lex was watching him with his undivided attention, his face otherwise unreadable.

"Was anyone hurt?" Lex prompted.

Clark shook his head and looked at Lex. "Amazingly, no, but apparently there was this sort of, well, meth lab in the back, so the fire got out of control and the smoke was pretty awful. My eyes are stinging like crazy."

Clark had dropped his eyes away, but raised them again when his friend didn't say anything. Lex was peering at him intently, searching the teenager's sooty face for something Clark couldn't guess at. Lex nodded suddenly, as if making up his mind about something, and ushered Clark toward the guest bathroom with fraternal concern.

"Take a nice, long shower. You've got plenty of time before your date gets here. Can I get you anything? Eyedrops? A drink? A doctor?"

Clark shook his head, stepping onto the cool clean tiles of the bathroom floor.

"No, I'll be fine." Clark looked down at himself with a shy half smile. "I don't know about these clothes, though."

Lex nodded. "I'll take care of it, just leave them on the floor in there." Lex hesitated by the door to the bathroom, his hands thrust into the front pockets of his slacks. "You sure you're okay?" He looked worried, and Clark wished he could reassure him, confess that it would take way more than a fire to do him any real harm.

"Honestly, I'm fine. Just . . . really dirty. It was one of those freak things . . ."

—"You should have called me," Lex admonished, his brows lowered in concern.

"I didn't want to interrupt your meeting." Clark glanced at Lex once more, at the clean tile floor beneath his filthy athletic shoes, then slowly closed the bathroom door, sensing Lex's distress following after him in worried waves.

Clark remembered the time when Lex had confronted him directly about the car accident that had jump-started their friendship, asking to be told the truth. It was after dark, and Clark had been outside repairing a fence on the farm when Lex drove up in his Porsche and began his umpteenth, but most earnest, inquisition on the matter. After insisting that he didn't think Clark had been completely honest with him, and asserting that he thought he knew why, Lex had spelled out exactly what really had happened, forcing Clark to protest the truth directly.

"You're the closest I've had to a real friend my whole life," Lex had confessed with real emotion in his voice. "You don't have to hide anything from me."

For once, Lex hadn't sounded accusatory or cunning. He'd said he needed to talk, and pacing around the farm in the dark that evening, he'd just looked hungry for connection, lonely, in need of the kind of intimacy only honesty can foster. Clark had been so frustrated with his own inability to tell the truth that he'd stormed off, matters not helped by the fact that he'd actually lost his powers in a freak lightning accident earlier that week and was living in vulnerable flesh for the first time in his entire conscious life. The next day at school he'd gotten into an altercation with the boy to whom his powers had mysteriously transferred and had taken a pretty bad beating. Lex had shown up at the hospital, and Clark hated the look of rueful concern on his friend's face as he limped away from Lex's apology, cut and battered and holding his painfully bruised ribs. He had eventually gotten his powers back, but he'd never forgotten how much of a fraud it made him feel to have Lex confront him so openly, then retract his assertions so diffidently. The truth was, he hadn't liked the way it had felt to be injured and physically defenseless in front of Lex, and he'd hated hearing Lex apologize for something he was perfectly right about. It had brought up all the strange boundaries of trust that existed between them. Lex surrendered his apparent emotional invulnerability the same time Clark had been robbed of his physical invulnerability, and Clark hadn't been able to meet him there. His own failure to be honest that night, his *disinclination* to, had troubled him ever since.

Though the smoke and soot strains from the fire scrubbed off, the feeling of duplicity persisted. He'd never been in any real danger from the fire, and outside the guest bathroom his friend waited and worried and doubted his own excellent instincts. As he dried off and changed into clean clothes for his date, Clark thought about the strange dream he had had, wondering again if there would ever be a time when the truth of who he was could be public knowledge, something he never had to hide, something emblazoned across his chest for all the world to see. And whether or not that would be a good thing.

He emerged clean and neatly dressed in a pair of chinos and a dark blue Oxford his mother had bought him for his last birthday. He had no choice but to wear his only pair of good shoes. As he emerged from the guest bedroom, Lex let out a low, appreciative whistle.

"You clean up nicely, Kent."

"Is this okay?" Clark asked, his voice dispirited as he raised his arms to either side, awaiting inspection.

"Perfect. You look great. And it won't matter anyway." Lex leaned in toward Clark with playful surreptitiousness. "Between you and me, your date's a first-class hottie."

Clark exhaled, blowing dark bangs off his forehead.

"I really wish you hadn't gone to all this trouble—"

"No trouble," Lex said with an enigmatic smile.

"How do you know her?" Clark asked with a nervous grimace, moving toward the kitchen to get a glass of water. His throat still felt raspy and dry from all the smoke. Lex sauntered back to the couch and switched off his laptop.

"We're in business together, actually," Lex said, amused with his answer. He lowered the laptop screen and sat down. "But really, she's a friend of a friend."

Clark poured filtered water into a tall glass, trying not to think about severed pinkies and exploding meth labs.

"How about you? Who're you seeing tonight?"

Lex rubbed the back of his neck as he lifted his legs and sank deeper into the couch.

"An old friend. Her name's Lorelei. She's part of the crowd I used to run with in my urban menace days."

"The Club Zero crowd?" Clark asked, leaning against the kitchen island as he drank his water. He could barely see Lex over the breakfast counter that separated the kitchen from the living room, but his friend's voice was close and clear.

"She might have been there once or twice, yeah." Lex

liked talking about Club Zero about as much as Clark liked talking about the Porsche accident. "So what really happened today? Where were you?"

Clark put his glass in the sink and frowned.

"Just what I told you. I got kind of lost, and I ended up in this shopping center in Neo-Tokyo looking at tattoos. Something weird happened with their storage back room, and the place caught on fire. I helped drag one or two people out, then I came back here." Clark paused and waited for Lex to say something. After a moment, Lex's disembodied voice rose from where he was stretched out on the couch.

"How can you possibly expect me to believe that?"

Clark drew up to his full height, slightly offended. That was pretty much what had happened, after all. He was about to defend himself when Lex sat up suddenly and turned to peer at him over the back of the couch.

"*You*? In a *tattoo* parlor? Martha Kent's little boy scopin' out the ink? The apple of *Jonathan Kent's* eye shopping for a tat?"

Clark grinned roguishly as Lex continued. He had no problem with Lex teasing him as long as he stopped prying for information.

"The Smallville Saint under the gun? Lowell County's favorite son pounding skin? The Conscientious Kansas Kid tacin' it on?"

"I was just looking." Clark shrugged with a smile.

"Yeah, and I spent my day at church," Lex sneered jokingly, calmly putting his shoes on before standing and moving toward the intercom system as a loud blat startled Clark.

"That you, Matt?"

"The young lady's here, Mr. Luthor."

"Thanks, we'll be right down." Lex turned from the intercom to beam at Clark. "Ready?"

Clark bit his lip and wished he could sink behind the counter.

"You're coming?" he asked weakly, hopefully.

"Just to make sure you kids get off okay." Lex smiled. "Then I've got to get ready for my own date."

"Lex . . ." Clark's voice was small, and he was looking down at the floor rather pitifully. Lex had to press his lips together tightly to keep from laughing, his heart going out to his quiet friend.

"Yes, Clark?" he asked carefully, eyes dancing with hilarity. He knew he was seconds away from busting up completely.

"I'm kind of . . . shy . . ." Clark confessed to the kitchen floor.

"I know, buddy, I know," Lex said, unable to suppress a slight chuckle. He walked over to where Clark stood behind the breakfast bar, put a reassuring arm around his shoulders, and led him to the door. "You're gonna be fine, I promise. Come on."

Clark took a deep breath and let Lex lead him out to the elevators. He was so distracted by his own dread that he didn't notice Lex snatch a compact Polaroid off the butler's table in the hall. They rode down to the lobby in silence, Clark's head held low, Lex's held high, an anticipatory smile enlivening his features. Together they walked out into the twilight and stood before a long, black, stretch limo.

Lex opened the passenger door and Clark saw two pretty but inexpensive-looking evening shoes emerge. Lex reached into the car with a smile to offer his hand,

and Clark was still staring at her shoes when the girl stepped out onto the pavement.

"Now, you two have met, right?" Lex prompted. Clark looked up in confusion and immediately lost his breath. He felt a flash go off in his face as he struggled for words.

Lana Lang smiled wide, her perfect little nose wrinkled.

"You didn't tell him?" she asked, turning to Lex, who was grinning as he waited for the Polaroid to develop.

"And miss *that* look? No way."

"Who did you *think* you were going out with?" Lana asked Clark, grinning and swatting playfully at his arm with a small clutch purse that matched her shoes. She wore a simple sleeveless lavender halter dress that showed off the soft curves of her shoulders, further accented by a matching wrap that hung from her slim arms. Her shiny, dark hair was swept up elegantly and her luminous brown eyes peered up at Clark, at once familiar and fathomless. Clark was amazed that no one was commenting on how loudly his heart was thumping in his chest, then thought that perhaps he was dreaming again.

Lex laughed and shook his head. "You'll have to give him a second, Lana. He's speechless."

Lana laughed as well, slightly embarrassed. Sensing their discomfort, Lex stepped in to finish breaking the ice.

"Hey, thanks for coming all the way to the city," Lex nodded to Lana. "I hope the ride was comfortable."

Lana, never terribly impressed with small talk, stood up on her tiptoes and kissed Lex on the cheek. This seemed to snap Clark out of his daze, and he moved forward instinctively to take her arm.

"It was very sweet of you to set this all up," she told Lex. "You're a good friend."

"Yeah, Lex," Clark finally managed to stammer, realizing that the soft warmth of Lana's arm was not something he was dreaming. "This is—I mean, *thanks!*"

An embarrassed flash of a smile told Lana that her compliment meant a lot to Lex, and she felt proud that Clark had insisted on befriending him despite everyone's misgivings about the Luthor family name. Lana had thought the pairing odd at first, but the two young men had clearly become good friends. There was no doubt in her mind that Lex sincerely liked and watched out for his younger friend, and that Clark appreciated Lex's intelligence and unpredictability.

"You look amazing," Clark gushed in her ear suddenly.

"Thank you, Clark," Lana replied, cocking her head slightly to one side as she smiled. She was carefully remaining poised and gracious when what she really wanted to do was throw herself back into the limousine to laugh hysterically for at least fifteen minutes straight. The look on Clark's face really had been worth its weight in gold, and even though it was no big secret that he liked her, Clark was not usually terribly forthcoming with his feelings.

"Oh, yeah, this is a keeper," Lex grinned, gazing at the Polaroid he'd taken before slipping it into his pocket.

"Let me see!" Lana grinned, but Lex just gave a chin nod in Clark's direction.

"It's right there," he laughed. And indeed, as Lana sneaked another quick peek at Clark's face, the initial expression of delighted shock had not yet left his face. Lana sighed quietly to herself, shivering slightly. She admired

Clark's chiseled bone structure and muscular build, not to mention his shiny, dark hair and vivid blue eyes. There was no question that Clark Kent was the best-looking boy in school. Unfortunately, he also happened to be the most puzzling.

"Hey, one of you two together before you go," Lex smiled, holding up the camera again. Clark was shaking slightly as he put his arm around Lana and smiled at Lex. She felt so warm and soft against his side, he half wished he could turn into the Clark in the picture, frozen next to Lana forever, instead of the one who was about to have to let go.

Lex snapped the photo, then ushered them into the car.

"The driver has all the directions," he told them matter-of-factly, "and the restaurant knows to put you on my account. Don't worry about anything, just have a good time. Lana, you still think you want to head back tonight? I've got a whole extra bedroom if you want to crash here, or we could put you up at the Centennial, if you'd prefer."

"No, really, Lex, that's okay, thanks. The car's plenty—I'll just stretch out and relax, and I'm sure I'll be back in my own bed before I know it."

Lex nodded, winked at Clark, and closed the car door behind them, waving the driver off.

Clark turned to Lana with a shy grin.

"When did he call you?" he asked.

"Yesterday." Lana smiled as the car pulled away. The backseat was large enough for half of their high school and included a minibar and a TV. "He said he needed his bachelor pad to himself for a few hours and begged me to help. I told him I'd be happy to."

Clark swallowed, fearing that her simple sentence was going to keep him up all night. Did she mean she'd be happy to as in "Sure, Lex, anything I can do to help you out," or she'd be happy to as in "A date with Clark? I can't wait!" Or maybe she just meant she'd be happy to as in "I was brought up to always be helpful and polite." Or maybe—

"How's city life been treating you?" Lana asked, her hands folded neatly in her lap. Clark shook himself back to the present, where life was really good.

"Did I tell you how amazing you look?" he asked, blue eyes wide.

Lana giggled, blushed, wrinkled her nose, and dropped her head all at once.

"Yes, you mentioned something like that." She laughed. "You look great, too."

"Oh, uh . . ." Clark hadn't been fishing for, or even anticipating, the return compliment and looked sheepish and shy. "Thanks. Hey, do you know where we're going?"

"Some place on the waterfront called The Vertical. It's up on the sixtieth story of Maggin Tower with 360 degrees' worth of windows. It's famous for its views. "

"Cool." Clark nodded, though truthfully he wouldn't have cared if they were going to a prison cafeteria to dine as long as she was sitting across from him.

"Are you having a good time?" Lana asked, starting to turn toward the window. Clark grabbed her other hand so that he held both of her hands in his own and slid closer to her on the wide leather seat, bringing his face mere inches from hers.

"Oh, yeah, *totally!*"

Lana laughed and moved one of her hands above both of his to pat them.

"I meant in the city, with Lex. Not right this second."

Clark opened his mouth to answer, let go of her hands, bit his lip, then hugged himself. He had no idea what to do with his hands if they weren't holding Lana's.

"Yeah, yeah, it's been great." Clark nodded. He didn't know why he was being such an idiot. There were times at school and at the coffee shop when he could manage whole, friendly, intelligible conversations with her, including segues, topic changes, and sometimes even jokes. But this was a *date*. Lex had said so, and Lana hadn't contradicted him. Clark wasn't sure why that made such a difference, but his eyes itched and burned with the intense desire to ignite something.

"What have you two been up to?" Lana prompted, as Clark rubbed at his closed lids.

"Well, Lex has been attending meetings at Luthor-Corp, and I've just been kind of bumming around the city, checking things out."

"Did you see the meteorites?"

"No, I haven't made it to the museum yet. Tomorrow, for sure. They're closed on Wednesdays, and I want to head back Thursday. Have you gotten in some good riding?"

Lana nodded vigorously, painfully aware that the conversation was flailing. Somehow she seemed to have once again touched on one of the many things Clark Kent didn't want to discuss, and all she'd asked was what he'd been up to! Honestly, he could be so *weird* sometimes!

"Yeah, I've managed to go out every morning. It's so quiet and peaceful, I really should do it more often. Listen—" Lana paused, and when Clark glanced at her it seemed to him that her expression was apprehensive and self-censoring. "We don't have to be all datey and weird here, Clark. I mean, we're friends, right?"

Clark swallowed and shifted slightly away from her.

Whoa! What did she say that for!? "*Were friends . . .*" *Just friends? Like friend-friends or like I'm-like-a-brother-to-her friends? And we don't have to be "datey"—what's that? What's she saying? Does she mean this isn't a date!?*

"Yeah, uh, yeah, of course we're friends."

"I just mean," Lana sat forward, laughing nervously. "I just mean it's silly for us to be all awkward with each other and everything. You seem stressed. I mean, I'm stressed. Are you stressed?" Lana had both of her hands resting on her chest and was leaning forward, peering at Clark with a self-consciously quizzical tilt of her head.

Clark nodded, swallowing, then made an attempt at a carefree laugh that didn't go off too well. All he could think about was kissing her. It was like someone was sitting behind him snatching every non-Lana-related thought out of the back of his brain before he could even utter one of them. He took a tiny bit of comfort in recognizing this as the normal young Earthling behavior it was and smiled ruefully, wondering if teens on his home planet had these problems.

Assuming it's even there anymore, he thought to himself, the smile fading. *You don't even know that much.*

Lana sat back in the seat again, brows furrowed. Clark realized he had just deflated in front of her and was scolding himself for the sudden descent into maudlin self-pity when Lana leaned in close to him and kissed his cheek. For a split second he was enveloped in the warm, exotic scent of vanilla, gardenia, jasmine, and musk that was uniquely Lana's. The light touch of her lips to his cheek tingled, feeling at once too light and too weighty. He sucked in a huge, fast intake of breath without realizing it and reeled, finally breaking into a huge grin.

Lana grinned back, satisfied with the complete transformation that spread across his face.

"There." She giggled. "That's better."

The laughter died on her lips when Clark turned to gaze at her. His eyes were depthless—she'd never seen that exact blue anywhere else. It was like the color of a deep, moonlit lake on some distant planet, galaxies away. Once she'd locked into his stare she couldn't break away from it, not even when he laughed suddenly, swallowed, and turned toward his window. She felt her heart catch in her throat as she stared at the back of his head, wanting suddenly to touch his hair. She cleared her throat and turned to look out the opposite window.

"Oh, uh, Chloe said to say 'hi,'" she murmured quickly, still looking away.

Clark turned his attention back to Lana, one eyebrow raised. "What did you tell her?" he asked.

"Just that Lex invited me to come spend an evening with you guys in the city." Lana glanced toward Clark with a smile. "I wasn't exactly sure what the plans were."

Clark nodded, frowning slightly. "So you didn't say it was a date or anything?"

Lana opened her mouth to speak, thought better of whatever she had been about to say, then shook her head, and started again. "You know, I don't remember what my exact words were. What should I tell her when I get back?"

Clark sensed something slightly accusatory in Lana's tone and was relieved when he thought of an evasive answer to her question.

"Tell her the truth." He shrugged. He had to hide a slight smile when Lana rolled her eyes.

The window separating them from the driver lowered

suddenly with a clean electric hum, and the car slowed to a stop.

"This is it," the driver said with a slight smile before exiting the car to hold the door for them. Clark stepped out onto the curb first, then reached in to help Lana. The smile she gave him as she took his hand was dazzling. "I'll be right over there when you're ready to go," the chauffeur told them, indicating a lot a few feet away. They both thanked him, Lana taking Clark's arm somewhere in the process, then, grinning with excitement and pleasure, they headed together down the red carpet that led into the restaurant.

"Whose name do you think the reservations are under?" Lana asked in the elevator as she clutched Clark's arm. It was clear that her excitement about the restaurant outweighed any frustration she might have been feeling toward Clark.

"I don't know," Clark answered. He was grinning back at her, relieved to see her having so much fun. "We'll try mine, I guess, and if that doesn't work, we'll try yours."

"And if that doesn't work, we'll try Lex's," Lana agreed, cuddling up to him more as they stepped out of the elevator together on the top floor and approached the maître d'.

"Mr. Kent, Miss Lang," he smiled, sweeping up two menus. "We're so glad you could join us this evening. If you'll follow me, please."

Clark and Lana exchanged astonished glances as they surrendered her shawl and his coat to a smiling hostess then followed the maître d' to their table.

"I guess this is what it feels like to be a Luthor," Lana whispered.

"Minus the everybody hating you part," Clark answered, waiting until Lana was seated before slipping into his own seat. Lana accepted her menu from the maître d' with another dazzling smile.

"You're a good person to see past that, Clark," she said, turning her attention back to him. Clark sat up a little straighter, beaming, and glanced out the floor-to-ceiling window at his immediate left, which was not unlike the glass walls in Lex's apartment. From where he sat, he could see the Queensland Bridge stretching out elegantly across the black waters of the West River. If he strained a little bit to look over his shoulder, he could see the lights of the Ordway Docks diffused by the hovering fog.

Wait a minute. The Ordway Docks. Pier 42 . . .

Clark focused his eyes more keenly, as he had the afternoon he'd been stargazing out his science classroom window in the broad daylight. He was able to pick out Pier 42, which seemed quiet, a scattering of flat-roofed warehouses casting long shadows over several small docked boats. Were Yakuza heading to it even now, ready to inform their gunrunners that there'd been a fire at one of their drug production labs?

"Great view, isn't it?" Lana exclaimed, looking out to her right. She twisted slightly in her chair, grinning. "I think Fort Hob's Park is right over there."

Clark was about to answer her when an attractive young woman about Lex's age approached their table wearing neatly pressed black slacks, a simple white blouse, and a black apron. Her blond hair was pulled back in a French twist, and her smile was warm.

Clark gazed at Lana as the waitress recited the evening's specials. Lana was hanging on to the waitress's every word, enjoying the atmosphere and the glamorous names of the dishes. Occasionally Lana would nod seriously or make some small sound of delight, as if to reassure the waitress that she had never heard of a more-wonderful sounding dish. Clark remembered how he'd been worried about hurting the feelings of the salesman in the fancy clothing store Lex had taken him to the day before and felt a surge of tenderness toward Lana. He didn't often have the opportunity to notice similarities between himself and his friends.

The waitress smiled at Clark. "Can I start you out with anything to drink this evening?" she asked.

"I'd love a soda," Clark said diplomatically.

Lana looked up with a nod. "Yes, diet for me, please."

"Certainly." The waitress seemed unconcerned with their beverage choices. "I'll be back in just a moment to take your order."

As Lana watched the waitress go, her foot brushed against Clark's shoes under the table, but she retracted it quickly. Clark felt the brief contact shoot up his leg like a bolt of electricity.

"It seems like everybody in Metropolis expects me to order alcohol or something," Clark smiled.

Lana's bright eyes met his. "You had alcohol?"

Clark shook his head. "No, but Lex had me in a bar the other night and seemed disappointed that I didn't want to try any."

"You guys were in a bar?" Lana sat back slightly, but tilted her head to one side, engrossed. "What did you do?"

"Well, he played cards with the Japanese Mafia while I drank chemically pasteurized milk and people-watched."

Lana's dimples appeared as she flashed another smile.

"Actually, that isn't true," Clark amended, glancing over his shoulder to squint at the pier. He was relieved to note no unusual activity there. "I didn't drink the milk," he confessed.

Lana chuckled and opened her menu.

"What are you thinking of getting?"

"The steak looks good, but I wonder where the cattle comes from here. It'd be kind of silly to come all the way to the city just to get meat they probably shipped in from Smallville."

"You sound like your dad," Lana commented. She looked up in time to see Clark's blue eyes light up.

"I do?" he asked, beaming.

Yeah, Lana thought. *Except weirder.* Their waitress approached their table with the two sodas and took their orders. After handing his menu over, Clark glanced out the window again, watching the pier. He noticed movement and felt his chest tighten. He wanted to find out why the Yakuza had been watching Lex, but not at the expense of his night out with Lana. After spending the whole day trying to stumble upon the Yakuza, Clark found himself hoping with all his heart that they'd remain hidden in the city for at least a few more hours.

Looking closer, he realized that there were people on the pier, but they didn't look like minions of organized crime. It was a young couple, only a few years older than Clark and Lana, walking hand in hand in the moonlight. Clark smiled with relief, hoping the young man out on the docks was having as much fun as he was in the restaurant.

"You know, maybe we should get something special to drink," Lana suggested. Clark turned his attention back to

Lana and noticed that her eyes were sparkling. "You know, to celebrate."

"Celebrate?" Clark's eyebrows went up.

"Yeah. This." She shrugged her slender shoulders, hands clasped before her on the table. "You. Me. The city."

"If you want to," Clark readily agreed. He was actually happy with his soda, but he couldn't imagine denying her anything that might elicit another one of her amazing smiles.

"Oh, it's silly. We don't have to," Lana decided suddenly, her hands fluttering up to smooth her hair as she scoffed at herself lightly. "I'm just getting kind of carried away here. It really is so lovely."

"Not half as lovely as you," Clark heard himself blurt out. He was mentally kicking himself when, to his delight, Lana blushed and smiled.

"Thank you, Clark." She laughed.

Embarrassed, he shot another glance over his shoulder. The young couple had stopped at the end of the pier and were gazing out across the water. Clark was about to look away when he noticed something else. He frowned as he watched three long cars drive up onto Pier 42 in procession, all cutting their engines at the exact same moment. There was no way for the young couple to exit the pier without passing the cars. Would the Yakuza let them walk by, or would they feel threatened by the presence of civilians near their exchange site? Clark remembered the man with the tattoos pushing the Japanese teenager into the path of an oncoming subway train just because Clark had followed him, and his frown deepened.

"What's the matter?" Lana asked. "What are you looking at? The docks?"

Clark stood abruptly, placing his napkin on his chair, as Lana watched him with surprise.

"Excuse me just a second, will you? I . . ." Clark looked around the restaurant wildly, hoping to identify something on which to pin his excuse. "I have to use the rest room."

Lana nodded, frowning as he raced toward the bathrooms. She'd just realized what the biggest problem was with Clark Kent.

He had a hard time staying still.

CHAPTER THIRTEEN

Clark bolted past the maître d', who watched him go with a look of confusion.

"Forgot my wallet!" Clark called over his shoulder, barreling into one of the elevators a second before the doors closed. The moment he started to descend he silently cursed himself for not taking the stairs, which he could have managed at easily ten times the speed of the elevator, maybe a hundred. Speed was everything. His plan was to run on and off the pier at superspeed, transporting the couple off the docks and safely away from the Yakuza one at a time. There was no reason they needed to see him. He figured they'd be confused and unable to explain their sudden relocation, but that was a lot better than getting shot.

At long last the elevator doors slid open and Clark bolted out the building's front doors. He ran across the well-manicured lawn of Maggin Tower, heading back toward the docks on the building's north side and opening up into a full superspeed run the moment he passed the streetlights illuminating the grass. He had to dart across one street that was chiefly used as a delivery road for the docks, quiet at this time of night, then bolt past three piers to get to the one he wanted. When at last he came to Pier 42, he stopped running to get his bearings, slightly breathless with anxiety if not exertion.

The dock area was cooler than the rest of the city, and Clark huddled against the wind, wishing he hadn't left his jacket with the coat check. He missed the pleasant Smallville evenings, although he was intrigued by the brackish smell coming off the water. He scuffed his good shoes as he wandered carefully down the rough, salt-worn wooden planks, occasionally reaching out to touch the waxy texture of a knotted docking rope.

The moment he'd stepped out into the dark, the city had begun to cry to him again. Clark was tempted to put his hands over his ears. He couldn't tell if he was actually hearing things or if his mind was racing so fast through potential crises and disaster scenarios that it was creating its own echo in his buzzing skull. Lex had been right when he'd asserted that it was a wholly different proposition to worry over the safety of over ten million people when you were used to keeping track of forty-five thousand.

Clark had to fight back the urge to start running up and down the gridded streets of Metropolis, stopping at every door to make sure everyone was all right. At the very least, he wondered if he should get back to Luthor Tower Two and check on Lex. For all he knew, Yakuza henchmen were in Lex's living room threatening to gun the young industrialist down while Clark played amateur detective in the dark. Of course, he did have a solid lead.

As quietly as he could, Clark scaled the fire escape of the warehouse above the three black cars. As suit- and sunglasses-wearing armed Yakuza started climbing out of the cars, Clark counted seven muscular Caucasian men emerging from one of the boats that had been docked at the pier all along. Clark realized with an uneasy flip of his stomach that he hadn't even thought to check the boats for signs of life when he'd been watching from the restaurant window.

Three of the Yakuza, all wearing variations on a shiny snakeskin suit Lex would have laughed at, walked to where the pier met the dock. Turning their backs on the cars, they pulled out some of the largest guns Clark had ever seen. At first he was appalled that they would display weapons so brazenly, but then he realized with a slow smile that he himself had interfered with Yakuza business twice in so many days. Was it possible that those were for him?

His smile faded as he saw the young couple stranded at the end of the pier. They had noticed the cars and the activity, but were hanging back, understandably hesitant to wander into the fray. Clark glanced over his shoulder at Maggin Tower, knowing that Lana waited on the top floor, unable to make out anything but the shape of the pier itself with her normal vision. Once again, he reminded himself to move quickly. He turned his attention back to the men on the boat, who were unloading crates onto the pier even as several of the Yakuza *kobun* unloaded smaller boxes from the trunks of their cars. One of the Yakuza and one of the men from the boat spoke quietly together. There was no question in Clark's mind that they were in the middle of an illegal exchange of drugs for guns.

Clark felt uncertain about his plan. Even though it would only take him about a second to pick up either member of the couple in a fireman's carry and run them off the pier, that was a second in which Yakuza attention might turn dangerously to the remaining member. Since they were on the river, Clark decided he could pass the

Yakuza first, pushing both the drugs and guns into the water before grabbing the couple, thereby rendering the weapons useless and also, he hoped, leaving something for the Metropolis police to find later. It wasn't a great plan, but it was better than doing nothing. Also in his favor was the darkness and the fact that once it was over, no one would be able to tell the local authorities anything about what happened without admitting their own involvement in the trade.

Clark waited until it looked like all the crates and boxes had been unloaded, then jumped off of the warehouse roof, landing in a crouch by the side of the structure. Moving as fast as he could—which was, he'd sometime ago established, faster than the human eye could follow—he launched himself at the three Yakuza guards, grabbing guns out of their hands and tossing them into the river before they could even register that something was wrong. From Clark's perspective, it was as if everyone was moving in slow motion. By the time he reached the end of the pier and had the young woman over his shoulder, even the speech around him had been reduced to gradual, drawn-out syllables.

He had already gotten the young woman to safety and was heading back for the young man when the half words spoken by those he was passing at superspeed began to come together in his head.

"—biiiiiig fiiiiiiiiiiirrrrre—"

"—beeee pleeeeeaaaassssed—"

"—luuuuthoooooor—"

Luthor? With the young man already over his shoulder, Clark hesitated, straining to make out the rest of the sentence.

"—Corp in broad daylight. Matsushita-san has his best men on it."

Clark realized with dismay that he was standing still. A few feet ahead of him, the Yakuza guards were noticing that they were suddenly unarmed, and the pier burst into animation like a fire dosed with gasoline.

Many began racing back to their cars or the docked boat.

"The field agent!" one of the men on the boat shouted. Clark heard the heavy click of a gun safety slipping off and saw a red laser dot appear on his chest.

"*Hai!*" someone affirmed in Japanese.

"That's a field agent?" someone else asked.

"Undercover," someone else asserted.

"Must be a *ninja*," another voice joked. "He appears from the darkness."

Clark caught his breath and dashed down the pier at superspeed, realizing he'd blown it. He placed the confused young man next to his girlfriend a few feet away from the docks and was already halfway back to Maggin Tower when he heard the metallic crack of a gunshot. He stopped in his tracks, glanced up toward the restaurant where he knew Lana still waited, then turned around to go back.

As he ran onto the pier again at superspeed, Clark tried to figure out what had happened. It seemed that one of the Yakuza had fired at another, but that didn't make any sense to Clark unless the shooter had assumed that Clark's presence on the docks indicated a setup. The bullet was spinning toward a young Japanese man standing near the first car. He was just beginning to turn his head toward the shooter, seconds away from noticing the fatal betrayal.

Clark knocked the bullet out of the air with his forearm and turned to hurl himself at the endangered Yakuza, knocking the intended victim backward and out of harm's way should the shooter fire again. The young man he was saving had shiny dark hair like Lana's, and a slender, expressive face. Clark realized that his teeth were gritted. He couldn't help himself. Two sets of gunfiring bad guys stood ready to kill him and each other, and Clark felt responsible for the safety of every last one of them. Despite the guns and the drugs, they were human. Clark couldn't let them get hurt.

Even though the action of saving the first Yakuza took him less than a second, two additional shots were fired as Clark scrambled back up to his feet. Still moving at superspeed and warning himself not to slow down this time, Clark raced onto the docked boat and pushed the primary gunman clear, taking shots to the back from two separate directions as he did so. Whirling around the deck, he grabbed every gun he could get his hands on and tossed them all over the side. Next he dashed back down to the pier, barely dodging shots to the chest as he grabbed guns away from the Yakuza, all of whom continued to try to fire with their empty hands for several seconds after Clark had tossed their weapons into the river.

Clark knew from his last encounter that the Yakuza were fast and decisive. They reacted without hesitation or mercy when they felt cornered. Clark realized he was lucky that they seemed to have agreed on a retreat. The car closest to the dock—a flashy black Cadillac—roared to life and started to back off of the pier, tires skidding violently over the damp plank boards. Reacting with pure adrenaline, Clark bounded over the other two cars to land on the roof of the retreating Cadillac. He dug his fingers into the metal of the car's frame and reached down to rip the hood off the trunk. After tossing the hood toward the second car on the pier, momentarily obscuring the view from their rear window as they also began trying to back up and race off of the pier, Clark reached blindly into the trunk of the car he was clinging to and felt his fingers close around a single crateload of guns. The Cadillac lurched forward, and Clark let himself be thrown backward toward the open trunk, holding the gun crate against his chest as he rolled off of the Cadillac altogether, hurtling down toward the pier. The crate crashed and broke open between the Cadillac and the second car in line for the exit, heavy black guns skidding across the pier as Clark fought to slow his own skid and struggle back to his feet.

He had managed to do so when the second car backed straight into him at over 40 MPH, rolling over the scattered guns as if they were twigs. Clark felt the force of the car engine try to push him backward and dug his heels in, stopping the car against his hip. The tires squealed and began to smoke as Clark held the car in place and tried to pry the trunk open. It proved a difficult task, though, as the back of the car looked as if it had hit a steel column, and Clark realized with a jolt of recognition that it was his own body that had folded the trunk in on itself like paper.

It seemed unlikely that anyone else was going to be able to get it open either, so Clark decided it was well past time to make himself scarce when the driver of the third car, which was still blocked on the pier by the second car, panicked and accelerated.

Clark could hear shouting from inside the third car—

a Lincoln—but couldn't understand what was being said.

Clark shot after the Lincoln, which seemed mere seconds away from pitching itself right off the edge of the pier, but in his recklessness, tripped over an abutment and found himself flying, facefirst, toward the end of the pier almost as fast as the car.

Stop, stop, stop, stop, STOP! Clark was screaming at himself, wondering if his invulnerability extended to self-caused accidents. He felt his shoulder crunch into the southeastern batter pile just as the Lincoln started to pitch headlong into the river. Gritting his teeth, Clark wrapped his left arm around the pile and grabbed for the sinking car with his right hand. He felt the cold metal of the bumper catch in the straining fingers of his right hand the exact same moment his left arm slipped from the damp wood of the pile.

Clark hit the cold water of the West River a fraction of a second after the Lincoln. He couldn't help thinking of the time Lex's Porsche had taken him over the side of the Old Mill Bridge in Smallville. Clark had hit the water before Lex's car that time, and had only had one person to save from drowning, but the image of a human face out cold behind the windshield of the underwater car was unsettlingly familiar. Banging as hard as he could on the glass windows of the sinking Lincoln, Clark felt full-blown terror.

There were three men in the car, and only one of them was still conscious. He had been in the backseat but was now scrambling into the front as if hoping to get control of the steering wheel and drive the car back out of the water. Clark recognized him as the one who had opened fire on his fellow Yakuza. Though the Japanese man was in his late forties and had an unusually impassive face even in the midst of his panic, Clark couldn't help but see Lex there in that sinking metal coffin.

I won't let you sink, Clark thought frantically. *I won't let you go down.*

Swimming with all his might, Clark made his way past the front of the plummeting Lincoln. He moved to put himself in front of it and push it back up toward the surface, but even his X-ray vision couldn't help him in the soft, endless blankness of the dark waters under the night sky. Disoriented and not entirely confident about where the surface was, Clark prayed that the car hadn't flipped over in the river and that its back was still pointing up. Holding his breath, he strained every muscle in his body, swimming as fast as he could with the car boring down into his shoulder.

In the cold depths of the river, Clark would barely have been able to prove his own consciousness to himself if not for the straining in his body and the frenzied echo of his own thudding heart filling his ears. He still wasn't completely sure he was heading in the right direction, and he didn't know how much oxygen was still in the car or how airtight the windows were. He had no idea what he was going to do when and if he was finally able to push the nose of the car back up through the surface of the water. The only thing he felt any certainty about at all was that he couldn't give up.

He couldn't have been underwater for more than a few minutes, but to Clark, it felt like hours. Even though he was fairly sure he couldn't drown, when at last he felt the pressure on his shoulder shift, Clark spent the last ounce of his strength fighting his own way up through the surface of the water just for the reassuring gulp of air it afforded him. Before the car could sink again, Clark punched through the windshield, shouting at the man who was still conscious to help him drag the other two out. It took the two of them, each hauling one of the unconscious men through the water, another incalculable handful of soaked, freezing minutes to climb back up onto the pier with their charges. The Lincoln began its second descent into the watery depths of the West River, this time empty of human life, while Clark and the Japanese man checked the pulses of the unconscious men they'd splayed out on the dock, then collapsed beside them.

The boat and the other two cars were long gone. Guns littered the pier. After catching his breath, Clark rose and kicked them into the water one by one.

"Are you all right?" the stoic Yakuza asked quietly from where he knelt shivering on the pier by his still-unconscious friends. According to the social customs of the Yakuza, these two men were his brothers, and he looked truly worried over their well-being. His accent was thick, and his voice was surprisingly kind. Clark hugged himself from the cold, his back to the man and the end of the pier.

"You shot at one of them," Clark heard himself saying. "One of your own people, you shot at him. I saw you." He turned to face the older man, suddenly intent on knowing what the rationale for such a senseless action could possibly have been.

The Yakuza gunman studied the face of his teenage rescuer for a moment, then nodded. "Things tonight did not go as planned. Masuji-san is in charge of the exchange. His death would make up for our failure."

Clark was sure he had misunderstood. "But it wasn't

his fault that everything went wrong all of a sudden! It was mine."

The Yakuza's expression remained impassive. "Your death would have been even better. But it was not within my power to arrange at the time."

Clark knew he had to get back to Lana, but an unfamiliar feeling of indignation was building in his chest.

"You mean every time something goes wrong, you kill one of your own people!?"

The man looked down at his two companions, who were both still unconscious. "There must always be retribution," was all he said.

Clark lifted his chin, intending to refute the man. Instead, without quite deciding to, he ran.

Clark ran the length of the dock and over to the base of the restaurant tower. He was exhausted, cold and kicking up a windchill factor against his wet skin, but he wanted to run until he met morning, wanted to run east until he crashed headlong into the rising sun, which would maybe give him light and warmth and quiet and strength. He'd never reach the sun, but if he hurried, he might reach Lana.

She was still sitting at their table when he reappeared in the restaurant, dripping wet, the back of his shirt torn from bullet holes. The water gradually pooling under his shoes onto the soft, dark carpet of the restaurant was oily and foul. Patrons looked up from their dinners as shocked by the smell as by the sight of Clark.

Lana took one look at him and rose to her feet. Grabbing her purse, she stood directly in front of him, eyes flashing.

"Clark, what happened? You left me sitting here alone for nearly twenty minutes, and I can't even *imag-*

ine how you're going to explain *this*!" She gestured at his appearance, and Clark could tell she was caught somewhere between anger, worry, embarrassment, and confusion. He couldn't think of anything to say that wasn't completely preposterous, and was beginning to attract unwanted attention as he soiled the expensive carpeting of the restaurant with river water.

"Lana, I'm so sorry," he finally managed, but she said nothing. Shaking her head, she headed for the elevators, not even bothering to retrieve her shawl from the coat check. Clark raced after her. "Lana, please, I—all I want is to spend this evening with you. What happened has nothing to do with you, try to believe that."

Lana turned to Clark with a glower. "That's where you're wrong, Clark. That's where you've *always* been wrong. Keeping secrets, disappearing in the middle of things, showing up soaked from head to toe and offering no explanation—that *does* have to do with me, because I'm your friend, and I'm here with you, and I'm part of your life. You can't expect to be one person when I'm around and someone totally different the rest of the time and not have it *matter* to me. This *does* have to do with me, Clark, and I can't believe you'd say otherwise!"

The elevator doors opened, and Lana stepped inside, pushing the button for the lobby. Clark thrust his hand in to hold the door.

Lana leveled her angry gaze at him, her arms crossed defensively in front of her. "I'm patient, Clark. If you can explain to me where you went and what you did and why you look like that now, I'll stay to hear it."

Clark took in a short breath as if about to speak, then looked miserably down at the floor. He couldn't think of anything to say. Nothing that came to mind made any sense, and they were all lies anyway.

"That's what I thought," Lana muttered from between clenched teeth, turning her glare from Clark to the control panel. Clark took his hand away from the elevator and watched as the doors closed, obscuring Lana's irritated expression. He tried to cheer himself up with the thought that at least a car was waiting for her, and Lex's driver would get her safely home.

After collecting his coat and her shawl, Clark walked slowly down the sixty flights of stairs that took him from the restaurant to the ground floor, shivering and despondent. Once outside, after confirming that Lana's car had left for Smallville, Clark wandered without direction or purpose, lost again in the city until he was too tired to take another step. Leaning against a telephone booth, Clark tried to calm himself, tried to think, but the strain of the past few hours was welling up inside him, and he no longer knew if he was shaking from the cold or from residual fear. He knew it wasn't yet late, but was still surprised by how many people were out, hurrying up and down the streets, honking horns, hailing cabs, *dying, minute by minute, weakness by weakness, drowning, all of them, every second, farther and farther down, into the noise, into the pollution, they just vanish, and more come to take their place . . .*

Clark stepped into the telephone booth and closed the door behind him, hoping to block out the morbid thoughts that were filling his head. He didn't feel like a hero. He didn't feel invulnerable. He felt like a sixteen-year-old boy, homesick, disheveled, and overwhelmed.

It was quieter in the phone booth, and a little bit warmer. With his back pressed against one of the glass walls, Clark slid down into a crouch, hid his face in his hands, and cried.

CHAPTER FOURTEEN

Lex slipped Lorelei's coat off her bare shoulders, smelling the sweet perfume on the back of her neck as his fingertips brushed her warm skin. He felt something inside his gut kick and tighten, and smiled to himself as he tamped it down. When he had been a little younger he'd assumed it was just lust. Now he was beginning to understand that it was something more desperate than that, some ache of cold grief that wanted only to warm itself in the heat of a sympathetic embrace.

Lex knew that such psychic wounds were potentially lethal. Lionel had told him so over and over again while pouring salt into them and assuring Lex that the pain would make him stronger. Lex was no longer certain whether his father had sincerely believed in his sadistic version of tough love or had been out to sabotage his son from the very beginning, but he did know without a doubt that he would sooner choke on the anguish than let anyone sense its presence.

He draped Lorelei's coat over one of the kitchen barstools while she stepped into the Metropolis penthouse, her eyes shining and her strappy pink shoes clicking pleasantly on the polished concrete floor.

"What a wonderful place!" she exclaimed with genuine approval. Lex might have appreciated the compliment if he'd had anything to do with the interior decorating, but, alas, he had not.

"Can I get you a drink?" he asked evenly, and Lorelei turned to him from the center of the living room with a smile, her auburn curls shining under the track lighting.

"Whatever you're having," she said agreeably.

Lex tried not to hold it against her. Obsequious geniality bored him to tears, but he knew it was a behavior drilled into most members of polite society, especially females. He wandered leisurely into the kitchen, fished two square crystal glasses out of a cabinet, and poured two healthy servings of scotch as Lorelei sat on the black leather couch, her long legs crossed.

"So where's this friend of yours?" she asked.

"He's on a date of his own," Lex answered, carrying the drinks into the living room. He handed one of them to Lorelei and sat down on the couch beside her with a slight smile. He thought he saw her already broad grin tighten but couldn't think why she should be so nervous. "The girl next door, his heart's desire. Knowing Clark, he'll walk her all the way home to Smallville."

"You sure he won't try to get a motel room somewhere?" Lorelei teased, taking a sip of her scotch.

Still smiling, Lex nodded. "I'm pretty sure."

"A little square, is he?"

"No. He's actually a really good kid."

"I can't believe you took him on vacation with you," Lorelei protested with a wrinkled nose.

"I like him," Lex said simply, then leaned back in the couch, closing his eyes as he rubbed his temples with the thumb and middle finger of one hand. "And I'm not on vacation."

Lorelei took what seemed to Lex to be an excessively

long swallow of scotch, then took off her heels, dropping
them onto the rug as she pulled her legs up under her
carefully toned body. She twisted to face him better.

"What *are* you doing here?" she asked, her tone suddenly serious. Lex opened his eyes and glanced at her
with wry amusement. Seductions were always entertaining, even if they weren't terribly challenging on an intel-
lectual level.

"Here in Metropolis, or here on the couch?"

"Just . . . here." She laughed.

Lex thought it rang false. She was after something,
and it wasn't necessarily his body. His eyebrows went up
as she began to run her foot along the inside of his thigh.
Instead of arousing him, her gesture made him feel
strangely numb.

Lorelei thought she saw a flicker of coldness in his
eyes, and was surprised when Lex leaned forward suddenly and locked his mouth against hers, his tongue forcing her lips apart with an almost calculated savagery.

He pulled back just as suddenly as he'd pressed forward, and Lorelei lost her equilibrium, along with her
breath. His heat, when he was close to her, was searing,
something she missed desperately the second it was gone.
Her body had begun to have a conversation with his that
her mind was not a party to. She could feel a throbbing
warmth begin to pool just beneath her skin, and his
steady gaze assured her that he was completely tuned in
to her pounding pulse. Flustered, she turned her face
away from him, fighting to keep her breathing in check.

She had always liked him more than she would ever
admit. It was absurd, really—they'd never been particu-
larly close. Back in Lex's wild days, she'd just been a
decorative accessory in his inner circle, tolerated but

never trusted. He had barely even known her name. But she had watched him, heard about his exploits, even shared the occasional drink or surprisingly warm laugh with him, and he moved her. There was a dark power in Lex Luthor. He made her feel safe, as if he could easily fight into submission anything the world threw at her. He also made her feel needed. He was the perennial bad boy on the brink of salvation, not yet too far gone. Could he be reaching out to her now? She hadn't thought there was any chance that he could be sincerely interested in her, which is why she had agreed to betray him. Lorelei wanted to call the whole thing off, beg Lex's forgiveness, and run. But it was clearly too late for that.

"Are you all right?" he asked with a tenderness that contradicted the aggressive challenge of his kiss. Lorelei swallowed and tucked a stray strand of hair behind one ear, then sat up abruptly.

"I'm fine," she said too quickly, then, barreling ahead with the subtlety of a Mack truck, she continued. "So . . . *how* long have you been in Smallville now?"

Lex's eyes narrowed, and all traces of kindness and amusement left his face.

"You obviously have something on your mind," he said coolly, shifting on the couch so that Lorelei now felt the presence of an invisible wall between them. "What can I do for you, Lorelei?"

Damn. This was not what she wanted. Lex Luthor, negotiator, was not someone she was qualified to be alone in a room with. She was counting on his considerate, gentlemanly nature, qualities she knew he insistently stifled when he was conducting business.

"No, I—" Lorelei floundered, then laughed lightly in

an attempt to recover. "It's just been a while. I want to know what you've been up to."

Lorelei looked up at Lex from under long, dark eyelashes and tried to gather her feminine wiles around her like barbed wire. Lex's expression darkened.

"I've been running a fertilizer plant," he said quietly.

"Are you turning a profit?" she started to ask. The question ended in a squeak when Lex suddenly slammed his glass down on the coffee table with such force that scotch splashed up in a mini tsunami. He rose to his feet so rapidly it made Lorelei woozy, no less so when he turned to her with burning eyes.

"Did my father put you up to this?" he demanded. His rage was both fierce and controlled. Lorelei wanted to run from him.

"Your—? No, no, I haven't seen Lionel for years."

"Who then?" Lex leaned in toward her with a snarl, one hand gripping the back of the sofa on either side of her head, trapping her against the black leather couch.

Tears welled in Lorelei's eyes. "Lex," she whispered, "I'm sorry, I—"

"Who?" Lex repeated.

She shook her head. "I don't know him. He said he was a federal agent." Tears of embarrassment and frustration began to run down her cheeks, and Lex sighed as he straightened up, pulling a white linen handkerchief from the front pocket of his slacks and offering it to her with a slight roll of his eyes. Lorelei took it from him gratefully, dabbed it against her eyes, and blew her nose. She took another swallow of scotch, hands shaking, then continued in a small voice.

"He was pretty average-looking. I mean, handsome enough, but not the kind of guy who'd stand out in a crowd. Late thirties, dark hair, green eyes, medium height. He had a . . . a small scar on his chin. He told me he needed information on you and the boy who was staying here with you, and that if I didn't cooperate he could have me arrested for obstructing justice, or something like that. I didn't know what to do. I figured if I asked you a few questions, maybe that would be enough. Then I could find out what he wanted with you when I reported back." She paused again, sniffing, then looked up at Lex with her large, wet eyes. "I'd never do anything to hurt you, Lex. You have to believe that. I—I've never said anything before, but I think you're . . . I mean, I wish we . . . ."

"Where'd you run into this guy?" Lex asked, calmer but apparently completely ignoring the emotional subtext of the conversation.

"He was waiting outside my apartment this morning."

"And how are you supposed to get back in touch with him?"

"I don't know. He didn't say. I guess he'll find me." Lorelei rose from the couch, swiping a stray tear off her cheek and taking a deep breath. "Did you understand what I was trying to say before, about us?" Lorelei frowned at the rug, annoyed with herself. "I guess I didn't really say it, did I?" She turned her green eyes back to him, and there was nothing but sincerity in her gaze. "I care about you, Lex. I have for years. I was just afraid to tell you because I couldn't imagine you feeling the same way about me."

Lex had begun to pace, and Lorelei wasn't sure if she was getting through to him or not. Feeling emboldened by the confession of her true feelings, she continued, her voice steadying as she allowed herself a shy smile.

"You'd laugh if you knew how often I think about you. I've really missed you since you left the city. We all have. It's just not the same without you. But you know how they say you regret what you didn't do more than what you did? Well, it's true. I always wished I'd told you how I really felt. I mean, not even because I thought you'd feel the same way, but just because . . . because I wanted you to know how special you are."

Lorelei reached out and gently rested a hand on Lex's arm. Lex didn't meet her eyes, but he stopped pacing, his eyes focused on the floor. Lorelei took this as encouragement. She knew how isolating his life was, how difficult it was for someone with his kind of money and power to trust people. She had always hated the way people judged him by his father's reputation without getting to know him, and had always wanted the chance to reassure him that his friends knew and valued his true worth. Smiling more warmly, her eyes still sparkling with tears, she continued.

"It made me so sad, thinking that maybe everyone was always afraid to tell you how they really felt about you. I know you probably won't choose to spend your life with me or anything, but at least I have this chance to tell you that I think you're . . . well, kind of amazing."

Lorelei allowed herself a timid grin as Lex finally turned to face her.

"When you see this bastard again, I want you to get some form of ID from him," Lex said. Lorelei blinked, the smile vanishing from her face. Lex squared his shoulders. "I'll have my lawyers prepare a subpoena you can hand him on the spot, but they'll need a name to fill in on their end."

"Lex?" Lorelei asked, shrinking back from him slightly. "Didn't you hear anything I just said?"

"I'll have you tailed, of course. But just go about your normal business. No one will interfere with you."

Lorelei tightened her grip on Lex's arm, looking at him pleadingly.

"I'll do anything you say," she agreed, "but please acknowledge what I just told you."

Lex stared coldly at her hand on his arm until, bewildered and almost frightened, she released him.

"You should go now," he said thickly.

Lorelei sat back down on the couch long enough to pull her shoes on, her emotions teetering somewhere between resentment and dismay.

"I understand that you're angry," she started, rising from the couch. Lex had her coat over one arm and was already holding open the door to the entrance hall for her.

"I'm not angry," he said straightforwardly. "It's not your fault."

Lorelei looked at him, confused, then moved forward to take her coat, embarrassed by how intensely she wished he'd help her into it. She hesitated in the doorway, wanting to say something more to him, but he took her by the elbow and led her toward the elevators.

"God," she said with a sad shake of her head as they waited for the elevator. "I'm just like everybody else in your life, aren't I? I mean, here I am telling you I care about you, but from where you're standing, it must seem like I just came here to stab you in the back."

Together they heard the tinny ping of the elevator chime, and the steel doors slid open, flooding the foyer with harsh, fluorescent light. Lorelei turned to Lex with one last, desperate attempt to explain herself, feeling raw and exposed.

"Everything I said was true, Lex. It had nothing to do with that guy."

Lex slipped one hand into the elevator and held the doors until Lorelei finally stepped in, not knowing what else to do. As she turned to face him, he removed his hand.

"You did hear what I said to you, right? Please tell me you heard me."

"I heard you." Lex nodded, as the elevator doors started to slide shut. Lorelei stepped forward, ready to press the HOLD button. "You said you're just like everybody else."

The elevator doors slid shut.

CHAPTER FIFTEEN

Clark stepped out of the elevator onto the top floor of Luthor Tower Two and stopped to look at himself in the mirrored entryway. His dark hair was matted against his forehead, his clothes were wrinkled and disheveled. Lana's shawl hung out of his jacket pocket. Although his jacket now hid them, bullet holes dotted the back of his shredded shirt. Dirt from the murky river water stained his face, hands, and throat, and his shoes still squished with every step he took. He had spent hours walking around in the city, hoping to get in late enough to find Lex already in bed.

Sliding the card key into the flat steel lock, Clark opened the door to Lex's penthouse as quietly as possible. The lamp in the living room was on, but Clark assumed that was just a thoughtful gesture on Lex's part and not an indication of his being awake.

He closed the door behind him, pressing it gently shut so as not to make much noise. He was past the glow of the lamp and halfway to his room when he noticed Lex sitting at the dining room table in relative darkness. With a swallow, Clark pulled his jacket around him tighter, hoping Lex wouldn't notice the state of disarray he was in.

"Clark, are you drowning?" Lex asked from the

shadows. There was the familiar hint of amusement in his voice, but something harder as well.

"Not anymore." Clark sighed. He turned toward his friend with a slight wince, wondering why Lex was sitting alone in the dark. "It's a long story. I'll tell you all about it in the morning. I'm really tired . . ." he pleaded softly.

Lex rose and flicked on the overhead light. Clark watched the smile on his face dissolve as if it had always been a mirage.

"Oh, my God," he said, obviously truly stunned as he looked Clark up and down. "I heard you squish in, and I figured maybe the lovely Miss Lang had thrown a glass of water in your face or something, but look at you! What the hell happened?"

Clark cursed himself for not thinking to come up with a plausible excuse for his condition on the way home.

"I . . . fell into the river, and . . ." he stammered.

"Where's Lana?" Lex demanded.

"On her way home, with your driver. She's fine."

Lex turned away, and his posture stiffened. When he turned to look back at Clark, his eyes were flashing dangerously.

"I don't know what's going on here, Clark, but I don't like it. Seriously, you're a minor, and your parents entrusted you to my care. You're my responsibility until we leave Metropolis. I need you to tell me what really happened, right now."

Clark gestured helplessly, caught between trying to convey, "I *did* tell you," and "I *can't* tell you." With a fresh wave of frustration, he remembered his father's words from the telephone call the morning before. *Lex*

*Luthor is the last person in the world you should be con-
fiding in.*

"What do you want me to say, Lex?"

Lex exploded suddenly, his jaw clenching as his hands
balled into fists.

"I want the *truth*, Clark. I can't be on goddamned sub-
terfuge patrol around the clock with you. I can do it with
my father. I can do it with my business partners. I can
even do it with my dates, but I'm not gonna do it with my
friends! Be *straight* with me." Lex paused, taking a deep,
measured breath, his voice shifting from volcanic to low
and hard and icy. "Be straight with me or get the hell
out."

Lex turned his back on Clark and waited.

"You . . . you want me to leave?" Clark asked meekly.

Lex's head dropped as he thrust his hands in his pockets and sighed. When he turned around again he looked
tired, which was as startling to Clark as seeing Lex angry.

"No. I don't want you to leave, Clark," he said quietly.
"But just tell me this much. Are you involved with the
agent who questioned Lorelei?"

Clark's eyes widened.

"What?"

Lex leaned forward slightly, peering intently into
Clark's face. He did not look friendly, or pleased. Clark
held his gaze, and then frowned to himself. He was hearing strange, high-pitched electronic reverberations again,
only this time they were getting louder. He didn't want to
point them out for fear that they were beyond Lex's audible range.

"No one's approached you about me lately? A federal
agent type, say? You're not in a deal with somebody?"

Clark's face registered shock as he turned his full attention back to Lex.

"What? No!" Without thinking, Clark reached up and tried to swat the electronic buzzing sounds away from his ear like a fly. "What are you talking about?"

Lex took a deep breath and rubbed at his forehead as if trying to subdue a terrible headache.

"My date earlier told me she'd been contacted by a man claiming to be a federal agent of some kind. He wanted intel on me—and you, maybe. She said he had dark hair, was in his late thirties and had a small scar on his chin. Ring any bells?"

Clark shook his head. "That could be almost anyone."

Lex nodded. "I know. I thought my dad might be behind it, but Lorelei swears he wasn't. At least, not as far as she knew."

Clark couldn't imagine the kind of life where, when something went wrong, the first person you had to suspect would be your father. His heart went out to Lex. It seemed that where the young billionaire was concerned, there was danger everywhere.

"Wait a minute!" Clark said excitedly, remembering the conversation he'd heard on the pier. "Something did happen tonight. I don't know if this has anything to do with Lionel or not, but I overheard one of the Yakuza mentioning LuthorCorp. He said something about LuthorCorp 'in broad daylight,' then something about some guy named Matsushita-san. That's all I caught."

Lex stared at Clark with a strangely impassive expression. "You 'overheard' the Yakuza?" he asked finally.

Clark realized he might have said too much and was about to try to put his eavesdropping in some reasonable context when the shrill keening noise in his ears intensified. He winced, and this time Lex noticed and erupted again.

"Clark, dammit! Tell me what's wrong!"

Clark shook his head, though he was still grimacing.

"No, I—I'm just really tired . . ."

Clark started to make an X-ray-assisted sweep of the apartment, wondering if there was some kind of electrical problem. "You know," he continued, talking mostly to distract Lex from noticing how intensely he was staring at the walls, but also because the thought had suddenly come to him in murky focus. "That description kind of sounds like that imposter doorman we saw."

Lex frowned, trying to recollect what a man he'd barely glimpsed at looked like. He couldn't bring any distinct features to mind. Glancing back at Clark, he noticed that his friend's blue eyes had suddenly gone wide. Clark's hand shot out and grabbed Lex's arm with surprising urgency.

"Well, it's probably nothing," Clark said loudly. His chiseled, open face was contorting itself in an effort to convey something to Lex, but aside from comprehending Clark's insistence, Lex wasn't sure what was being indicated. He felt the younger man's fingers biting into the flesh of his bicep, though, and watched his friend carefully. "We should just turn in," Clark continued, with slightly exaggerated enunciation. With his left hand still gripping Lex's arm, he pulled the young billionaire closer, his right hand circling in the air between them in some sort of "keep it rolling" gesture. "I'm sure we're getting all worked up without reason."

Lex frowned in confusion, but went along with Clark attentively.

"Yeah," he said out loud, glancing around the penthouse

uncertainly and turning his attention back to Clark. "You're probably right."

Clark was nodding at him encouragingly. Still standing toe to toe with him, he let go of Lex's arm and made some kind of weird flying gesture by his stomach with one hand. Lex shook his head at him and turned up both palms to indicate he didn't get it, but Clark quickly placed his own hands over Lex's and pulled them back down.

"Okay, well, good night!" Clark said cheerfully, surprising Lex by releasing his hands and suddenly embracing him. Clark smelled like salt water and sewage, and his flesh was as unyielding as steel. At a loss, Lex started to hug Clark back, then felt his friend's mouth centimeters from his ear.

"Bugs," Clark whispered urgently. "And cameras."

Shocked, Lex patted Clark's shoulder fraternally and released him, stepping back.

"Sleep well," Lex said loudly, eyes beginning to rove the penthouse frantically. Clark's eyes made a quick, darting survey of the apartment, and Lex followed his every glance: the mobile, the wall sockets, the light sconces, the phone . . . Lex nodded very subtly, though he himself saw nothing out of the ordinary.

Clark began to move toward the bedroom, unsure of what else to do. Lex remained standing in the middle of the living room for a moment, staring at the floor, his expression darkening. Clark shot him a pleading glance, and Lex pulled himself up.

"No, wait a minute," he said suddenly, his voice dark again. "This is all just a little too weird for me. I think it would be better if you grabbed a few things and got out."

Clark gaped at Lex and studied him to see if there was

some secret meaning to his words. Lex met Clark's eyes and stared into them coldly.

"Okay," Clark said quietly, his stomach dropping. "If that's what you want."

"I'm going out for a drink," Lex snapped, grabbing his cell phone, wallet, and keys. "I want you gone by the time I return."

Clark nodded, still taken aback. He felt miserable and confused as he watched Lex slam the door of the penthouse behind him. He stood alone in the apartment for a few minutes, thinking, then changed his clothes and collected his few belongings. He put the card key Lex had given him on the coffee table and left the penthouse carrying his backpack and duffel bag.

He had barely stepped foot outside of the building when Lex's Porsche pulled up at the curb.

"For someone who can see invisible spyware, you sure are a slow packer," Lex quipped.

Clark blinked at his friend in confusion, causing Lex to get out of the car and grab his duffel bag. "What am I gonna do with you?" Lex muttered as he tossed Clark's bag in the backseat. "Feel free to get in anytime now."

Clark let himself into the Porsche, placing his backpack by his feet, and waited. Lex jumped back into the driver's seat and drove away from Luthor Tower Two significantly faster than the speed limit allowed.

"Did you really think I was just going to leave you?" Lex asked incredulously as he stopped the car for a red light. "Two people were *killed* in that building last night! And now you're telling me the whole place is bugged? Clark, I've got a credit card or two. We don't need to stay there."

Clark smiled at him weakly. "I . . . thought you were

really mad at me," he confessed. "I mean, you've got plenty of reasons to be."

Lex glanced at Clark, then shifted his car back into drive as the light changed to green. "I'm not mad," he said quietly, his eyes on the road. "Just a little paranoid, maybe." Lex drove quietly for another minute, and added, more to himself than to Clark, "Though it isn't paranoia if everyone *is* out to get you."

Clark smiled, exhausted beyond words, and turned to look out the window.

"Is a hotel all right?" Lex asked after another few minutes had passed. "I've still got meetings I have to get to in the morning, then I want to get to the bottom of whatever's going on here."

"Yeah, a hotel's fine," Clark answered. "Whatever you want to do."

Lex nodded and pulled up to valet parking in what looked to Clark like a very expensive five-star hotel. Clark followed Lex into the lobby, numb with insecurity and fatigue, then up the elevator to the fourteenth floor. Lex stopped him outside one of the rooms and handed him a card key.

"I'm right here," he said, indicating the next room over.

Clark nodded wearily and opened the door to his hotel room. "Lex?" he called suddenly, sticking his head back into the hall.

Lex appeared from his room with a concerned look on his face. "Yeah, Clark? What is it?"

Clark felt foolish, but also overwhelmed and emotionally off-balance. "You're . . . you're really not mad at me?" he asked. He was remembering the scowl on Lana's face, the furious flash of Lex's eyes, all the lies he had and hadn't told that night.

Lex smiled softly, but Clark noted that it looked a bit strained.

"I'm really not mad at you," Lex insisted. "Now get some sleep, okay? I'll see you in the morning." He carefully kept his smile in place as Clark waved good night to him and disappeared into his room, but let it fade as he put out the DO NOT DISTURB sign and locked his door behind him.

Lex leaned against the hotel door and stared at the ceiling. He thought about Lorelei, the doorman, the security guard, the electronic bugging devices in his apartment, his father, and Clark. Especially Clark. He wanted so badly to be able to trust his friend, but so many secrets stood between them. He knew Clark was moral, guileless, and even naive. But he also knew that Clark had a secret life, and that somehow, unalterably, he had decided Lex was not someone with whom he could share it. *He doesn't trust me*, Lex thought painfully. *And really, why should he?*

He honestly wanted nothing but health and happiness for Clark and his family, but that hadn't stopped him from circling the Kents like a bloodhound, shadowy and persistent and surreptitiously obtrusive. He wanted Clark's trust. He wanted it so badly that he was willing to lie, cheat, and steal for it.

With a sigh, he started getting ready for bed. Lex Luthor was brilliant, meticulous, and self-aware. Following the trajectory of his hopes and desires, he saw all too clearly the sharp twist they took when they began to burrow back into his own dark heart. He watched the twisting the way sailors watched the stars and the swell of tides.

He knew it was treacherous, and that bad weather was coming.

But it was all he had to navigate by.

CHAPTER SIXTEEN

By ten-forty the next morning, Lex sat alone at the head of a large, oval table in the LuthorCorp central offices, sipping a cup of cappuccino and reading over the notes his father had faxed him concerning his first meeting with Multigon. According to a note he'd left with the front desk at the hotel, Clark was already long gone when Lex had checked out around ten, so there had been no opportunity to touch base about the strange events the previous evening. Maybe just as well. Without any new information, there was nothing new to say.

Lex finished Lionel's fourteen-page meeting brief and mulled it over. He had at least ten more minutes before the attendees started filing in, and was thankful for the quiet. He hadn't managed even an hour of quality sleep the night before, and felt mind-numbingly tired. He drained his cappuccino and fished his cell phone from his pocket.

"Lionel, London," he said into the phone, and waited while a recording of his own voice confirmed the command and initiated the call.

"LuthorCorp, London," answered a pleasant female voice.

"Hey, Cynthia, it's Lex. Could you put me through to my dad, please?" Lex stretched out in the comfortable

conference room chair while he waded through pleas-
antries with his father's European secretary.

"Lex! What a nice surprise. Let me see if he's still
available, dear. Can you hold for just a moment?"

"Sure." Lex stood, walking over to the conference
room buffet table to refill his coffee. He smiled at the as-
sortment of pastries and croissants his office catering
firm had laid out, thinking that Clark would be pleased to
see him surrounded by so many breakfast options, even if
he fully intended to ignore them all.

"Lex?" Lionel's voice was suddenly in Lex's ear, pretending fatherly concern. "Is everything all right, son?
Did you get my notes?"

"Got 'em right here," Lex affirmed. "Just have a few
quick questions for you if you've got a minute."

"Of course, Lex. What can I do for you?" Lionel
sounded pleased. Lex figured he was laying a trap of
some kind.

"In table four, did you mean to short-circuit the feed-
back loop between Vrtis and the Scenario Analysis Com-
mittee? I know you were concerned about keeping your
CPM event driven, and with Vrtis out of the loop, the
SAC won't have timely access to strategy formulation or
forecasting."

Lionel laughed as if Lex had just handed him a cute
finger painting.

"Vrtis won't be with us much longer. I'll make sure the
SAC has what they need. Anything else?"

"Yeah. I was wondering why you're having my apartment bugged."

"*Your* apartment?"

"Fine." Lex gritted his teeth. "*Your* apartment that you
gave me to use whenever I'm in Metropolis."

"Honestly, Lex, I have no idea what you're talking about."

Lionel's voice sounded sardonic and amused, as usual. Lex frowned and rubbed the back of his neck, trying not to let it get to him.

"Cut the crap, Dad. I've got Clark with me. Whatever *Art of War* head trip you've got planned for me is gonna have to wait until he's safely back home."

"As I recall, Lex—and this would be from your own accounts as well as a few of my personal experiences— your little friend spends more time protecting you than the other way around."

"Yeah, well, be that as it may, I don't want him getting sullied by your unique brand of confidence erosion, even by proxy. Got it?"

Lex could hear his father settle back into some large, cushy office chair and knew with a sinking sense of distress that whatever Lionel was after, Lex was playing right into his hand.

"What exactly is your relationship with this boy, son?"

"We're friends. I'm sorry, let me translate that for you. A friend is someone you trust, enjoy spending time with, and wish safe from harm."

"No, Lex. A friend is a liability waiting to happen, a luxury—"

"—you can't afford. Yeah, yeah. I heard you the first nine hundred times."

"Well, apparently you weren't listening carefully enough. Now tell me what's really bothering you, son."

"*You* are, Dad!" Lex practically shouted. He caught himself and took a deep breath to regain his composure. "*You're* bothering me. And the penthouse. And Lorelei

Lasser. And the two employees found dead the other morning at Luthor Tower Two."

"Yes, well that *is* an alarming development," Lionel conceded. "Which is why I'm so grateful to have you there in the position to look into things. Do you have any leads?"

"No," Lex answered tightly. "Not yet."

"You know, Lex, I was really beginning to admire the way you've been standing up to me lately, toe to toe, a real opponent."

Listening to his father, it was all Lex could do not to hurl the cell phone down at the carpet floor of the conference room and begin smacking his head against the wall as hard as he could. Lionel's most hurtful lectures always started as tempered compliments, and Lex let himself get sucked in every time. Only a few months before he had been standing in his father's hospital room after Kansas twisters had brought half the family home down on top of him. Lionel had looked frail and defenseless as he called Lex to his bedside with what sounded like genuine need in his voice. Lex had decided to risk an emergency operation to alleviate pressure building behind Lionel's optic nerves. After acknowledging his awareness of Lex's decision and starting what sounded like a compliment as Lionel admitted that he would have done the same thing had their positions been reversed—*I saved him the way I couldn't save Mom, and he's going to thank me for it, tell me I'm not a complete disappointment to him*, Lex had thought emotionally at the time, letting his guard down as he reached out to his injured father—Lionel had smoothly switched gears without warning, squeezing Lex's hand tightly in his own as he told his son that the operation had been a failure, leaving him blind, and that he would have been better off if Lex had left him for dead.

Now as Lex stood in the LuthorCorp Metropolis nineteenth-floor conference room, his wish to find something vulnerable in his father that he could connect with was tarnished by feelings of guilt and worry. Lionel was blind, after all, and Lex believed that it was partly his own fault. Lex knew he was still hoping that Lionel would reach out to him. Instead of wishing for something that would never happen, Lex resolved to listen for the moment when Lionel's compliments switched to criticism.

"You've grown into an interesting young man." *Wait for it.* "And it's not impossible for me to imagine a bright future for you at LuthorCorp." *Wait . . .* "I really mean that, son." *Now.* "And that's why I'm so concerned with this paranoiac streak you've developed. I'm not saying that your path isn't strewn with danger—I know it is. And as we've just been discussing, I'm not advocating naïveté. But these flights of fancy have to stop. It's just not healthy, son. Bugging the Metropolis penthouse? I mean, really! When I need intel on you, I have much subtler ways of attaining it. You'd never even know. If I've said it once, I've said it a thousand times—keep your eye on public perception. That would preclude killing employees, you understand."

Lex stood in front of the banquet table, seething, as Lionel continued.

"Now listen, I know an excellent doctor in Metropolis who could talk to you—confidentially, of course—and determine whether it might be in your best interest to look into therapy of some kind. Now, I would hate to have you committed involuntarily, but I am your father,

Lex, and with the kind of symptomology you've been displaying lately, I'd be remiss if I did nothing to help you."

Lex tried to catch his breath as Lionel waited, patient and silent. Have him committed to a psychiatric ward? Stunning, even for Lionel. It had to be a bluff. PR like that would be bad for LuthorCorp. Unless Lionel then made a big show of hiring him back on after treatment, the compassionate father always willing to stand by his black sheep son. Lex felt his mouth run dry and was just about to end the call unceremoniously when Jolene, the LuthorCorp receptionist, flung open the meeting room doors and began ushering in the attendees with the same smile she'd had plastered on her face when Lex had first walked in that morning.

"Yeah, funny, Dad. Listen, I've gotta get this meeting going. Thanks for giving me the heads up on Vrtis."

"You sure you'll be all right, son? Now I feel bad about burdening you with the extra responsibility of running these meetings . . ."

"Oh, it's probably best that I keep busy. Idle hands and all that."

"Well, I'm glad you feel that way. You'll be my little Neoptolemus over there, sacking Multigon's Troy."

"And here I thought I'd be playing Isaac to your Abraham."

"Let's hope it doesn't come to that, Lex."

Lex held his breath and closed his cell phone. He felt less than an inch from the edge, felt like screaming at the top of his lungs. If he was Neoptolemus, that made Lionel Achilles, and oh, how he ached to give his father a swift kick in the heel. Maybe he'd report the penthouse security breach to the Metropolis police and let his father handle the follow-up questions. Maybe he'd use the meeting to sell LuthorCorp shares to Multigon at half of market value. Lex was smiling once more as he took his seat and cleared his throat, his hands folded neatly on the table before him.

"If I could ask you all to please take a seat, I'd like to get started."

Lex could feel the members of his father's board of directors sizing him up, along with the Multigon representatives. "I'm sure most of you are familiar with my father's fourth quarter projections, but if I could have you turn to page fourteen in your prospectus, I'd like to take you through the new management model he's proposing for—"

Lex was being so careful to stay confident and cool that he was the only one who didn't react when a gunshot rang out directly behind him. Still in his chair at the head of the conference table, he turned calmly toward the door as several of the meeting attendees jumped to their feet; some threw themselves under the table, two screamed, and one spilled coffee all over his freshly pressed suit.

Five Yakuza *kobun* stood in the entranceway of the conference room, their dark hair slicked back and their guns all trained on Lex. They were not the same men Lex had played cards with, but he had no trouble identifying them as part of the same clan.

At their feet, Jolene lay in silent shock, blood oozing from her shoulder. Lex rose and moved toward her, ignoring the cold, steel muzzle that was pressed against the back of his head the moment he knelt beside her.

"Jolene," he called softly, pressing two fingers against her warm throat to check her pulse. The attractive receptionist seemed unable to move her head, but her eyes darted toward him pleadingly as she tried to speak through lips Lex could tell felt thick and noncompliant to her.

"So sorry, Lex," she said weakly. "Tried to stop them, I . . . ."

Lex pulled his cell phone out of his pocket with his left hand as he gently hushed her, taking her trembling hand in his right one.

"You did great. Don't worry, Jolene. I'm not going to let anything happen to you."

The words had just left Lex's mouth when a second shot rang out. Lex managed not to drop his phone, but was shocked into silence as a small, perfect little hole appeared dead center on Jolene's chest, then slowly began oozing blood. Her eyes remained riveted on his face, but comprehension vanished from them instantly, as if someone had flipped a switch behind her neck and simply turned her off. Feeling blood on his face and murderous rage beginning to boil within his own broad chest, Lex glared at the men standing above him. Behind him, he could hear gasps and crying and murmured prayers.

"Everyone in this room is my guest here. For your own sake, I hope you're not planning on hurting any more of them."

Lex meant what he said, but the man closest to him laughed low in his throat as another sent a quick snap kick straight into Lex's jaw. Pain bloomed across his jawbone as Lex fell backward on the carpet. The blood he tasted at the corner of his mouth as he struggled back up to his elbows had a strangely calming effect on him. It was as if that little tang of salt on the tip of his tongue was all it took to set free a darkness that came flying out from behind locked doors in his heart to swamp everything sympathetic and warm in him.

Two images sparked in his mind. A gun, and Clark. He rose to his feet and began charging the man who'd kicked him in one fluid movement. He was so fast and focused that no one in the room noticed his left hand opening his cell phone. Blindly, he pressed two buttons with his thumb and then let the phone, still open, slide back into his jacket pocket before bringing both hands forward to reach for the gun in front of him.

Four guns were now pointed at Lex's face. He heard someone bark out an order in Japanese, the smell of blood and cordite burning in his nostrils. With clenched teeth, his fingers closed around the cold steel of the handgun he'd launched for. He was carefully imagining the actions it would take to initiate the death of each and every one of the intruders one by one when he felt something hard and cold smash into the side of his skull. Everything spiraled down into a soft, painful blackness.

Twenty-three blocks away, the phone began to ring in Lex's penthouse. Agent Green watched with narrowed eyes as the answering machine clicked on.

The machine's loud electronic beep was followed by a strange shuffling sound, then snatches of conversation that seemed to be coming from some distance away.

"Somebody do something!"

"Is he unconscious?"

"Is she dead?"

"*Chikushō!*"

"*Chotte matte kudasai . . .*"

"*Ki o tsukete!*"

"Where are you taking him?"

"*Shōganai . . .*"

"Where the hell's security? I thought LuthorCorp was fully protected!"

Agent Green frowned. Half the voices spoke in English, but the other half were in Japanese. It was the Yakuza, the same people who had killed Tad. It had to be! The alien had been working with them all along, and now they were taking him in, closing protectively around him and his friend to keep Agent Green from getting any closer. Agent Green was surprised he hadn't put it all together before. Now time was running out and he could no longer afford to passively observe his prey. Although he knew he might pay dearly for taking on the extraterrestrial directly, Agent Green feared that delaying the inevitable confrontation would prove even more costly. He had no doubt that, given enough lead-time, the Yakuza could help the alien disappear completely. It was time to act.

Popping his briefcase open on the desk, Agent Green pulled out a highly specialized tracer and attached it to the bottom of the answering machine, which was still recording the incoming call. The tracer would help him identify the origin point of the cellular call using a covert S.T.A.R. Labs satellite for triangulation. That done, he snapped his briefcase shut and swiftly exited the penthouse, a dark anticipation growing inside him.

For the first time in his life, Agent Green knew exactly who he was.

He was the man who would kill the alien.

CHAPTER SEVENTEEN

Lex awoke to the smell of stale smoke and launched into a coughing fit. He was tied to a chair, and his left temple throbbed violently. The room he found himself in was dusky, with high ceilings and a decidedly industrial feel. A few feet in front of him, the same group of Yakuza *kobun* who had violently snatched him from the Luthor-Corp offices sat around a long, rectangular table smoking cigars and playing cards. If not for the guns, tattoos, and the quiet menace of their bearing, they would have looked like a group of Japanese clubgoers pretending to be Mafia soldiers from the Prohibition era.

One of them—a man Lex didn't recognize as he squinted at him through the murky, smoke-filled room— was speaking into a cell phone as he leaned against the card table, his English lightly accented but otherwise perfect. He wore a tight, shiny suit of dark red snakeskin and had bragging rights on all ten fingers.

"Well, now I'm telling you ten million."

Ten million was enough to pique Lex's interest. *Unless he means yen*, he thought with a derisive sneer. He saw the man's eyes dart toward him. Realizing that Lex had regained consciousness, the man in the red snakeskin suit sauntered over to him with maddening casualness.

"Consider it interest." The man's hand shot out and slapped Lex suddenly and with such force that Lex drew in a hissing breath of pain despite himself. "Say hello," he commanded, thrusting the phone toward Lex.

Lex glared up at him and forced a carefree chuckle.

"Another beer would be great, thanks," he said between clenched teeth. The man in red only smiled, pulling the cell phone back up to his own ear.

"He has your obstinacy," he said silkily, and Lex's heartbeat quickened. Wait a minute—was he talking to Lionel? "And your earning potential. It would be a shame if your selfishness destroyed him."

He was—he was talking to his father! Lex laughed, a real laugh this time, his eyes regaining their customary spark.

"He won't pay you a dime for me." Lex grinned, addressing his adversary with a casual shake of his head. "Hang up the phone."

From where he was sitting with his hands tied behind his back and his ankles tied to the legs of the chair, Lex couldn't hear the other side of the phone conversation. It was clear, though, that Lionel was giving Red Snakeskin Suit an earful. The man smiled coldly at Lex as he listened, eventually covering the mouthpiece to address his captive.

"He says he'll pay," he said with a toothy grin. "Perhaps you underestimate your father."

"Or perhaps you overestimate him," Lex replied, feigning boredom.

Red Snakeskin Suit snapped his phone closed abruptly, his mouth pulling into a hard, thin line.

"It is not wise of you to try my patience," he hissed.

Lex looked up at him, bemused. " 'It is not wise of you to try my patience?' " he repeated in a mocking tone.

"That's good. I'm gonna have to remember that. They teach you that in supervillain school?"

As he expected, the man reached out, slapping him hard in the face again. Lex turned with the punch this time and straightened up with a smile.

"All right, let's get serious," Lex continued straightforwardly, the smile vanishing from his face. "Hitting me is beneath you. It's the sign of a desperate negotiator. I'm losing respect for you by the second, and you need my respect if we're going to enter into integrative bargaining. Understood?"

His captor looked vaguely shocked but said nothing. Lex continued calmly, trying to adjust his posture so that he almost appeared to look comfortable in the chair he was tied to.

"First of all, I need something to call you. All the nicknames I'm coming up with are uncharitable." Lex searched his memory and then met his adversary's eyes. "For argument's sake, I'll just use Matsushita for now, okay?"

Lex saw a flicker of surprise cross the man's face and nodded.

"Great. So, Matsushita-san, I don't know what kind of deal you think you've got going with my father, but he's toying with you. Tell me, how much do you think he's worth?"

Matsushita frowned. The other Yakuza turned their attention from the card game to Lex. Lex turned his head so that he was addressing all of them.

"Seriously, I'm curious. Did you do your homework on Lionel Luthor? What do you think he's worth?"

"That is not our concern," Matsushita said with a

bitter frown. "He owes us. We want back only that which he is already obligated to pay."

Lex let out a laugh, his eyes disappearing momentarily behind his eyelashes. When he looked up again, there was so much amusement in his gaze that three of the Yakuza from the card table moved their chairs closer to his, slight smiles pulling at the corners of their mouths.

"Then why'd you raise the price on my ransom?" he asked offhandedly.

Matsushita stiffened.

"I take my orders from *Oyabun*," he said fiercely.

"Sure," Lex nodded agreeably. "And for your loyalty, *Oyabun* is doing everything he can to protect you and ensure your future." Lex didn't even bother trying to hide a smile of satisfaction as the rest of the cardplayers moved to get closer to him. "That includes milking my father for all he's worth. Now come on. Someone, take a guess. What do you think Lionel's worth?"

"Eight hundred million!" ventured one of them. After consulting with another in Japanese, a second guessed two billion.

"Two billion. Anyone else?"

"Ten billion!" shouted out the youngest with an enthusiastic grin. He was missing the top joint of his pinkie finger and had a badly capped tooth.

"Ten billion . . ." Lex scoffed. "*I'm* worth ten billion. Is that all you've got?"

"Twenty billion!" came a shout from the back. Lex nodded sagely.

Sensing the control Lex was beginning to have over the room, Matsushita pistol-whipped his captive hard against his jaw. Lex couldn't hide a wince of pain as his already beleaguered jaw took another hit, but he managed to stay calm as he spit blood from his mouth and slowly raised his head to look at his tormentor.

"You do not speak unless I tell you to!" Matsushita growled in a desperate bid for control. Lex smiled ever so slightly, but before Matsushita could ask why, the youngest *kobun* called out petulantly, followed by one of the middle-aged men.

"Let him tell us how much Lionel is worth."

"We want to hear!"

Lex held his gaze steadily on Matsushita, who frowned down at him, then nodded to save face.

"You may continue," he said darkly, realizing he had just undermined himself by silencing the charismatic captive to begin with. Lex bowed his head slightly.

"With your permission, then," he said before raising his head. He could not be faulted for his manners, but Matsushita did not at all like the gleam in the young Luthor's eyes.

"Let's see, where were we? Ah, yes. Based on Luthor-Corp's current stock price," Lex confessed quietly, forcing everyone in the room to lean in toward him. "Lionel Luthor is worth approximately forty-three billion." Lex let that sink in a moment before adding with a teasing smile, "But, you know, ten million *is* a lot to pay for the return of your only *kobun*."

Lex held a practiced smirk in place as he met the eyes of one or two of the Yakuza, until within a matter of seconds, they were all chuckling along with him.

"So"—Lex nodded, still grinning, after allowing another moment to go by—"are we ready to get down to business?"

Several of the Yakuza continued laughing, but Lex

held the eye of Matsushita, who continued to watch him warily.

"There are three principles of negotiation we have to keep in mind here. The first is that LuthorCorp always builds agreements from the bottom up. That means Lionel's gonna want to deal in *specifics*: price, protocol, delivery time, and conditions. The general principle behind the deal—that he owes you money and you want it back—means nothing to him. You'll have to start by working with that reality."

By now the Yakuza were collected around him like grinning schoolboys, all but taking notes. Matsushita moved behind Lex's chair, still clutching his silver cell phone in one hand. But he, too, was listening.

"Second thing is to get clear about your bottom line. You need to know—either from *Oyabun* or by consensus here—what you'll compromise and what you won't. And once that's been decided, you've got to stick to it absolutely. That means follow through; if you tell Lionel you're willing to kill me if he doesn't pay up, you'd better mean it. Which brings us to our third and most important point, and frankly, I'm surprised you guys don't know this one."

Afraid of losing face again, Matsushita turned his back on Lex and the Yakuza who had gathered around the bound Luthor.

" 'Therefore, I say,' " Lex began, quoting from memory. A few of the older Yakuza exchanged quick smiles with one another, recognizing the Western translation of Sun Tzu's *Art of War*. " 'Know your enemy and know yourself; in a hundred battles, you will never be defeated. When you are ignorant of the enemy but know yourself, your chances of winning or losing are equal. If ignorant, both of your enemy and of yourself, you are sure to be defeated in every battle.'"

Lex stopped and waited until he heard the rustle of Matsushita's pants that indicated he had turned back to his hostage.

"Now we know what Lionel's worth, but that only begs another question—a question absolutely critical to this deal. Knowing what he can pay means nothing unless we also know what he's willing to pay *for*."

Lex paused and met each pair of eyes in the room, one by one.

"Fortunately," he continued, "I know what that is. Unfortunately"—he craned his head around to meet Matsushita's eyes, and gave him a friendly wink—"I'm a little tied up at the moment."

CHAPTER EIGHTEEN

"Lex?"

Clark let himself into the penthouse with a mixture of relief and trepidation. Now that he knew the place was bugged, he was anxious about what he said and did there and who might be recording it. Even under such stressful circumstances, however, the calm orderliness of Lex's apartment was an oasis after time spent on the hectic city streets below.

"Lex?" he called again. No answer. Clark knew Lex had meetings to attend and had been counting on his friend's absence. After watching the sun rise over the harbor that morning, the fiery yellow ball bathing him in a lonely amplification of strength as it climbed up into the sky, Clark had headed straight to Luthor Tower Two. He wasn't exactly sure what he intended to do, but he wanted to take a closer look at the surveillance equipment and see if he could come up with any clues as to who might have put it there.

A blinking light on the answering machine distracted him. Clark didn't want to invade Lex's privacy, but he felt he had to check the message. It might be a lead, information he could bring back to Lex. Wincing slightly, Clark pressed the PLAY button.

The voices all sounded muffled and distant, but Clark's panic was unambiguous and immediate. Something

awful had happened to Lex, something involving the
Yakuza. The call was a message for him, a plea for help,
an open phone line Clark had no idea how to trace. Had
Lex known Clark would come back to the apartment?
Did he think Clark would know what to do? Clark
glanced at the window, the breathtaking view filling him
with dread. Lex had become one of the millions of voices
in Metropolis, calling to be saved from somewhere in that
overwhelming sea of distress. Clark didn't even know
where to start.

*Think! If they grabbed him at LuthorCorp, maybe they
left a clue there. . . .*

The message was still playing, now a barely audible
recording of feet running down a stairwell, as Clark raced
out the penthouse door and down the stairs, bypassing the
elevator. He shot past the doorman and out into the street,
figuring that cars would be no harder to dodge than
pedestrians, and more prepared for the impact should he
miscalculate. Still, there had to be a better way to get
around the city!

Fortunately, Clark knew where the LuthorCorp Tower
was located, having been there once in the past. It was
across the street from the *Daily Planet* building, which
had a unique globe on top that made it easy to spot and
identify from almost any vantage point in New Troy.
Traffic was so congested downtown that Clark found it
easier to run at superspeed over the tops of cabs and cars,
few of which were actually moving. Though the drivers
of the vehicles he raced over might have thought they
heard something on their roofs, there was no way they
could see him with their naked eyes. Besides, by the time
they thought to look up, Clark was blocks away.

He was finally forced to a stop by the automated slid-

ing glass doors of the tower, which took a frustrating two
seconds to open for him. He ran at normal human speed
to the receptionist desk guarding the elevator banks, but
noticed that the elevators themselves were already under
heavy guard.

"I'm sorry, sir," the receptionist called to him as he approached, "but we're under temporary lockdown. I can't
admit you."

"Where's Lex?" Clark demanded, earning an extra
scowl from a security guard stationed immediately behind the young redheaded receptionist.

"Mr. Luthor has had to cancel his afternoon appoint-
ments," she started nervously, but the security guard cut
her off.

"Who are you?" he asked, leaning forward toward
Clark. He was holding a military rifle and evidenced absolutely no sense of humor.

"My name's Clark Kent. I'm his friend. Look, he
called his apartment from his cell phone and I heard the
message, but I don't know how to trace the call. I just
want to help find him. Do you have any idea where he
was taken?"

"I'm sorry, sir," the security guard answered, not looking the least bit sorry. "We're not at liberty to release any
information at this time."

Clark persisted, brows furrowed in worry.

"I have information that might help. Somebody
bugged his apartment, and—and both the security guard
and doorman of Luthor Tower Two were killed the other
morning. What if it's all connected?"

"I'm sorry, sir," the security guard repeated, and
Clark's shoulders tensed. He glanced at the receptionist,
who was listening to him with wide eyes but was

obviously in no position of authority, before turning his attention back up to the cold, appraising stare of the security guard. "We have to follow a certain protocol here, established by Mr. Luthor himself . . ."

"Yeah, but you mean *Lionel* Luther, and it's a *PR* protocol. Lex's life is in danger. I think we have more important things to worry about than LuthorCorp public relations!"

"I'm sorry, sir," the security guard said again, his voice thick with irritation. "We are not at liberty to release any information at this time."

Clark blew his bangs off of his forehead in frustration and turned to exit the building. Since it was broad daylight, it seemed highly unlikely that the Yakuza still had Lex in the building. Would they have taken him back to Neo-Tokyo? Could they have made it back there yet?

With the powers of a superbeing and the reasoning of a sixteen-year-old boy, Clark decided his best bet was to move toward the Takashi Plaza in Neo-Tokyo by way of the Ordway Docks, checking every car and building on the way. And since he already knew he couldn't race at superspeed through foot traffic, he'd try going across the rooftops, using his X-ray vision to see into the apartments and cars beneath him.

Across the street, the *Daily Planet* lobby was a bevy of activity, and no one paid any attention to him as he walked quickly in and headed for the interior stairwell. He ran into only three people on his way up to the roof, and all of them were too busy to take any notice of him. He used a combination of X-ray vision and his exceptional sight to keep track of the goings-on as he passed each floor.

He felt confident that he could recognize Lex, even

skeletally, and that the Yakuza would be carrying guns, which would stand out in an X-ray-vision scan. He hadn't, however, put any thought into what he might see besides that for which he searched.

The images came in almost too fast to process, the expected ones blurring into a textured backdrop for the startling, unexpected deviations to pop up against as Clark combed the city in search of Lex. If looking out over the Metropolis landscape and imagining all the people moving through it was daunting, searching through them one by one was unbearable. Within two minutes, Clark had glimpsed into the private lives of more people than he'd met in his entire life.

As he dashed from building to building, wanting wholeheartedly to help all those he saw in need, he could hear his father's alarmed voice in his head.

"What if someone *sees* you? But what if someone *sees* you?"

Clark imagined himself arguing back, trying to explain. *I had to help Lex, Dad. And if I could have, I would have stopped to help every single person I passed. Isn't that what you taught me to do?*

The image of Lana's face when he'd returned to their table from the dock fight swam into his head, and he wanted to scream with frustration. Would the people he loved always be balanced against the safety of strangers? Clark knew that every millisecond he could spend helping someone else was a millisecond in which Lex could be killed. He knew every act of charity he might perform would be a chance for someone to notice his special gifts and use them to take him away from his parents. He knew every risk he took was another evasive lie waiting to be told to one of his best friends. What he didn't know was how much of the world he had the right to expect to change.

By the time the penthouse answering machine message cut off, Agent Green had used a secret S.T.A.R. Labs satellite to isolate and track the signal of the cell phone that had left the strange message. Whoever had placed the call had not hung up, and although the answering machine eventually stopped recording the incoming static, the cell phone signal was still open for the S.T.A.R. Labs satellite to locate. The satellite itself was a piece of technology that Tad had told Mayer about years before, and at the time Mayer hadn't believed such invasive tracing was possible. Now Agent Green knew better. He knew better about a lot of things.

While the satellite worked with the Global Positioning System to locate the cell phone's unique radio signal, Agent Green dialed into the Infinity receiver to listen in at the penthouse. One of the two young men was there, playing back the message, but Agent Green couldn't tell which one, only that he left in a hurry.

Before being distorted by some obstructive change in location, the cell phone signal led Agent Green to an upscale, modern section of Neo-Tokyo, which confirmed his hunch that the Yakuza were involved. That was just what he needed—Japanese control over alien intelligence! Or worse . . . alien control over Japanese technology. Agent Green's jaw tightened. He understood more clearly than ever what was truly at stake, and knew he'd have to be willing to sacrifice his life to achieve his homeland's security. That was what America stood for, after all; the clash between safety and freedom. Sometimes, however, the two dovetailed beautifully. Agent

Green knew he was free to kill the alien and the Yakuza as a matter of national security.

That made the rest of the hunt a matter of playing his S.T.A.R. Labs connections just right. With the help of a Metropolis field agent—*another* Metropolis field agent, Agent Green corrected himself—he isolated six addresses that had been noted for heavy Yakuza traffic, including the private residence of the Metropolis *oyabun*, a seventy-three-year-old spitfire who lived in a towering high-rise just north of Murakami Plaza. Agent Green began checking the addresses methodically, first performing casual sweeps, then employing new equipment he'd picked up from the lab—including an ultrawideband "radar flashlight" that allowed him to detect human respiration and movement through walls up to eight inches thick, and a portable thermal-imaging scanner to scrutinize the locations more carefully. He moved with confidence, knowing it was just a matter of time before he found what he was looking for. Fate was on his side. He'd been sure of it ever since Tad Nickels's death.

"New terms, Dad." Lex was still tied to his chair, but Matsushita held a cell phone up to his ear as he and his fellow Yakuza gathered around him in a tight circle. "Price just doubled. Now my friends want twenty million, transferred directly into *Oyabun* Koike-san's personal account."

On the other end of the line, Lionel's voice sounded strained.

"Don't be foolish, Lex. I overheard you acknowledging that I was unlikely to pay a dime."

Lex swallowed despite himself, then drew in a deep breath. Knowing your father would do nothing to save your life was one thing. Actually hearing him say it was quite another.

"Ah, but that was when it was me up on the auction block. Now all we're trading is our silence."

"So am I to understand that you're in on this with these malefactors now?"

"According to them, Dad, you got in bed with them a long time before I did. And that's exactly why you need me in the deal. Does you no good to buy their silence if I talk, does it?"

"Silence about what? You're really trying my patience, Lex." Lionel dropped his voice and moved his mouth closer to the phone. "These people are out of your league, son. Why do you think I cut my ties with them? Even if I do pay them, I can't guarantee your safety."

"Yeah, well, let me deal with covering my own ass, as usual. All I need from you is twenty million—"

"That's utterly preposterous. You can't for a second think I'll—"

"—In return for which, we fail to go to press with the story of how you arranged your own son's kidnapping as an excuse to pay out debts to a known criminal organization." Lex clicked his tongue scoldingly. "Bad PR, Dad. Your Achilles' heel."

There was a momentary silence on the other end of the line, then Lionel's bemused chuckle set Lex's teeth grinding.

"Naughty little Neoptolemus . . ." Lionel's laughter stopped abruptly, and Lex could hear the steel in his tone as his father sat forward, causing whatever chair he was seated in to squeal. "This is all your doing, Lex. I had this under control before you started playing your pitiable little games. When this turns into a bloodbath, I just want you to remember that it's your fault. That is the price you pay for defying me. Good luck to you, son. I hope you can get out of there alive."

Lionel's phone clicked off and Lex stared at the concrete floor of his industrial prison for a moment, jaw flexing, before he spoke.

"He's thinking it over," he told Matsushita.

Matsushita looked at the cell phone, then at Lex, then at a knife sheathed at the side of one of his associates, and smiled.

"Untie his left hand," he commanded. Lex went pale.

CHAPTER NINETEEN

Clark made it all the way to Neo-Tokyo without seeing any sign of Lex or the Yakuza. Takashi Plaza was still closed down while the Metropolis police looked for further evidence of drug production, so Clark had to sneak in and search the place from top to bottom. It was his best guess about where the Yakuza might have taken Lex, and when it became apparent that he wasn't there, Clark had to fight off a wave of despondency. What was he going to do, check every building in Neo-Tokyo?

He wound up doing just that, at least with seventy-six of them. Working north from Collyer where the plaza was located, Clark used an improvised combination of superspeed, X-ray vision, and furtive prowling to case the buildings of upper Neo-Tokyo. He would have checked even more, but luck was with him on the eighth block. In the basement of a tall apartment building on Dorfman, his X-ray vision picked up the solid metal mass of guns and finally came to rest on the specific thoracic curvature and proudly held clavicle he had come to associate with Lex.

Clark's relief was short-lived. He knew Lex would most likely be under guard, and so the gun held to his friend's skull did not surprise him. What he couldn't figure out was why someone was holding Lex's wrist in order to keep the young millionaire's hand flat on the only table in the room. If they thought Lex capable of pulling a weapon, they would have had both of his hands secured. The position made the bones of Lex's left hand look strangely exposed to Clark, who remembered Lex's history lesson on *yubizume* at the exact same second in which he registered the shape of a sharp metal knife being held above Lex's pinkie.

Clark raced into the lobby of the building so quickly that he broke the sound barrier, the two large glass panels on either side of the double wooden doors shattering in their panes behind him and falling to the floor like raindrops. He wrenched the stairwell door off its hinges without meaning to and took the narrow steps down to the basement so quickly that his shoes barely touched the ground once during his descent.

The stairs led him down to an empty laundry room with dark cement flooring and only one hanging bulb for illumination. He raced back into the room's darker shadows, quickly finding the door that separated the Yakuza's secret storage room. The door was locked from the inside, and Clark realized that there must be an external entryway from the alley; but he didn't have time to go back and find it. As he broke the door open, he saw the heads of eleven Yakuza start to turn toward him in slow motion, guns coming up at almost the same measured pace. Lex had also started to glance over his shoulder and the only ones who did not turn to look his way were the man holding Lex's wrist, and a man in a dark red snakeskin suit who was wielding the knife.

Clark could see that the blade had already penetrated Lex's flesh. The blood that must have been pouring from his finger now seemed to Clark's eye to be seeping out from under it at an almost imperceptible rate. The fifth middle phalanx bone just above the first joint had been nicked, but not yet severed by the time Clark was close enough to push the knife out of the way. Still moving at superspeed, he turned his attention to his friend's injury, unleashing waves of heat from his blue eyes, instantly cauterizing the wound. With a strange mixture of remorse and relief, Clark watched Lex as, in slow motion, he began to pass out from the pain, beads of sweat emerging from his abruptly overheated skin.

Lex had felt the knife slice into his finger, acutely aware of both a hot, screaming protest of nerve endings in his pinkie and a cold, lurching clench in his abdomen. He had barely had time to process either of the sensations as pain, however, when he heard the door break behind him. He managed to crane his head around far enough to see a flash of color when a new jolt of pain shot through his body like a bomb, originating in his finger and blazing up the back of his neck so quickly that he felt himself pitch forward into an anxious and agonizing darkness.

He sank under for a moment, trying to hold on to consciousness, the room, the present. His stomach told him in no uncertain terms that any attempt he made to rise back up would be unhelpfully mimicked. Still, he grabbed on to the sounds he heard around him—something metal being hurled across the room, a gunshot, the impact of one human body against another, a second gunshot—and tried to use these to climb back up from out of his pain-tinged oblivion. He was about to let go and slip all the way down into soft nothingness when he heard a word in Japanese he thought he recognized. *Nōjō*. He had been forced to look it up more than once when negotiating from Smallville with foreign investors, and eventually it had stuck with him. *Nōjō*. Farm. They were saying something about a farm boy. A secret agent farm boy.

Clark?

Lex fought his way tooth and nail to full consciousness, finally opening his eyes. He was still tied to his chair, his chest and head slumped over the table, facedown. The cloying scent of burning flesh hung in the air. With the sickening fear of having lost a part of his body, Lex swallowed and slowly turned his attention to the hand still splayed out on the table, unsure whether the tip of his pinkie had been completely lopped off, or was still dangling precariously from the rest of his hand. All around him he could hear the sounds of a titanic struggle, the phrase "farm boy secret agent," repeated several times in various frustrated curses.

His pinkie was still there. Lex sat up, blinking, and flexed his hand. Pain shot up his arm, but his pinkie was still there! He pulled up his other hand, realizing, as he did so, that he had been untied. Spreading both hands out on the table, Lex counted ten fingers, then counted again, more slowly, just to be sure. *Yes, ten!*

Lex examined the pinkie of his left hand more closely. The flesh was raw and burned, as if it had been very recently cauterized. How long had he been out? He got up from his chair and turned to look behind him.

Four Yakuza were on the ground, moaning, and several guns had been scattered into far corners of the room. Matsushita stood in the middle of the carnage, lashing out at some strange disruption in the air, the moving blur of color Lex had noticed right before he passed out. Lex couldn't imagine what it was, or what made Matsushita think he could hit it. But then all at once Matsushita did seem to make contact, smashing his elbow into something hard and solid before stumbling back clutching his arm with a howl of pain. It almost looked as if he had broken it on impact.

The Yakuza who still had guns were firing them almost randomly, panicked. Lex was about to wade into the fight to try and secure a gun for himself when he noticed the room expand with additional light, a faint breeze stirring the stale air. Someone had opened the alleyway door.

Almost as soon as he had taken note of it, Lex heard something roll into the center of the room from the direction of the door. All at once, the room was filled with a loud hissing sound and plumes of chemical smoke. Coughing, Lex closed his eyes and grabbed on to the table to steady himself. He started to move toward the current of fresh air but was stopped by the nuzzle of a gun pressing into his ribs.

"You're coming with me," a distinctly American voice said directly in his ear. Lex let go of the table and raised his hands slightly above his head, wondering if the CBI had finally shown up to take down the Yakuza and were first shepherding him out of the room for his own safety.

It seemed unlikely, though, that the CBI would use such force on a known civilian. Lex's sight was still obstructed by the smoke, which he coughed his way through as the man with the gun grabbed him roughly by the shirt collar and began pulling him from the premises.

"Who the hell are you?" Lex finally asked between coughing fits.

The voice in his ear was low and threatening.

"Call me Agent Green."

CHAPTER TWENTY

"Mind telling me which agency you're with?"

Lex was being hurried through the Metropolis streets with chemicals still stinging his eyes, his pinkie throbbing from a second-degree burn, and a gun pressed to his back. From what he'd been able to make out, his new captor fit the description Lorelei had given him of the man who had approached her: late thirties, brown hair, green eyes, average-to-tall build, and a small scar on his chin.

"CBI," the man answered curtly.

Lex wondered if maybe this guy was the secret agent the Yakuza had been cursing. "Yeah, that's what I figured," he continued. "So maybe you can clear something up for me. Why, in a room full of known international criminals, did you put a gun to the back of the only civilian present?"

"You're under arrest, Lex Luthor."

"I am? You're kidding me. On what charges?" Lex stopped walking until Agent Green's gun urged him on. "Did my father put you up to this?"

"Lex!"

About twenty feet behind them, Lex suddenly heard Clark calling to him anxiously. He twisted his head over one shoulder to shout back to him, much to Agent Green's obvious displeasure.

"Clark! Over here!"

Lex had no idea where Clark had come from or how the teenager had found him, but as strange as it was, it was also oddly predictable. Clark had pulled Lex out of more disasters than Lex cared to count, and although he'd been able to return the favor once or twice and believed unwaveringly that it was his job to protect the younger boy, the more panicked Lex was, the faster the name "Clark" rose to his lips.

"Leave the kid out of it," Agent Green grumbled, burying the gun more deeply into Lex's back.

Easier said than done, Lex thought.

He was quiet for a moment, wondering where he was being led and whether he might be able to flag down a cop. When neither answer was forthcoming, he turned his charms on Agent Green, smiling sociably.

"Seriously, you're gonna have to help me out here, buddy. I can think of about twenty—mm, make that twenty-one—questionable activities I've participated in over the last few months. For which am I being detained?"

"Don't play smart with me," Agent Green snarled.

Lex thought what he did every time his father said the same thing. *I'm not playing, you moron, I am smart.*

"I know your real story," Agent Green continued. "I know all about you. You may be able to fool everyone else, Mr. Luthor, but not me. You're *evil*."

Lex frowned. Agent Green had made his proclamation with utter certainty. Indeed, Lex sometimes wondered if what the man had said was, in fact, true; if his heart was darker than most, his soul more twisted. A young friend of Clark's had once accused him of seeing only "in shades of gray," and Lex had to acknowledge the truth of the statement. He was never quite sure he knew where to draw the line, for instance—a completely altruistic act and a completely unforgivable act were equally difficult for him to imagine. Even Clark, toward whom he felt more fondness and benevolence than any other being on the planet, was cloaked in shades of gray, the pure innocence and compulsive decency sometimes giving way to steely secrecy and tight-jawed lies.

Still, even if he were evil—whatever that really meant—who was this guy with the gun and how would *he* know?

"Would you mind telling me what you're basing your assumption of my evilness on?" Lex asked. He wasn't entirely sure whether he wanted Agent Green to say something absurd and ignorable or something undeniably conclusive. He just knew that he was tired of the allegation.

Agent Green forced him down a flight of stairs toward the subway. When he turned to glare at him, Lex could see the revulsion in the man's eyes and felt the gun jab more insistently into his lower back.

"It's not enough that I found you consorting with underworld criminals? How far does your influence reach now?"

Lex's eyebrows lowered in bewilderment.

"If you're talking about the Yakuza back there, in case you hadn't noticed, I was their captive, not their business partner. That association traces back to my father. How about you? Are you a minion of the great Lionel Luthor?"

"I know what happened in Kansas that October in 1989," Agent Green said, walking more quickly. Lex looked around at the crowd disparagingly, wondering when someone was going to notice the gun. "How little nine-year-old Lex Luthor was caught in that meteorite shower. Knocked down flat in the cornfields, his hair gone."

Lex scowled. It was not his favorite memory. Every time someone mentioned it, his mind raced forward to the moment when Lionel had found him quaking on the ground and refused to lift him in his arms.

"That's all public record," he said, a bit more tightly than he meant to.

"Yes," Agent Green nodded, "just as it's public record how much money your family sank into that godforsaken town after that fateful day, and how you yourself moved back there just last year, buying up control of everything from fertilizer plants to coffee shops. Nothing happens in that town that you don't know about."

Lex peered quickly over his shoulder and established that Clark was still in frustrated pursuit. Clark was being followed by several angry, gun-toting Yakuza, all running down the stairs of the subway along with the rush-hour crowd.

"Also on public record are several of the inexplicable events that occurred between that day and this one," Green continued. "How you should have plunged to your death in your Porsche but instead emerged unscathed, deflecting your salvation onto a fifteen-year-old boy—"

Lex interrupted with a wry laugh. "Yeah, that one throws me, too."

"How you robbed a bank and got away with it . . ."

"I was cleared of that," Lex frowned. "All charges were dropped. What kind of files have you been reading?"

"That poor old woman in the nursing home who died

the minute after you visited her. They say she could tell the future. What else could she tell, I wonder?"

Lex was silent. Cassandra had clamped his hand in hers and began to tremble, her eyes wide, as if she was watching the unfurling of a future too terrible to voice. He'd asked her what she was seeing, then realized she was no longer breathing. Clearly a case of bad timing, but something he still felt strange about.

"Then there was the time you managed to deny the existence of a Level Three at the fertilizer plant, even after a former employee took high school kids hostage in the building to prove that there was one . . ."

"That was my father again." Lex sighed. "I had no idea that was there, and I still have no idea what it might be or why he's still denying its existence."

"Then there was your fiancée, Victoria Hardwick, who was attacked several times in your home and finally driven, along with her father, to financial ruin . . ."

"I'm not sure I'd say she was ever my fiancée." Lex smiled. "Though I will take credit for her financial ruin. Are you going somewhere with all of this?"

Agent Green shook his head, frowning bitterly. "Evil, Mr. Luthor," he repeated. "You're evil."

"I'm starting not to like you very much, either," Lex muttered, as Agent Green hurried him on.

Clark had noticed Lex's abduction through the smoke just in time to unleash an unfettered charge against the Yakuza who still stood, coughing, covering their mouths, and aiming their weapons haphazardly in the thick smoke. Still moving at superspeed, he'd snatched all their guns away, crumpling them up together between his hands into one large metallic ball that he'd then swiftly bank-shot into a trash bin in the now-accessible alleyway. Yakuza backup arrived from upstairs at almost that exact moment, and Clark cast a quick look over his shoulder and began running after Lex as a fresh wave of ten or more angry, armed Yakuza followed. Unlike the Yakuza Clark had knocked out in the basement, the new wave of gunmen had a clear target to pursue. Clark even recognized some of them from the incident at the pier, and it was apparent that they recognized him, as well.

The man who had Lex roughly by the arm was wearing a dark business suit, but Clark couldn't see his face. Out on the open streets of Metropolis, Clark didn't know how to get closer to Lex and his captor without hurting any of the hundreds of people who swarmed between them. Glancing behind him, Clark confirmed that the pursuing Yakuza were having the same problem. It was difficult to move through the crowd, and even more difficult to keep track of anyone in the constant stream of humanity, though Lex's height and the late-afternoon sun shining off his bald head were a boon to Clark. He could see that Lex and the man were talking, but couldn't follow what was being said as he struggled to catch up to them.

Behind him, one of the Yakuza shoved a woman that was in his way into oncoming traffic and Clark stopped and held his breath. He was afraid to get too close to her, both because it would take his powers to do so and because the Yakuza might open fire if they had even a partially clear shot at him. The driver of the car she'd been pitched in front of hit his brakes hard, and although there was a minor fender bender with the two cars behind him, the woman was uninjured. Clark turned his attention back to the abduction, searching for Lex's head in the bustling crowd.

Glancing back once again, Clark was amazed to see one of the Yakuza aiming for him in broad daylight, amidst a crowd of hundreds. He pushed his way farther into the crowd, then looked over his shoulder once more. The gun lowered. Clark exhaled and pressed forward, his shoes pinching his feet as they hit the pavement again and again. He realized with alarm that he'd lost sight of Lex and his captor, and that businesses were beginning to let out for the day, the streets thicker and thicker with people every second.

Clark had to use his X-ray vision to find Lex and his captor in the growing crowd. Looking through walls was bad enough, but peering intently through a mob made Clark feel dizzy. The sea of marching skeletons was like a chilling presentiment, a grisly reminder of the fragility and mortality of everyone around him. When at last he found Lex, he was alarmed to find his friend shrinking until he realized that he was heading down a flight of stairs.

The subway again. *Great.*

Clark broke into a run, almost careening into a pretty businesswoman, who dropped her briefcase. Clark picked it up for her, apologizing profusely, but she barely stopped walking as she took it back from him and continued rushing to wherever she was going. Clark sighed and picked Lex out from the crowd again, rushing forward as the Yakuza gained on him. There was no doubt in Clark's mind that they would willingly endanger innocent people to achieve their goal. But what *was* their goal?

The Yakuza were chasing Clark because they rightly

thought he had interfered with several of their recent operations. They also might have thought he had something to do with freeing Lex. He still wasn't sure why they wanted Lex, though, or what the man who had Lex wanted. Somehow, he had to protect his friend and convince the Yakuza to back down. As he struggled through the crowded corridors of the subway, Clark remembered the words of the man at the pier: *"There must always be retribution."*

Agent Green looked nervously over his shoulder, then turned his attention back to his captive, leading Lex through the underground tunnels with determination.

"Your friend is very persistent," he grumbled.

"That he is," Lex agreed.

"The stories about you—I could go on and on."

Lex was confused. "But they're just that, stories. Are you telling me you have a government file on me, and it's filled with my misadventures in Smallville? Not to make my situation worse than it already appears to be, but is anyone looking into my tax status or my business holdings? If you perceive me as some kind of threat, it seems like you could do better than bringing up a bank robbery I was formally cleared of or a meteorite storm I got caught in when I was nine."

"I know the truth," Agent Green said ominously.

Lex stopped where he was, causing a minor traffic jam in the tunnel, and turned to face Agent Green. He could feel the gun twist into his side.

"Keep walking!" the agent snapped.

"What is it? What's the truth? Tell me."

"I have a picture," Agent Green said secretively. He forced Lex to continue walking, but Lex glanced behind them and saw that he'd bought Clark some much-needed time. Not that he was sure what Clark could do about any of this.

"A picture of what?" he asked. It suddenly occurred to him that there was something familiar about Agent Green's face. He had seen this man before, but where?

"Your *spaceship*," Agent Green hissed, imbuing the word with so much heated disgust there was no doubt that he considered himself serious.

"My *what*?" Lex laughed with a combination of total shock and delight. He turned to his captor, ignoring the gun pointed at his stomach.

"You killed Lex Luthor in that field and took over his body, " Agent Green insisted.

A strange expression crossed Lex's face. "So I'm not even a humanoid alien?" he asked, looking almost serious. "Just somebody dressed like one?"

"I *will* shoot you," Agent Green warned.

Lex, however, refused to take one step farther. He looked genuinely intrigued. "Would that matter?" he asked. "I mean, seriously—can you just shoot me, do you think? Can you possibly know what that would really do to me? Remember, I am an alien."

"You're a what?" Clark asked, catching up with them, pretending to be breathless.

Lex turned to Clark with a strange smile on his face. "He has a picture of my spaceship," he told his friend, indicating Agent Green.

"He has a gun," Clark added, alarmed.

Agent Green, frustrated, whipped the gun around and pressed it against Clark's head. The gun didn't concern Clark one bit, but was it possible that this man actually had a picture of his spaceship? And what had he told

Lex? And what had Lex made of it? The crowd around them continued rushing up and down the corridor, streaming around the trio as if they were rocks in the middle of a river.

"Cooperate, or your friend here gets it," Agent Green said threateningly, his eyes on Lex and his gun held against Clark's head.

Clark saw Lex's eyes go wide with worry, but could say nothing to reassure him. Truthfully, it would be a million times better for him to get shot than Lex, but Lex had no way of knowing that.

Passersby started to notice the gun. People all around them began to scream and back away as Agent Green kept the barrel pressed against the teenage boy's head. Lex's eyes narrowed and went strangely cold. Clark didn't like the look one bit.

"You know what I think?" Lex asked menacingly. Clark was amazed by how quickly he had gone from amused to incensed. "I think you're as much a secret agent as I'm a decorated Boy Scout, and I will take you apart with my bare hands if you hurt a hair on his head."

Lex took his eyes off of Agent Green's gun just long enough to note that the Yakuza had caught up with them. They had trained their guns on Clark, and most of the civilians in the subway were backing away from the standoff. Lex gritted his teeth and lunged for Agent Green's gun.

The agent was clearly taken by surprise, and Lex pressed his advantage, grappling with Green until the gun was pointing toward the floor.

"Run!" Lex shouted to Clark. Still grappling with Agent Green for the gun, Lex twisted with all his strength until he was sure the gun was pointing toward Agent

Green's leg. Ignoring the burning pain in his finger, Lex forced Agent Green to pull the trigger.

Two separate gunshots echoed through the subway tunnel. Lex looked up, fearful for Clark's safety, as Agent Green fell to the tiled floor by his feet. Lex's breath caught in his chest as he watched Clark crumple to the floor beside him. One of the Yakuza held a smoking gun.

And then, with no warning, one of the lights overhead began to sputter and flash. A second later, the underground passageway was plunged into total darkness.

CHAPTER TWENTY-ONE

"Clark!" Lex went down on his hands and knees in the dark, panicked, trying to find the body of his injured friend. Right before using his heat vision to overload the interior lighting circuit, Clark had made careful note of Lex's location. The second the tunnel was plunged into darkness, Clark leaped up and put himself between Lex and the Yakuza as a precautionary measure. But as he had hoped, the Yakuza had seen him go down. Satisfied that they had their retribution, Clark could hear them agreeing to disperse. They were eager to use the unexpected darkness for cover.

Groping through the pitch-black tunnel at superspeed, Clark managed to grab twelve guns. He threw them down into a pile near Lex, pretty sure that he'd snatched a few keys and soda cans from passersby by accident as well. Better safe than sorry, though. He was back on the floor of the tunnel by the time the emergency generator lights flicked on. Closing his eyes, he listened to the resulting confusion with satisfaction. The only person he was still worried about was Agent Green. Lex had apparently shot him in the leg, and Clark wanted to secure medical attention for him as quickly as possible.

"Clark!" Lex was shaking him urgently by the shoulder, and Clark felt bad for making his friend so worried. Still, he could tell his plan was working. Subway security was arriving on scene, and although the Yakuza were no longer armed, the Metropolites in the tunnel were making sure that the security officers knew to detain them.

Slowly, Clark opened his eyes and looked up at his friend.

"What happened?" he asked with exaggerated uncertainty.

Lex frowned and began checking him for gunshot wounds. "That's a good question."

Clark squeezed the bullet he had caught in his hand until it flattened out into an unidentifiable metal disk, then casually tossed it aside while Lex was distracted.

"You . . . shot that guy?" Clark asked, sitting up.

"Yeah, in the leg. And the Yakuza shot you . . . I thought. You're not hurt?" Lex was still patting Clark down, not quite able to believe he was uninjured.

Clark smiled sheepishly. "I heard the guns go off and I guess I just . . . fainted," he confessed. Lex fixed him with a penetrating stare, then merely shook his head.

The subway security officers were calling for police and paramedic backup. The man whom Lex had shot appeared to still be conscious. He was on the floor groaning and muttering what Clark hoped everyone would take for gibberish.

"Don't . . . let him get away," the agent panted. "Controls the lights . . . He'll kill us all!"

Lex followed Clark's gaze to Agent Green. "Sad, isn't it?" he commented. "It took me a while, but I just realized where I've seen him before. He used to work for my father in an R&D capacity, wanted to be a secret agent of some kind even then." Lex stood and reached down to help Clark up.

"What do you think of his theory?" Clark asked with a

slight smile as he rose to his feet. "Would he make a good secret agent?"

Lex's eyes flashed into Clark's. "I think it's dangerous to pretend to be something you're not," he answered.

A uniformed policeman approached Clark and Lex. "I need you gentlemen to move back," he insisted. Clark started to step away, but Lex met the policeman's eyes.

"That maniac tried to abduct me," he said calmly, indicating Agent Green. Paramedics had arrived and were setting up a transport cot. "He just dragged me twelve blocks at gunpoint. You'll need to take my statement."

The policeman looked over his shoulder at several other cops, who were in the process of handcuffing the Yakuza. "Stay here," he nodded. He motioned for a detective.

"What did he want with you?" Clark asked, peering toward Agent Green again. "For that matter, what did the Yakuza want with you?"

Lex smiled. "What can I tell you? I'm just a popular guy."

The detective singled out by the cop approached Lex and offered his hand, which Lex shook.

"I'm Detective Ross Salter," he informed them. "You say that man abducted you?"

Lex nodded. "I think he may also be involved in the recent murder of my security guard and doorman."

Clark could tell the detective was excited by Lex's words. "Mike Morganson and Ralph Harley?"

"Yeah, that's them." Lex thrust his hands in his pockets, and Clark realized that he hadn't mentioned the cauterization.

"We also think he was involved in the death of an elderly couple in the building across the street from where

Morganson and Harley worked," the detective continued. "Do you know anything about that?"

Lex frowned. "No, I'm sorry to hear that. Before this afternoon, I hadn't seen him in over a year, and then only once. I can't tell you much about what happened, but I can help you pin a breaking and entering on him. He covered my apartment in spyware earlier this week."

"Can I ask you to come down to the station with me?" the detective asked. "It sounds like you could be very helpful."

"No problem." Lex nodded. The detective excused himself, promising he'd be right back, and Lex turned his attention to Clark.

"How'd you find me?" he asked, hands still in his pockets. Clark gave Lex his most innocent look. "The other day, you couldn't even find your way back to the Towers without me, and today you're running around Neo-Tokyo like a pro."

"I heard the message you left on the answering machine at the penthouse," Clark answered. "There were Japanese voices on it, and it just seemed like this would be a good place to start looking. Besides"—he smiled—"you're not the hardest guy to pick out of a crowd."

Lex ran a hand self-consciously over his smooth scalp, but he was grinning. "Yeah, I guess I do stand out a little. That whole alien thing wasn't really such a bad hypothesis, I guess. I do have a secret weapon, after all."

Clark frowned at his friend. "You do?"

Lex held Clark's gaze for a long moment, offering him his most enigmatic smile. Then he gave a short laugh and walked toward the police detectives.

"Lex!" Clark called suddenly, panicked.

Lex turned to look at him with one eyebrow arched.

"What time is it?" Clark called anxiously. Lex glimpsed at his watch, then back up at his friend.

"Five-twenty, why?"

Clark deflated, frustration and exhaustion finally showing through his chiseled features.

"I missed the museum," he groaned. "And they're closed on Wednesdays."

Lex smirked.

"Well, you'll have to use *your* secret weapon, I guess."

Clark blinked as Lex turned back to the detectives. Shaking their hands, he began making plans with Detective Salter to tell him his story, *or*, Clark thought wryly, *as much of the story as he feels like sharing*. What had he meant, though, by his "secret weapon"? There wasn't any way he could know about Clark's X-ray vision, was there? Or about any other of Clark's extraordinary powers?

Clark sighed and leaned against the wall, watching the paramedics take Agent Green away. He'd worry about that later. Just then, all he could think about was getting out of the city.

CHAPTER TWENTY-TWO

Lionel Luthor rose from his leather office chair in a less than pleasant mood. He'd been trying unsuccessfully to get ahold of his Metropolis office all day, and had received some bad news about a hoped-for land acquisition in Yokohoma earlier that afternoon.

He shouldered on his gray linen suit jacket, grabbed his walking cane, and walked briskly to the door of his office.

"Cynthia?" he called testily, annoyed by his inability to see. "Cynthia, where are you?"

"I sent her home," he heard his son answer affably. A magazine rustled from a few feet away.

"What are you doing in London, Lex?"

Lex unfolded himself from his chair, coming to stand toe to toe with his father.

"Aren't you going to ask me how my flight was? I came a long way to see you, Dad."

"Lex." Lionel's voice held a nasty edge of warning as he flashed a wolfish grin. "I'm a very busy man."

"This won't take long. I just want to know why you felt the need to drag me into your dealings with the Yakuza."

Lionel glanced off to the left, rubbing his beard thoughtfully.

"As usual, I don't know what you're talking about, Lex."

"As usual," Lex replied, "I don't believe you."

"The first contact I ever had with the Yakuza was when they phoned me about having kidnapped you." Lionel paused, a slight smile tugging at the corner of his mouth as he lifted one eyebrow in a quiet challenge. "Of course, I was terribly concerned for your safety."

"It showed."

Lionel forced a light chuckle, stepping back from his son. Lex caught the small gesture of retreat and smiled. The phone at the reception desk began to ring. Lionel glanced in its general direction with a frown, pretending it was the excuse for his having given ground.

"We must stand strong in the face of threats, Lex. I've taught you that. If I'd have given in to their demands, who knows what they would have asked for next." Lionel's voice rose and fell dramatically as he spoke. He was a master of oration.

And lying, Lex thought dryly.

"Funny, it sounded to me like you had a prearranged price worked out with them. Frankly, Dad, I was a little insulted. Six million? Is that all I'm worth to you?"

Lionel laughed. The phone stopped ringing, then started again almost immediately.

"They wanted ten million—*twenty* once you got involved—and as you're no doubt aware, I refused to pay it."

"Meaning I'm *not* worth six million?" Lex's voice was low, and he realized he was losing focus. He shook his head slightly and lifted his chin.

"I never said that." Lionel offered his boy another cold smile as the phone continued to ring. "Son, if you came all the way to London to get me to admit to something I didn't do, I'm afraid you've wasted your time."

"Oh, no, Dad, not at all." Lex had regained control of his emotions, and now his eyes danced as he sauntered over to the receptionist's desk and leaned against it, reaching behind his back to lift and then drop the phone receiver, hanging up on Lionel's caller. "I'm actually extremely gratified to hear you deny any connection with the Yakuza. After all, as you yourself just pointed out, they were never paid."

Lex pushed away from the reception desk and headed across the dark blue carpet toward the elevators. Lionel could hear his son turn back to face him.

"After everything that happened this week, I wanted to make sure to stay on their good side," Lex continued. "So I posted their bail." He turned his back on Lionel and pressed the DOWN button. The elevator doors opened instantly, and Lex turned once more to look at his father. "I'm just glad I won't have to worry about any of them coming after you." He smiled.

Lionel clutched his walking cane tightly and stood perfectly still as Lex entered the elevator and the doors slid shut.

"I had the whole museum to myself for four hours!" Clark gushed, as his mother poured him another glass of milk. His father sat across the long maple table from him, listening with a smile. "Lex even had the geologist curator come in and talk to me about the achondrites!"

"That was awfully nice of him to get them to open the museum for you on a Wednesday." Martha smiled, putting the milk back in the refrigerator.

Jonathan shook his head, caught between disapproval and awe. "Imagine having that kind of pull," he sighed.

"He said the Lex Luthor Space Exploration Wing had a nice ring to it," Clark grinned. Martha laughed.

"I'm just glad you're home in one piece." Jonathan smiled, reaching across the table to ruffle his son's hair affectionately.

"We'll lay those pipes first thing tomorrow, Dad," Clark grinned back.

"So you had a good time?" Martha asked, coming to sit next to him. The wood-shuttered windows behind her helped keep their little yellow house on Hickory Lane cool in the summer and warm in the winter, as did the large barn in front that shaded it from wind and sun. The house was always full of light, though, and as an autumnal sun stream edged slowly across the table, Jonathan moved a small vase of sunflowers to allow the soft petals to feed in the radiance.

"Yeah, it was . . ." Clark trailed off suddenly. His parents were the two people on the planet he never had to lie to. He took a deep breath. "It was a little much, actually," he admitted, eyes shyly focused on the table. "I'm really glad to be home." His depthless blue eyes darted up to look at his mother, who smiled back at him lovingly. "It's hard to imagine you living there, Mom. Before you met Dad, I mean." Clark turned all the way toward her, his handsome face animated with curiosity. "I mean, it stays with you, doesn't it, once you've really spent some time there? I keep thinking about all those people, and how fast their lives are moving. How they have all these problems and all this violence in their lives . . ."

"We don't have enough trouble for you here?" Jonathan interrupted with a laugh.

Clark smiled, shaking his head. There was no question his dad was right—Smallville was a hotbed of activity, sometimes too much so.

"Yeah, but . . . it's different. Being back here I just have this weird sense that I'm missing something, but I don't really want to go back. Not yet, anyway." He turned back to his mom. "Do you know what I mean?"

Martha cocked her head slightly, considering.

"I used to think about those sort of things a lot." She nodded. "I guess I still do. There's something exhilarating about living like that, and I admire the people who stick with it."

"It kind of gave me a sense of how big the world really is," Clark confessed. "I mean, if there's that much going on in Metropolis, and Metropolis is only one city, in one state, in one country of the world . . . of *one* world . . ." He glanced at his dad, then at the flowers on the table, and finally back toward his mother. "I don't know, it just seems like there are an awful lot of people on the planet, and they all want such different things."

"No, son," Jonathan corrected warmly, shaking his head. "Essentially people all want the same things. To be safe, to have enough to eat, to have a place to call their own and be able to protect and provide for their families."

"To be loved," Martha added, smiling.

Clark shook his head.

"Maybe. Maybe at their core. But I saw people who enjoyed inflicting pain, and people who didn't value life, and people who were so lost, I don't know if anyone could ever lead them back to themselves. I mean, that's sort of what was different. Here, as bad as things got, I always assumed that everyone means well. But I don't know, I'm not sure that's true anymore."

Jonathan pressed his lips together and nodded.

"You're right, Clark. There are people in this world, maybe even a lot of them, who take those needs I mentioned and use them as an excuse to go after more than their share."

"And there are people who get so hurt or twisted somehow," Martha agreed, "that they end up inflicting the kind of pain they were originally running from."

"But how do you know who's who?" Clark asked.

"You develop a sense of people," Martha said thoughtfully, "an instinct."

"Or sometimes you'll have information, like someone's reputation," Jonathan added in a slightly darker voice.

"And sometimes you'll be wrong," Martha concluded, patting her son's arm.

Clark shook his head again, overwhelmed.

"It's so much easier when you think you can rely on everyone." He turned to his mother. "But knowing there's all this despair in the world, too—not stuff that comes from meteor-rocks, but things that are already with us, things that come *out* of us. Doesn't it ever scare you?"

Martha's eyes shone with tenderness as she reached out to draw her son close.

"Not now that you're here," she said with a soft smile. Clark closed his eyes as he returned his mother's embrace, feeling the warmth of his father's hand as Jonathan reached across the table to squeeze his own.

"Hope is always stronger than despair, son," he said deeply. "And you're the best hope we've got."

They held each other for a long moment. Clark sighed

deeply, opening his eyes. His mother let go of him, stood up, and kissed the top of his head.

"Now, maybe you want to go have a word with Lana before dinner?" she suggested in her most sensible, straightforward voice.

Jonathan let go of his son's hand with a laugh as Clark almost knocked his chair over jumping to his feet.

"This could take a while," Clark warned, grabbing his jacket.

"Take your time, son." Jonathan chuckled. "Take all the time you need."

Agent Green woke up in a hospital bed, his left leg in traction. He was gratified to see a uniformed police officer guarding the door to his private room. He was sure it was something the agency had arranged for his protection. He just couldn't quite remember which agency. As a field agent, though, he was sure he must work for some sort of agency. It only made sense.

His eyes darted up to the flat fluorescent light above his bed.

"Officer?" he called.

The cop looked over her shoulder at him with a slight frown. "Yeah?"

"Turn the light off. He controls the lights. I don't want any artificial light in my room."

The police officer rolled her eyes but reached over and flipped off the overhead. "Happy now?"

"Am I in Gotham?" he asked.

"Metropolis," she answered, pointing to the city insignia on her jacket. "But I think you're headed to Gotham as soon as you're stable enough to move."

Agent Green nodded, satisfied. "It'll be nice to be back where I belong."

"You've been in an institution before?" she asked with a raised eyebrow.

"An institution?"

"The asylum," she nodded, checking the chart on his door. "That's where you're headed, pal."

Agent Green frowned. "Is that where you took the alien?"

The cop pursed her lips together, thinking. "The Alien? Hm, I'm not sure. I know there are some people there with strange names, but I'm not sure I've heard of anyone called the Alien."

Agent Green tried to sit up, but the pain in his leg forced him back. Wincing, he raised his head off the bed.

"I don't understand. You caught him, didn't you? In the subway? He was right there! He's the one who shot me!"

"Lex Luthor shot you," the police officer corrected.

Agent Green nodded. "Yes, exactly!"

"In self-defense," she added, leveling her gaze on him.

"What? No, something's wrong. I arrested him. I had him there, under arrest, and he shot me, and the police came."

"You should get some rest," the cop said with a hint of condescension in her voice. "Do you want me to get a nurse?"

Agent Green lowered his head back onto his pillow, but did not close his eyes. Was it possible that the alien controlled the entire Metropolis Police Department? Would his influence extend into Gotham as well? Was the whole country already under his control?

Agent Green swallowed hard and resolved never to close his eyes again.

Clark smiled broadly the minute Lana opened the door to Chloe's house. He wasn't looking forward to the conversation they were about to have, but seeing her safe and less than completely furious with him filled him with relief.

Lana pushed through the screen door and joined Clark on the small porch. Her arms were folded across her chest, and she wouldn't meet his eyes, but at least she was standing next to him.

Clark cleared his throat. "Lana, I want to apologize again for what happened in Metropolis. More than anything, I wanted to spend that whole evening with you."

"Then why didn't you, Clark?" Lana asked irritably. She was staring across the street, still refusing to meet Clark's eyes.

"Someone was in trouble, and I was in the position to help," Clark said carefully. He'd thought about what he could tell Lana during the entire drive back to Smallville, finally deciding to keep his explanation as simple and truthful as possible. "It . . . got a little more complicated than I was prepared for, but in the end, no one was hurt."

"Did you know this person?" Lana asked, turning to him with a frown.

Clark thought about the young couple at the end of the pier, the Yakuza gunman, and the men he'd saved from the sinking car. "No," he answered honestly. "At the time, though, I thought they might have something to do with some trouble Lex was in."

Lana considered what he said. "Did you tell Lex what happened?" she finally asked.

Clark glanced at Lana's profile, unsure of what kind of answer she was hoping for. She lifted her gaze to the sky and watched the stars begin to emerge.

"No," he admitted. "Lex could tell that something had happened, just like you could, but I didn't tell him the whole story." Clark paused, glancing up at the sky. "I'm not sure it's my story to tell, Lana," he added quietly. "I was just trying to help out."

Lana sighed and moved to sit on the front steps. She met his eyes for the first time that evening as she sat down, inviting him to join her. Clark immediately moved to comply.

"You know, you have this funny habit of putting strangers before your friends," Lana said. Her voice didn't sound as angry as it had at the beginning of the conversation, and she wrinkled her nose the way she always did when she was deep in thought. "No one can fault you for wanting to help people out, Clark, but I wonder if there's more to it." She turned to look at him, holding his gaze. "If you're always there for everybody, you can never be completely there for any one person. I'm not saying that's good or bad either way, but it does seem . . . limiting. Do you know what I mean?"

Clark's eyes widened, and he slowly shook his head. Lana turned her attention to the street and tried again.

"No one person can ever have you as long as you belong to everyone. In the end, everyone will really *like* you, but will anyone be able to *love* you, Clark?"

Clark swallowed, dropping his eyes.

Lana hurried on. "I just mean, it's almost like something you do on purpose. Like some kind of defense mechanism to keep anyone from getting too close." Lana took his hand suddenly, and Clark lost his breath. "What are you afraid we'll see, Clark? You're one of the nicest people I know, but you keep everyone at this distance, as if you're afraid we'll find out that you're really a monster or something." Lana offered Clark a small smile. "Can it really be that bad?"

Clark squeezed Lana's hand, then released it. He stood up and walked down to the curb, shoving his hands into his pockets. The sky was dark, and full of stars.

And planets, Clark thought miserably.

Lana leaned forward on the steps, speaking intimately. "Sometimes, even though I know better, I catch myself thinking it's my fault that my parents died. Like if I'd been better, or smarter or something, maybe they'd still be with me." Lana got up from the steps, moving to stand next to Clark on the pavement. "Do you ever think about your parents? Your birth parents, I mean."

Clark met Lana's eyes and nodded. "Yeah," he admitted. "I wonder about them a lot."

Lana nodded as if satisfied with his honesty. "Do you know why they gave you up?" she asked.

Clark shook his head. "No idea. I'm not even sure if they're alive or not."

"Do you think maybe that has something to do with what I've been talking about?" Lana asked, her shoulder lightly touching his. "Like maybe you secretly think they gave you up because there's something wrong with you, or you weren't good enough?"

Clark thought about that, unsure of how to answer. He was grateful when Lana continued. "If it does, I just want you to know that it's not true. You might never know who they are or why they made the choices they did. But I'm sure they'd be proud of you if they could see you now. You're a really good person, Clark. Nobody could ask you to do more than you already do. I mean, you get good grades, you help out around the farm, you're nice to everyone you meet, and you're always trying to learn about new things. But even more than that, you always put your full effort into everything. I've never seen you hold back when you thought you could help someone. What more could anyone possibly want from you?"

Clark didn't answer right away. He was thinking about Metropolis and how different it was from Smallville. After helping somebody at home, Clark usually felt some degree of contentment. At the end of the day everyone headed off to their own little plots of land, and Clark could look around the modest town and know that basically everything was okay.

The city, though, wasn't like that at all. Every problem opened up into another one. There were always people moving through the dark, too many people, and somehow their lives never fully untangled. Mayer Greenbrae had had financial problems that ended up connecting him to the Yakuza, who ended up trying to hurt Lex to get back what they'd lost. The cause and effect barely made sense to Clark, who knew that he'd have to figure it out if he intended to continue actively helping people he didn't know. He had a fairly good sense of what Smallville needed from him, but when he tried to apply that same code of conduct to the city, the troubles in the world seemed to grow exponentially. Or at least, his awareness of them did.

"I think usually parents want their kids to live up to their full potential," Clark noted after a short pause.

"Exactly!" Lana exclaimed. She let out a short, embarrassed laugh and knocked her shoulder against his a little more forcibly. "And that's exactly what you're doing, right? So relax already, will you?"

Clark smiled softly but without conviction. Lana turned to look up at the night sky again, leaning her weight against his. He felt her warmth beside him but kept his eyes on the stars.

Lana was right. All he had to do was live up to his full potential.

Clark slipped an arm around her shoulders, and tried not to feel afraid.

ABOUT THE AUTHOR

Devin Kalile Grayson grew up in the San Francisco Bay Area and currently resides in Oakland, California. After earning a degree in English Literature from Bard College, Devin was working at a normal day job and taking post-graduate writing classes at U.C. Berkeley when she read and fell in love with her first comic book. She has worked for DC Comics ever since, in 2000 becoming the first woman to serve as the regular writer of a Batman series. Recent work includes the *X-Men: Evolution* comic for Marvel, the graphic novel *Batman/Joker: Switch*, and her monthly writing gig on *Nightwing*.

FIND OUT HOW IT ALL BEGAN . . .

BY WINNING ALL EIGHT BOOKS IN THE SMALLVILLE SERIES!

Here's your chance to win the entire *Smallville* series. Just fill out the coupon below, and you could be one of ten winners randomly selected in a drawing to receive an eight-title *Smallville* set! So enter anytime between March 1 and April 28, 2004—your entry must be postmarked by April 28, 2004—and you could own the saga from beginning to end! Winners will be announced on or about May 15, 2004.

NO PURCHASE NECESSARY TO ENTER. See details and official rules on next page.

Complete this entry form or send us a 3x5 index card with the following information:

(Please Print)

Name: _____

Address: _____

City: _____ State: _____ Zip: _____

E-mail:_____

Mail to: SMALLVILLE SWEEPSTAKES
c/o Warner Books
Dept. JA/EG, Ninth Floor, Room 953B
1271 Avenue of the Americas
New York, NY 10020

Official Contest Rules

PURCHASING DOES NOT IMPROVE YOUR CHANCE~

Official Rules. No Purchase Necessary, Residents of the continenta~ Canada only, age 18 or older. Void in Quebec, Vermont and where pro~ by law. Substitution for any prize may be necessary due to unavailability, ~ which case a comparable prize of equal or greater value will be awarded. To enter, follow the instructions on the entry form or hand print your name, address and e-mail address, if you have one, on a 3 x 5 piece of paper and send to: Warner Smallville Sweepstakes, c/o Warner Books, Department JA/EG, Ninth Floor, 1271 Avenue of the Americas, New York, NY 10020. Mechanical reproductions or use of automated devices not valid. Mailed entries must be received by the specified date. One entry per household. In the case of multiple entries, only the first entry will be accepted. Warner Books is not responsible for technical failures in entry transmission, or lost, late, misdirected, damaged, incomplete, illegible or postage due mail. Warner Books reserves the right to cancel the sweepstakes if it becomes technically corrupted. Winners will be randomly selected from all entries received by Warner Books, whose judging decisions are final. Winners will be notified by mail or e-mail within 30 days of the drawing. In order to win a prize, residents of Canada are required to answer a skill-testing question administered by mail. Any prize or prize notification returned to Warner Books as undeliverable will result in the awarding of that prize to an alternate winner: Odds of winning depend on number of entries received. Except as required by law, Warner Books will not share entrant information with any third parties. Warner Books may contact entrants in the future with offers we feel may be of interest and will add all entrants e-mail addresses to our science fiction newsletter mailing lists. Employees of Time Warner Book Group Inc, and affiliated companies and members of those employees immediate families are not eligible. Drawing governed by laws of United States. Any claims relating to this sweepstakes must be resolved in the United States. For a list of prizewinners, send a self- addressed envelope to Warner Smallville Sweepstakes, c/o Warner Books, Dept. JA/EG, Ninth Floor, 1271 Avenue of the Americas, New York, NY 10020 between end date of contest and one month later. Winners are responsible for all applicable taxes.

Entry constitutes permission (except where prohibited by law) to use the winner's name, hometown, likeness, and any text submitted for purpose of advertising and promotion on behalf of the sweepstakes sponsor without further compensation.